HARD LOVE

Meredith Wild

FOREVER

NEW YORK   BOSTON

Forever
Hachette Book Group
1290 Avenue of the Americas
New York, NY 10104
hachettebookgroup.com
twitter.com/foreverromance

Printed in the United States of America

RRD-C

First Forever Edition: September 2015
10 9 8 7 6 5 4 3 2

Forever is an imprint of Grand Central Publishing.
The Forever name and logo are trademarks of Hachette Book Group, Inc.

The Hachette Speakers Bureau provides a wide range of authors for speaking events. To find out more, go to www.hachettespeakersbureau.com or call (866) 376-6591.

The publisher is not responsible for websites (or their content) that are not owned by the publisher.

ISBN 978-1-4555-9176-3 (trade pbk edition)
ISBN 978-1-4555-6641-9 (signed edition)

HARD LOVE

Also by Meredith Wild

Hacker Series

Hardwired
Hardpressed
Hardline
Hard Limit

For my three little miracles . . .

HARD LOVE

CHAPTER ONE

Dublin, Ireland

ERICA

We stepped through the black painted doors of The Widow and into the energy of the pub. Laughter rose above the steady murmur of its patrons crowded together in small booths that lined the walls. With Blake's hand in mine, I led us farther into the room that wrapped around the old square bar, the centerpiece of this place made for spirits and revelry.

Around the corner, a face lit up with recognition, a smile mirroring my own.

"Professor!"

I broke contact with Blake and made my way toward the man I'd known all my years at Harvard as Professor Brendan Quinlan. He rose and greeted me with a tight embrace. The texture of his green sweater was rough under my hands, his salt-and-pepper hair a tickle against my cheek.

"Erica! Wonderful to see you. How have you been?" His Irish brogue had become more pronounced in the months since I'd seen him.

How could I possibly sum up everything life had thrown at me since graduation months ago? Still, in this very moment, I was…

"I'm great." I smiled broadly and felt Blake's warmth behind me, then his hand gently at the small of my back.

I glanced up at the man who'd completely stolen my heart since the last time I'd seen Brendan. Blake's dark brown hair was trimmed neatly for our recent wedding. His lean, muscular torso was hidden under a light sweater, but his jeans strained in all the right ways over the contours of his thighs. Maybe I was a smitten newlywed, but I wasn't alone in my admiration. Blake turned heads, even in the few minutes since we'd walked into the pub. And because he was mine in all the ways that mattered, I no longer cared who looked.

The professor extended his hand to Blake. "You must be the lucky lad."

Blake shook his hand, his deep hazel eyes crinkling at the edges with a smile. "I certainly am. It's a pleasure to meet you. Erica speaks very highly of you."

"And she of you. You two are quite the pair now." He darted his gaze between the two of us. "The maven and the mogul."

I laughed and leaned into Blake. "Maven? I'm not sure if I'm quite there yet."

The professor motioned toward the worn wooden table where we took our seats. "Don't doubt it! Might be a good title for a book in any case. I may have to steal it."

He winked, and the gesture tugged at my heart. I'd missed his friendship and guidance. Once so steady, and then suddenly gone after he'd left for sabbatical and I ventured out into the working world for the first time. I smiled inwardly, remembering how we'd spent hours going over my business plan and turning over ideas, all the while figuring out how I was going to satisfy my major between business-building efforts. I'd never forget what his support meant to me then and how it had set me on a journey that would challenge me beyond my wildest imagination.

He'd left for Ireland nearly as soon as Blake had come into my life. He'd had his reasons, of course. Despite his focus on business studies at the university, he'd left to pursue a different kind of dream and one I was eager to hear more about.

"How is the novel going?"

"It's going grand. Plenty of characters around here to inspire me. Isn't that right, Mary?"

The waitress, a woman with thick black curly hair pulled back into a clip, arrived at the table. She'd brought with her a dark pint filled to the frothy brim. She set it down and straightened, resting her hands on her hips over the strings of her small black apron.

"Is he pestering ye? I can toss him out. Wouldn't be the first time, would it, Bren?" She winked.

He shook his head with a smile. "No need, love. I'll be on my best behavior."

We ordered a couple more pints, and hours later I was warm from the beer and laughing, listening to Brendan's stories about his local friends and adventures. We talked about Harvard too, reliving the best of my college memories. I was careful to skirt past the others. Brendan would never know about those shadows, and I truly hoped he'd never know how close Max had come to repeating history. Perhaps when Brendan was back in Boston he would get wind of the assault charges that had been brought against his former student, but at least for now, he was far enough away that he likely wouldn't find out.

Blake and Brendan were chatting about one of Blake's business ventures when Mary returned to clear our empty glasses.

"There she is. My bride to be," Brendan muttered, his accent somehow thicker than it had been when we arrived.

"Oh, you." She smacked his arm, barely concealing a smile.

He beamed with a grin and turned his focus back to us. "Will you have another?"

I glanced at Mary's tray of empties. We could go a lot longer and regret it. I shook my head. "I'm good. You two can go ahead, if you want."

Blake leaned back and slid his arm over my shoulders. "No, we should head back. It's getting late."

Brendan nodded. "Of course. Let me see you out, then."

"I'll take care of the tab and meet you two outside," Blake said.

Brendan protested, but Mary ignored his pleas to pay. When he'd finally given up, he and I left the noise of the pub together for the much quieter clatter of the street outside. People walked in small groups past us, in and out of the surrounding establishments. A half-moon cast a sheen on the street. The cobblestones were misted with evidence of a brief rain shower we'd missed while inside.

I stuffed my hands into my pockets and took in all the details of this new place.

"Beautiful night, isn't it?" Brendan took a deep breath of the evening air.

"It is. I'm so glad we could catch up, Professor."

He chuckled. "Brendan! I beg you, call me Brendan. At least until you get to graduate school, and then we can work it out."

I laughed. "Not likely, but fair enough."

"I suppose what you've been through has been your education." His smile faded a little and his gaze wandered past me. "I'm sorry about yer man Max. I had no idea that he'd be such a disappointment for the cause, Erica. I'd seen a glimmer of hope in the boy...Thought for sure he'd straightened up from his younger days."

I looked down, not wanting to let on what a grave disappointment he'd ultimately been.

"It's okay. Ancient history," I said quietly, thinking back to the email update I'd sent the professor days after learning that Max and my ex-employee, Risa, had stolen company information and used it to launch their competing business. I hadn't wanted the professor to feel guilty, only to save him from sending any other unwitting students Max's way for help or support.

Max had proven far more dangerous than I'd given him credit for initially. Perhaps if I hadn't become so involved with Blake, he wouldn't have taken such an interest in ruining me in every way he could. But I wasn't about to make excuses for him, and I didn't want anyone else to have to go through what I had.

"Perhaps it worked out in a way, with you meeting Blake. Silver lining, as they say."

"Very true. The past few months have been hard, but I couldn't have gotten through them without him."

I'd always prided myself on my independence. I'd been left, hurt, and abandoned. I'd been underestimated and brushed off. Never had I thought I'd become so committed to another human being. I couldn't imagine having come through the past few months the same without Blake by my side, though. And I couldn't imagine today or any of my tomorrows without his love and support. Saying yes, sharing vows, and giving him my trust had come easier after everything we'd been through.

"Ready?" Blake had stepped through the doorway of the pub and come to my side, effectively sidelining my thoughts and our conversation.

I couldn't say I minded one bit. I'd loved meeting with my old friend, but I was ready to be back in Blake's arms, in a quiet place with just the two of us. We were on our honeymoon, after all.

I bit my lip, smiling. My honeymoon, with my *husband*.

I turned to the professor for a last hug, and we said our goodbyes before parting ways.

Blake and I began to walk the now familiar path back to our hotel, through the dark uneven streets out of Dublin's city center. A hint of rain and the lingering scent of the fresh flowers that had been sold on the streets hours earlier filled the air.

I held Blake's hand, admiring the details of the building architecture framing the old streets, greeting the bright-eyed faces that met us on the sidewalk. It was almost midnight, but our schedule was a mess, and I was in no rush to be anywhere as long as we were together.

Seeing my old professor again had been a flashback to a simpler time in my life. So much had happened since that first meeting in the Angelcom boardroom that Professor Quinlan arranged with Max's initial support. I never could have known then that I'd fall head over heels for the cocky investor sitting across from me...that I'd become his wife. But here we were, bound together as closely as two people could be.

Blake caught me closer to his side and brushed a soft kiss over my cheek. "I like Brendan. I can see why he's become a friend."

I smiled. "It seems odd to call him a friend when he's been so much more, but it's true. He encouraged me to build the business when I had so many doubts. He's the reason I took the path I did."

"A path that led you straight to me." He squeezed my hand. "Lucky me."

I glanced up and kissed his cheek as we walked. I was lucky too. I couldn't deny it.

But for all my early dreams, imagining where entrepreneurship would take me, I could have never imagined traveling the road I had. With Sid's and Alli's help, I'd built a business that had grown and had attracted outside partners that promised to take it to the next level. Days after signing over my stake in the company, I'd learned that Isaac Perry and Blake's ex would control the reins. The devastating development had sent me into an emotional tailspin—one I hadn't fully recovered from yet.

I thought back to the last day I set foot in the Clozpin office, none the wiser for what I'd done, what I'd signed away. I reminded myself that no matter what happened now, if the business flourished or crashed and burned, I'd never be able to go back.

"You're quiet. What are you thinking about?" Blake asked.

I blew out a breath and shook my head. "The business, I guess. Sometimes I still can't believe I'm not a part of it anymore."

"You can't let that eat away at you," he said quietly. "It's in the past, and you have a bright future ahead of you."

"Most of the time, I try not to think about it."

He was silent a moment before he spoke. "I know it still hurts. And I hate that you had to leave something you poured so much of yourself into. But you're free now. You have the world at your fingertips. Despite everything that happened, that's not a bad thing."

Maybe he was right, but so much was still unknown when it came to my professional future. "Clozpin gave me purpose. I can only hope Geoff's new projects will make me feel the same way. At least most of the team is still there, so it won't feel completely foreign."

Thanks to Blake appointing me to the board at Angel-com, I'd had the opportunity to invest in new projects that could fill the void. Geoff Wells was a programmer and had the same entrepreneurial spark that I recognized in myself. Enough that when things fell through with Clozpin, Sid, Alli, and I saw enough promise to rally around his concept as our next venture.

"I've been investing long enough to recognize passion when I see it. I see it in Geoff, and I've always seen it in you. You're going to give everything you have to make this venture successful. It's your nature. Believe me. One opportunity that didn't go according to plan isn't going to change that."

The memory of disappointment, of a soul-crushing failure, echoed through me. The more time passed, the more I could emotionally distance myself from what Isaac and Sophia had done. The more I could see the experience for what it was—a chapter . . . a learning experience that I'd not soon forget. While being ripped from the business that had meant so much to me wasn't as excruciating as it had been at first, the wound was still tender.

"Maybe. I can't help but feel like I . . . failed somehow." The guilt niggled at me like a bad dream I couldn't shake.

He glanced down at me. "You didn't fail. You learned."

I scuffed the sole of my boots against the stones as we walked, avoiding his stare.

"I've been around the block a few times, you know. You should trust me."

I smirked. "That's why I married you, of course. For your business acumen and wealth of knowledge."

He lifted an eyebrow.

"And your mountains of money," I added quickly.

"You're trying to tell me you didn't marry me for my dashing good looks? I might be insulted."

I pursed my lips, trying to look serious. "If I had to pick one thing that tipped the scales, I'd say it was your exceptional skills in bed. I think that's where you really excel."

"Well then"—he laughed, his eyes twinkling—"at least *my* purpose is clear."

He gave my ass a firm squeeze. Laughing, I pushed him away as we approached a street performer who was crooning for the barest of audiences. A small group of French-speaking tourists stood nearby, and an older man, dirty from the streets, sat on the opposite side of the street with a sloppy grin.

We slowed to listen as the tourists dispersed. The song was sad, but rich with love—raw and emotional the way he delivered each verse. Blake turned me to him, bringing us chest to chest. Our fingers laced, his breath warm against my hair, he led us into a simple nameless dance. I swayed toward him and closed my eyes, clinging to his frame the way I clung to every magical moment between us.

Straining for the lyrics through the singer's thick accent, I caught the verses.

> *When misfortune falls sure no man can shun it.*
> *I was blindfolded I'll ne'er deny.*
> *Now at nights when I go to my bed of slumber,*
> *the thoughts of my true love run in my mind.*

Another moment passed as the young man's voice faded into the night. The song was a somber one, made light only by his passionate delivery. Like so much of life, the pain was what you made of it. He'd made something sad beautiful.

I sighed and settled against Blake's chest. His body emanated warmth. His heartbeat was a steady reminder of his support, his love—a force that had saved me, changed me, and healed me in ways I'd never thought possible. He tipped my chin up, the glint in his eyes matching the passion in my heart. He parted his full lips, but hesitated, a wordless moment passing between us.

"I'm going to show you the whole world, Erica."

"I can't imagine enjoying a minute of it without you," I whispered.

He stilled our slow dance, tracing a fingertip over my lips, his countenance now serious in a way that threatened my next breath.

"And I'm going to make you fall in love with me all over again. Every morning and every night. In every city and at the edge of every ocean. I'll remind you why you're mine and why I've always been yours."

I drew an unsteady breath, feeling his promise all the way to my soul. Swallowing hard, I found my voice. "I think you're on the right track."

I arched toward him until our lips met. Soft and slow at first, the kiss went deeper, stealing every thought that didn't revolve around his taste and touch.

We broke apart slightly when a gravelly voice interrupted us.

"Go make love to her, lad, before she changes her mind entirely."

Behind us, the man who'd made his home for the night in the entryway of a high-end store offered an imperfect grin, pairing his words of wisdom with a friendly tip of his small bottle of liquor.

I smiled, and Blake, by the dark look in his eyes, seemed to immediately accept the stranger's challenge.

"I plan to," he murmured, his tone all velvet and delicious threat.

My skin tingled and he took my mouth again with a kiss that promised so much more.

CHAPTER TWO

BLAKE

I sat alone in the darkness, unable to quiet my thoughts. Outside the water lapped against the pillars that held our luxury bungalow safely above the crystal-clear ocean. The moon lit up the horizon and the waves rolled in uneven strips toward us. Then the inevitable crash of the salty sea meeting the shore. I could no more stop the motion than I could stop time.

The meditative rhythm of the sound should have soothed me, but I was far from soothed, far from sleep. Hours had turned to days, and somehow the days had melted into weeks. We hadn't wasted a moment, but I couldn't fight the unsettling feeling that hit my gut every time I thought about the honeymoon ending. In our busy lives, a month was an eternity. But somehow a month wasn't enough, and now I resented that life in Boston would be calling us back in a matter of days.

We'd touched down in Malé a week ago, and almost instantly I'd sensed the shift. Maybe because we'd both seen it coming. Maybe because there was nothing but peace on the island. No bustling cities, no friends to meet. No sights to take in, nothing excessive to buy. Just our bodies and an easy silence between us set against the backdrop of this beautiful place. The silence was natural, comfortable, but also weighted by the reality back home that neither of us was ready to face.

I released a tired sigh and reached for my laptop, unable to shake an uneasy feeling. My screen lit up the nearly black night around me. As our honeymoon days dwindled, my thoughts had wandered further from the simple life we'd enjoyed here. More and more they circled around the life we were going back to.

In the bedroom, Erica slept and I hoped it was soundly. She'd been restless most of the night. I wasn't sure if my restlessness was having the same effect on her, or if the same brand of anxiety riddled us both.

We'd promised to unplug, yet here I was, unable to ignore the reality that we both had enemies, and the most important responsibility I had as Erica's husband was to protect her. Keeping her safe as we navigated halfway across the world was one thing. Keeping her safe back home was another.

I wanted to be the one to fight for her. For her safety and her happiness. Erica was young, but she'd survived more than anyone should ever have to. I may have tried to keep the upper hand between us, but I never doubted her strength for a moment. Still, I'd made a promise to protect her.

I skimmed my email, ignoring the instinct to start clearing out the list of things to do that had amassed over the past few weeks. The list was too long to consider at this late hour. No, work would have to wait.

I pulled up another tab for the news. We'd caught snippets of world news at the various places we'd been, from Paris to Cape Town, but nothing about Boston had made its way to those channels. Now, front and center, was the familiar home page of *The Globe,* the headline proclaiming that Daniel Fitzgerald had won the Massachusetts governor's seat. A landslide victory.

"Prick," I muttered before clicking the link to read more.

I hated the man. I hated that in a very real way he was the only family Erica had, and still he'd brought nothing but terror to her life. If she needed protecting from anyone, it was from him. I tried like hell to keep my opinions to myself, not wanting to see the pain in her eyes whenever the topic of Daniel came up. But I believed it was the years of his neglect and all the ways he'd failed her over time, more than my words, that cut her deep in those moments.

No matter what she said, or didn't say, I wasn't going to let him come between us again, and I was going to make sure he stayed far away from our lives.

The article touched on the trials of the past few months of the race, the tragic death of his stepson Mark—the man who'd raped Erica years ago, a fact only a handful of people were privy to. Then the very public discovery of Erica, his biological and illegitimate daughter, and, lastly, the shooting...

I closed my eyes and my stomach lurched as I relived the memory of Erica's bloodied body in my arms. I stayed strong for her then, those few terrifying minutes that I thought would be our last together.

She was everything to me. Everything. A kind of desolation had swept through me when her eyes fluttered closed and her warmth began to fade. I thought I'd lost her. I'd held her, refusing to leave as I shook with rage and despair. Everything inside me fought the urge to scream, to find Daniel on the street and take my vengeance on him.

Daniel had pulled the trigger on the man who'd shot her, but he could never protect her. He would only cause her more pain, more of the heartbreak she'd tried valiantly to hide from me. I'd fantasized about a thousand ways I could ruin the man, but I knew better. I bottled up those plans, confident that a man like him was more than capable of ruining himself given enough time.

By some miracle, Erica had survived. The moment she'd lost consciousness, it felt like my heart had stopped beating. I was living and breathing, but existing only on the verge of survival until the doctors promised me she was going to be all right. And the moment in the hospital room when she opened her eyes again, warmth flooded my heart. New heat hit my veins, and the world became a place that I could live in again. She was with me. Safe, mine. But never the same.

I didn't know then what else could be lost. I opened my eyes. Unclenching my fists, I tried not to think about what her wounds could deny us.

I slammed the laptop shut and leaned forward, shoving my hands through my hair. Christ, five minutes online and my mind was running amuck, lost in a sea of dark thoughts. Resentment of what had been lost, lingering fear of what we still faced.

A second later, Erica's quiet footsteps padded across the cool marble floor of our bungalow. I turned toward the sound. The moonlight provided just enough light to see the outline of her body in the darkness.

"Hey." She slowed beside me, her questioning gaze landing on the laptop in front me.

"What are you doing up?" I asked.

"I thought you weren't going to work until we got back."

"I wasn't working." I reached for her hand, brushing my thumb over her knuckles. "Promise."

Her skin was warm, almost hot to the touch. No surprise in the balmy climate of the Maldives, but I didn't take for granted that was why.

"You all right?"

She answered with a silent nod.

"Another dream?"

"I'm fine," she murmured.

The way her voice became small gave me pause. Tension coiled in my gut, my resentment for the people who'd taken the peace from too many of her nights lodged tightly there. Instinctively, I wanted to pull her to me, save her from those demons. But in the wake of the night terrors that had faded considerably over the past few weeks, she could sometimes mistake me for the worst of them. Before I could question her, she pulled away, breaking our connection.

"I'm going for a quick swim. I'll be back."

Walking away, she tugged off the loose shirt that clung in places to her damp torso. She slowed at the edge of the infinity pool that blended the edge of our space with the endless ocean beyond. Her panties slid to the ground. The sliver of moonlight hit the curves of her body. The blond waves that fell to the middle of her back floated as she descended into the water and then submerged entirely, out of sight.

My body prickled with lust, but something far deeper took hold of my heart.

I rose and followed her to the edge of the pool. She stood in the center of the water, her hair slicked back, her breasts barely covered by the shallow water. I itched to touch her, every splendid inch of her. I'd had her plenty, but somehow it was never enough to sate my daily hunger for her.

"Mind if I join you?" I could barely hide the tone suggesting that I wanted more than I was asking for.

She smiled. "Of course not."

I stripped and stepped into the water, just cool enough to be refreshing. I walked toward her and stopped before we touched. We were inches away. I wanted her desperately. I wanted to haul her against me and show her exactly how much. But I waited, harnessing my patience.

After a long moment, she reached for me. Her fingertips trickled lightly up my torso. I caught her hand gently, holding it against my heart where it raced beneath my ribs. Every bittersweet ache, every rush of love felt there belonged to her.

Her lips parted and a single step closed the small distance between us. Unable to hold back any longer, I reached for her, gliding her against me. The water rippled around us. I brought her arm around my neck and she repeated the motion with the other, clasping her hands at my nape, holding us close. Her warmth radiated against me, and I released a breath I didn't realize I was holding.

"Erica," I murmured, capturing her lips in a slow kiss. My wife. The twenty-two-year-old beauty who'd taken over my life and made everything else fade into the background. I wanted to give her everything, and if I couldn't, I had to give her enough to make up for what all the others had taken away.

I swore it, a silent vow made when I slid the ring onto her finger and made her mine forever. I wanted to give her the solace that I could only find when we made love.

Every time meant more than the last.

Thoughts circled around the crazy love I felt for her, channeled into the gentle melding of our mouths. She hummed, nibbling my lip, sending a surge of blood south. I pulled back a fraction, catching my breath, but she pulled me to her again. I groaned, pressing against her firmly. I wanted her now, here. But something stopped me.

I cupped her cheek, gazing into her eyes now clouded with desire. I searched for an answer to a question I hadn't been able to ask her yet. I didn't want to see the hurt there, in the pale blue depths that matched the ocean around us.

A small wince wrinkled her brow. "What's wrong?"

My beautiful wife... I ran my thumb across her lips. "I want to ask you something, and I want you to tell me the truth."

"Ask me."

"Erica..." I paused, the words knotting in my throat for a moment. "Do you really want a baby?"

She stilled and tried to look down, but I wouldn't let her. I tipped her chin, lifting her gaze to mine.

"Tell me," I whispered. "I want to know if this is what you really want."

She swallowed and slid her hands down to my chest. "I want to share every possible experience with you, Blake."

"I want that too."

"I don't know if we're ready, but..."

"But what?" I asked, keeping my voice steady, objective. I wouldn't let on how my heart thundered in anticipation of her confession.

She drew in a deep breath. "I'm scared that if we wait...that we'll never get a chance." She pulled the edge of her lip between her teeth. "It's so soon. Maybe too soon. I don't know if it's something you could possibly want right now. And, also...I don't want to disappoint you."

I grasped her hand in mine and squeezed gently. "That's impossible. You know that, right?"

Her gaze flickered to mine, a hint of a smile playing on her lips.

Meanwhile a hundred disjointed thoughts whizzed through my mind. I'd narrowed my vision of the world to encompass only work for so many years. Then my relationship with Erica had changed how I saw everything. Widening that view further to accommodate the possibilities of parenthood was new. Not unwelcome, but unsettling in its own way. The question of having children was never one I'd had to answer until circumstances threatened the possibility altogether. Then suddenly, the resounding answer in my mind was *yes*. I wanted to give Erica a baby. I wanted to watch her grow round with our child. I wanted that experience, as thrilling and terrifying as it seemed.

Everything was uncertain now. When, how, if... Worst of all, so much of it was beyond my control.

I could hack my way into some of the most sophisticated systems in the world, but I had no control over the science of her body and the damage that had been sustained there, the consequences of which still remained to be seen.

If the prospect of having a child with Erica was new and a little mind-boggling, being helpless to ensure she could have that experience turned everything upside down. I had wealth, influence, and technology at my fingertips. I'd worked for all of it and in many ways took for granted the level of control over my world that came with it. Now I had the woman I loved in my arms, and despite everything, we were at the mercy of chance and nature's whim.

The fact both frustrated and emboldened me. I'd do whatever I possibly could to bring us closer. Come hell or high water, I'd meet every need, wish, and desire she had. I tightened my hold on her a fraction, the fervency of my silent admission wreaking havoc on my emotions. "If this is what you want, it's what I want. And I'm ready if you think you are."

A small smile crept over her lips. "We'll never be ready. I think we just have to be crazy enough to try."

I locked my gaze to hers. "Believe me, I've been trying."

Her breathing sped up, and a shiver worked its way over my skin. I'd never said it before, but I'd been trying like hell since she'd healed enough for me to have her again. She hadn't gone back on the pill, and I'd been inside her every night. I'd fucked her deeper and harder than I ever had, secretly hoping that doing so would give her what both of us feared we'd never have.

The two of us would be enough. I'd never need another, only her in my bed, in my arms, every day of our lives. But this is what she wanted, and deep down, I wanted it too. This would be more, so much more than I could really comprehend right now.

Hope glimmered in her eyes, hiding the sadness I'd seen there before. "How can you have that much faith, after everything we've been through?"

I shook my head. "I don't know. I feel like if we want it enough, it'll happen. Or maybe I'm just not used to taking no for an answer."

Overcome with all the things I couldn't completely make sense of, I held her against me and kissed her again, more deeply this time. The soft press of her body was the sweetest kind of torture. The kiss became urgent, our tongues tangling. Her taste stirred my hunger. Her hips brushed against me, and I hardened. I wanted to claim her then, to sink deep inside her, again and again.

A groan left me, and I lifted her legs around me. She clung to me tightly as I walked us out of the pool.

Fingertips sliding over my scalp, thighs gripping my waist, she took over my senses as she'd done so completely, so many times before. I forced my eyes open between her kisses to find my way to the cabana next to the pool. I laid her down on the white terry sheet that hugged the lounging bed, and she tugged me down over her.

★ ★ ★

ERICA

My touch trembled over Blake's shoulders. Rivulets of water trailed over his skin and down the strands of his hair onto me. Behind him, the night sky was an endless blanket of navy. Stars shimmered through the sheer fabric draped around the cabana.

Moments ago, I'd been scrambling to escape from my unconscious, wrapped up in scenes I'd relived too many times. Now I was in Blake's arms, healed and whole, and the magnitude of what we'd shared moments ago had left me breathless. Could this be real?

I wasn't convinced that what he'd just asked me hadn't been a dream. I'd thought about it, of course. Every time we made love there was a possibility, but I'd never imagined that he was wishing for a baby too, that he was trying...

I wound around him, tangling our limbs as a surge of wanting coursed through me. He took my mouth, moaning. I could taste the love in our kiss, sweet against his tongue as he tantalized me with tiny delicious licks. His body was firm against me, every muscle flexing and taut as we moved over each other. Had there been a moment when I'd loved him more than I did now? I couldn't remember. My heart swelled against the walls of my chest, flooding my veins with a rush of potent emotion.

"I love you," I said, breathless when we separated. "God, I want you so much right now."

He trailed kisses along my jaw, down my neck, to the tender place below my ear. He sucked and nipped, sending shivers over my skin.

"Erica," he whispered against my neck, "I want to give you a baby tonight."

The sweet proclamation stole the air from my lungs and the words that wanted to follow. My doubts. My fears.

He'd wash them away anyway. He'd make them seem small and impossible in the face of what he wanted, *we* wanted.

"I want that too," I said quietly.

He drew a damp stroke across my cheek, holding me with his gaze. Moonlight glittered off the droplets on his skin. "I know you're scared."

I didn't want to admit to all those unspoken thoughts, but he was right. I only nodded, not wanting to give them a voice. Not tonight.

"I am too. If we're going to try...if we're really going to do this, I need to see it in your eyes. When I make love to you, I need you to believe it."

"I want this, Blake." My voice quivered, and my heart seized with emotion. "Make love to me...please."

I smoothed my hands over the hard planes of his chest and over his taut abs. His erection throbbed against me, hot and demanding. Grasping it, I circled him and stroked the soft flesh to the tip. He hissed, gliding between my fingertips with a slow thrust.

I grew slick, evident when he shifted so his erection slid against my folds. He repeated the motion, sending jolts of pleasure over my clit until I could no longer stand it. I pivoted my hips, hoping to guide him inside me. He grasped his erection, teasing the tip against my opening. I bit back a frustrated moan. The man loved to tease. Then, his focus riveted on the intimate place where we joined, he pressed into me slowly.

"Christ, you're beautiful."

He caught me by the knee, holding me open as he pushed in. I gasped for breath. The sensation of him filling me, of my body stretching for him, unraveled me every time. I pressed my fingernails into his forearm, a silent plea for him to claim me deeper.

"Watching my cock slide into you...it's almost too much. Makes me want to lose it every time."

I arched against him. "I want you deep."

Palming my breast, he groaned and covered my body with the heat of his own. The hair on his chest teased my nipples, now hardened and hypersensitive. He kissed me, thrusting deeply. Then he gave me exactly what I asked for, as he had every night since I'd become his wife.

Nothing had ever felt so completely right.

I sank my head into the pillows behind me and pulled him down to me. I wanted us as close as we could be. Nothing but the sound of the waves and my cries as he made love to me filled the air. I closed my eyes tight, waiting for the rush of sensation to take me over.

"Erica...look at me."

I opened my eyes, and the face of the only man I'd ever loved filled the frame of my vision. His lips parted with ragged breath. Each muscle flexing with effort. The vision was intoxicating...breathtaking.

We were all too human then, the vast ocean surrounding us and the tiny island we inhabited. We were two small beating hearts in this world, yet what we sought now seemed enormous. What we wanted and what could be created between us, a spark of life, so small and fragile, was too overwhelming to fully comprehend. My heart beat heavily in my chest with the weight of what we were trying for.

Energy radiated between us, heightened when he

closed his hand tightly over my hip, the other threading possessively with my own. His gaze held me, too intense to break away, except I was unraveling a little more each second. Possessed by his potent stare and the fierce way he claimed me, I clung to him in every way I could. Like a thread growing taut and tense, my body strained toward release.

"I've never wanted anything more than I've wanted you. Nothing in my entire life has ever possessed me the way you have," he said.

"I'm yours."

"Forever," he rasped, meeting my lips with a bruising kiss. He banded an arm around my hips, leveraging his weight and changing the angle of his thrusts.

"Blake!" His name was a plea on my lips, a desperate kind of praise for the perfect way he felt inside me.

His expression weakened. An almost painful vulnerability swept his gorgeous features as he took us closer to that heaven we found in each other.

"Now, baby. Let go. Come apart, just for me."

That quickly, the thread snapped. He was incredibly deep. In my heart. In my body. Lips crashing, skin afire, bodies one, we came together. Together we fell into that perfect place, landing safely in each other's arms. The sensation rippled over me, vibrating between us until we were both still.

We lay tangled in each other, the air perfectly warm around us. The low rolling of the waves against the beach was the only sound against our steadying breaths.

Closing his eyes, Blake exhaled heavily. "God, do I love you."

I sighed, surrendering to the warm weightless comfort of being in his arms. I danced my fingers lazily over his skin, over his broad shoulders, replaying what had just happened between us.

Tonight had been different. Tonight we'd shared something I couldn't name. Hope, or maybe faith. Grasping for a dream only we could make together, and believing that somehow it might come true.

A rush of emotion hit me, maybe harder than it normally would have in this vulnerable postcoital state. I closed my eyes to calm the burning behind them. Drawing in a deep breath, I slowed my caresses.

"I should go clean up," I said quickly, hoping to buy a few minutes to pull myself together. I didn't want to ruin this moment with my tears.

"No," Blake said, his body still nestled above me, inside me. "We need to let my little guys do their work in there. Stay put for a while."

I laughed quietly, trying not to consider the possibility that it could be a lost cause. I pushed the hair back from his face. His gorgeous eyes twinkled in the moonlight.

I shook my head. "You're determined, aren't you?"

He smiled under a tender kiss and laced our fingers together. "Oh, Erica, you have no idea."

"Oh, I think I do." I arched against him, all too aware of how determined he could be. So determined that ever since I'd met the man, my nights were long, and the mornings always came too soon.

He hummed, his eyes darkening anew. "You're making me hard again."

I trailed my toes up his calves until my heels met the

backs of his strong thighs. I lifted my hips and drew him into me fully again. His erection hadn't flagged at all since he'd come. He met the motion with a small thrust of his own, solid proof of his lingering desire. I tightened around him and relished the delicious friction that I'd tasted so recently.

"Then let's try again," I murmured.

CHAPTER THREE

ERICA

The honeymoon had been an escape. A beautiful, decadent escape. Then real life called us back home.

A week later, bronzed from the sun and restored from the last leg of our trip on an island that was beginning to feel like ours, we touched down in Boston.

Thin gray clouds obscured the sun and the threat of the impending winter greeted us. I shivered when a gust of chilled air whipped across the tarmac. A reminder of the inevitable passing of time.

As Blake and I disembarked, I spotted a black Escalade parked in the distance. We approached, and a tall thickly built man circled the vehicle. Clad in all black, he was a forbidding figure, but one I knew well.

"Clay!" I lifted high on my toes to hug the beast of a man who'd made it his job to protect us for the past several months. "We missed you."

He cracked a shy smile. "How was your trip?"

"Incredible, but we're glad to be home." Paradise couldn't last forever, after all.

"It's good to have you back." He looked to Blake. "Home?"

Blake nodded once. "Home."

Clay drove us north, putting the skyline of the city

behind us. The highway gave way to the one-lane roads curving along the coast through smaller towns. I took it all in. The steady flow of traffic, the familiar signs, rows of seaside homes overlooking the deep blue sea. Everything was home, yet somehow foreign. Even the destination, a house we'd yet to make a home, would seem strange after such a time away.

Here and there campaign signs still dotted yards as we passed them, some bearing the Fitzgerald name and slogan. Daniel was maybe the last person I wanted to greet me on my first day back, but he was everywhere. As our new reality set in, memories flooded me in an unwelcome rush.

After years of not knowing who my real father was, I'd found an old photograph of Daniel with my mother. I could still remember my anxiety about reaching out to him. I'd been a mix of scared and hopeful as I sat across from his desk and told him who my mother was. As intimidating as that experience had been, truly knowing the man behind the expensive suit, the high-rise offices, and the political machine driving his campaign had proven far more frightening. And yet fear wasn't all I felt when I saw his name and remembered his face.

There was disappointment, too, and beneath that, anger. After all those years, I had expected more. I'd hoped for so much more. A knot formed in my throat, and I suddenly wanted to rip the signs out of every yard we passed.

Blake reached across the space between us and caught my hand. "What are you thinking about?"

I stared blankly ahead. "Nothing." Nothing that he

wanted to talk about. I didn't hate Daniel, as much as maybe I should have. But I knew that Blake did. He'd understand my anger, but commiserating with Blake about it wouldn't bring me any closer to peace.

"He won, you know," he muttered.

Daniel had won. I rolled that news around in my mind a few times, imagining all the pomp and glory, streamers and symbols of patriotism, and the false pride. And then I thought about the darkness under the celebration, where all the things he'd done to secure his victory were hiding.

I wasn't sure how I felt about any of it. What could I really say? *That's good? That's too bad?*

Blake and I rode the rest of the way in silence as I contemplated whether to mourn or celebrate Daniel's news.

Clay deposited our luggage in the foyer, and a quick exchange with Blake guaranteed he'd be back to collect us for work in the morning. We meandered upstairs to the bedroom, where we quickly collapsed.

★ ★ ★

I woke to the bright morning sky and an empty bed. According to the note left on Blake's pillow, he'd left for work early. I groaned and contemplated sleeping more, but the thought of catching up with Alli and the rest of the people at the new office spurred me to action. I took my time getting ready, switching on the news to lure me away from the bed, where I could have easily slept for another eight hours. I poured my coffee, pausing at the mention of Daniel's name. The newscaster was reporting a recap from the election that had taken place the previous week.

Even though I hadn't spoken to Daniel in months, he'd surfaced in my thoughts often enough. We'd parted ways. Well, he'd decided to remove himself from my life. Mercifully? Perhaps. Sometimes I wondered what he would say if I tried to reach him again. Would he insist on keeping his distance?

Now that he'd won the governor's race, maybe he wouldn't say anything at all. Winning the election was everything he'd been working toward since before he'd loved my mother. I was certain that any importance I'd held in his life had faded well into the background of current events.

I switched off the television, determined not to devote any more thought to it. Despite my serious jet lag and mourning the end of our blissful honeymoon, I was looking forward to throwing myself into work—something I hadn't been able to do since selling the company.

The caffeine hit, and I took that as my cue to head in. Clay drove me into the city and dropped me at Mocha, the cafe that I'd often frequented at the old office. I hadn't been back since Blake's ex, Sophia, had fired Alli and I walked out, but I couldn't stay away forever. I scanned the sidewalks, half expecting to see Sophia, but I didn't recognize any faces.

Inside though, I immediately spotted Simone. While she served a nearby table, I found my usual spot empty and sat down. My phone buzzed as I waited and I read a text from Marie welcoming me home. I wrote her back, making tentative plans to catch up in the next week. I knew she'd want to hear all about the honeymoon and I couldn't wait to tell her. I'd missed her more than she knew.

Simone came up to me, her eyes wide. "Holy shit, who are you and what are you doing in my cafe?"

I laughed. "I came for my caffeine fix. And to see you, of course."

"Damn right." She joined me, sidling up on the opposite stool. "So what's up? I haven't seen you since the wedding."

"Nothing yet, really. Just catching up at work today, probably. How about you?"

"Same old scene here," she said, gesturing to the bustling cafe.

"How are the new neighbors?" I couldn't help but ask, since Mocha was steps away from the Clozpin office, but I braced myself for an answer that would hurt. Good or bad, any news would be salt on the wound.

Simone shrugged. "From what I can tell, the big boss, Perry, is in only a couple times a month. I haven't seen the girl at all. They hired some new programmers. Can't complain about that, though. They've turned into excellent caffeine-dependent customers."

"I guess they're still up and running, then." I wanted to be unaffected, but I couldn't hide the listlessness in my tone.

"Seems that way. I'm glad James didn't stick around. He's a lot happier working with the old crew."

James had been the last to jump ship after the change in ownership. The last news I'd heard was that Clozpin had been hacked and damaging information had been leaked about Isaac and Sophia that could spell the end of the venture. Apparently they had recovered and moved on. Maybe it was time I did the same.

"What's this?" I asked, pointing to the artfully designed heart drawn in fresh black ink down Simone's inner forearm.

"Oh, just some new ink." She touched one of the ornate details that curved around a black keyhole in the heart's center.

"It's beautiful. The detail is incredible."

Her cheeks suffused with pink. "James designed it. He's an amazing artist. He got one too. A key."

I dropped my jaw, blown away by the unmistakable meaning behind the two symbols. "Wow. That's permanent, you know."

She laughed. "Well, it's supposed to be. That's kind of the point."

"I'm so happy for you both." After everything I'd been through with James, I was incredibly grateful that he and Simone had found something real that I hoped made them as deeply happy as Blake made me.

Her eyes went soft as she traced the design back and forth. "I honestly had no idea if we could have a future when we first started hanging out, but that man has worked his way into my heart so deep that if something ever broke us apart, I'd want this memory anyway."

"He's lucky to have you, Simone."

She released a sigh, sounding as hopelessly in love as I often felt.

"He's been through a lot. So much that he probably never told you, Erica. But I've never met a man in my life who opened his whole heart up the way he has. It's like, when we stopped dancing around the friendship thing and just committed to giving the relationship a chance, nothing could come between us. No games, no bullshit. It's just us."

I swallowed over the emotion thick in my throat. "Jesus, you're making me cry. Knock it off."

She smiled, blinking away what seemed to be the beginnings of happy tears too. Stepping off the stool, she came around to hug me.

"I missed you," I said. The words threatened to set off the waterworks for real. I'd loved my great escape with Blake, but I'd missed my friends too, more than I realized until this moment.

She gave me a squeeze. "I missed you too. You and all your fucking drama."

I laughed when she pulled away. "Sorry about that."

"No worries. Keeps things interesting in my otherwise tedious life of coffee and croissants. No more getting shot and all that, though, okay? I kind of need you alive. Business suffers when you're not around feeding your habit."

I rubbed my fingertips under my eyes, catching any remnant moisture from my mini breakdown. "I'll do what I can."

She brushed her hand down my arm. "You'd better. All right. I have to get back to work."

"Me too. I have a ton to catch up on."

"No doubt. Hey, do me a favor. Slap James on the ass while you're there. Tell him it's from me."

I rolled my eyes with a smirk. "I'll save that one for you, Simone."

She laughed and waved me off.

I walked the few blocks to the new office in the building that Blake and I now shared. I climbed the stairs to the second floor and paused a few seconds in front of the frosted door that read *E. Landon, Inc.* I smiled inwardly.

Mrs. Erica Landon. I was enjoying the ring of it. I'd taken Blake's name with no objections, but professionally he hadn't made an effort to bring my projects under the umbrella of his company. And in a time when I was fast losing hope, he'd arranged for the office space that would allow me to work on new projects to fill the void.

Determined to keep the past in the past and embrace this next chapter in my life, I opened the door to it. Inside, the team—a mix of old and new—worked at their desks.

Alli squealed loudly when she saw me. "You're back!" She rushed to me and hugged me tightly. "And so tan!"

I laughed as we separated. "A week on an island will do that."

"I'm insanely jealous. But what are you doing here? I thought you'd take a couple days to settle in first."

I shrugged. "I couldn't wait."

Geoff and Sid caught my attention from their workstations nearby.

"How is everything going? What did I miss?" I asked.

Geoff's eyes lit up. "Tons. Where do you want to start?"

"Wherever you want. Bring me up to speed." A giddy feeling bubbled through me—a familiar eagerness to speak the language of business and technology, and being thrown into the flurry of details surrounding a cutting-edge project.

Sid rose and leaned against his desk. "We've got two new apps you can test out."

"Awesome."

"Hey, stranger." A deep voice rang out from behind

me. James appeared through the door. His nearly black wavy hair was disheveled and matched his long black T-shirt and jeans. He leaned in and kissed me on the cheek. "Glad you decided to come back."

"Well, I couldn't stay away forever. Anyway, I'm not sure I'd know what to do with myself without you guys keeping me busy."

"Happy looks good on you," he said, playfully tapping the tip of my nose.

His deep blue eyes seemed to see right into my soul, the way they always had. My friendship with James had morphed into something far more meaningful than anything I might have expected when I hired him to join the original Clozpin team. Our brush with romance had been brief and misguided, but I was grateful we hadn't lost the connection that had brought us there to begin with.

"Thanks," I said, giving him a little shove. "You too."

He brushed his hand through his hair, revealing the underside of his forearm and the fresh ink that matched Simone's so perfectly—an ornate vintage key, designed in black and white.

"Nice ink." I winked.

"Thanks." His slanted smirk broke into a wide grin. He nodded toward the back of the office. "Come on, let's meet in your swanky office. We've been dying to break it in."

"Sure."

The five of us spent the rest of the morning going over the progress that had been made. Geoff, the brainchild behind the wearable technology venture that I had decided to fund months ago, led me through the latest builds.

True enough, the team had covered a lot of ground in my absence, but gaps needed to be addressed and improvements had to be made before we could bring the apps to market. Hours passed, and I lost myself in the details.

When we broke for lunch, I tinkered around my office, the space that I hadn't had a chance to settle into yet. But for the first time since I'd come back, I felt like this was truly what I was meant to do. Despite everything that had happened to throw me off course, I was as ready as ever to dive back into work and try again.

"Happy to be back?"

I swiveled in my chair to find Alli leaning against the doorframe.

"I am," I admitted.

"We're happy to have you back. The family too, of course. Catherine and Greg are having a welcome-home dinner for you guys tonight."

"That's sweet of them."

Alli's lips quirked up as she twisted a strand of her straight brown hair.

"What's up? You look like you want to tell me something."

"Well, there will be an extra seat at the table tonight."

"Oh? Who's that?"

She dropped down into the chair across from my desk and lowered her voice. "Do you remember that hot bartender from the club, the one who you sent back to Sophia with those awful drinks?"

"Vaguely." The passing of time along with my slightly inebriated state that night had made the details foggy. I distinctly remembered Sophia's brief appearance the night of my bachelorette party, however.

"That's Fiona's new man."

I lifted my eyebrows. "Wow. Him?"

"I guess they've been seeing each other for a while, but now she wants to introduce him to the family."

"That's a big step." Considering I hadn't met or known of any of Fiona's boyfriends, I couldn't imagine how her new beau might be received. Then again, her family had been nothing but welcoming and kind to me.

"I know. I can't wait to see how it goes down."

I leaned back in my chair. "I feel like I've missed a lot."

"That's bound to happen when you leave the country for weeks and don't read any of your emails."

"No kidding. It'll take me a month to weed through everything. Even if it does, though, it'll have been worth it."

My thoughts skipped through any number of the incredible memories that Blake and I had shared on our trip. A part of me wanted to tell Alli about our baby discussion, but I wasn't completely ready to share all my hopes and fears around that topic yet. Time would tell, and no matter what happened, I knew she'd be there for me when I needed her.

"Maybe you can give me the highlights over lunch."

"Sure." Alli fidgeted with the hem of her shirt.

"What's up?"

"Um, well..."

"Alli..."

"You just got back. I don't want to bombard you."

"I came to work prepared to be bombarded. Fire away."

Her pretty brown eyes dimmed slightly. "It's about Max."

I waited for her to continue.

"He had his sentencing...for the assault."

"Oh." I'd made my statement months ago, and with everything else that had happened between the time he attacked me and now, I'd put the trial out of my mind. I'd said my piece and could only hope for justice now. "So what did they decide?"

"They found him guilty."

"Wow. I never realized how good it would feel to hear those words."

Relief washed over me, but the peaceful sentiment quickly mixed with the hundred other emotions that I'd attached to Max and what he'd done to me. Anger and uneasiness that so many people in our worlds knew what a compromising position he'd put me in. The smallest recognition of guilt even, that Max was facing justice because of my cooperation. His life would be changed forever by this. And yet, I reminded myself that I'd done nothing to instigate his attack. He'd drugged me and cornered me alone. If Blake hadn't intervened, Max could have raped me. Even though he hadn't, I believe that he would have.

"He got two and a half years."

My throat went tight, and I closed my eyes. My body seemed to react to the news before my head had a chance to really comprehend it. A minute passed and I found my voice. "That's half the maximum sentence."

"I know," she said quietly.

Nodding slowly, I straightened the papers on my desk that were already neatly ordered. "Well, that's justice for you."

"At least they're going to put him away. Even if it's not as long as he deserves."

Max was losing his freedom, at least for a little while. I wanted to celebrate that small victory, but a part of me couldn't trust that it would be enough to atone for what he'd done.

★ ★ ★

BLAKE

"Oh, I've missed you two!"

My mother clapped and went in for a hug. I bent to accommodate her shorter stature. One would think I'd just come home from war, but I could never blame her for loving too much. That was her way, and when she switched her attention to Erica, I was all the more grateful for it. The two women swayed side to side a bit, and any last-minute regrets I might have had about buying our forever home a few houses down from my parents' disappeared.

Erica deserved a family, and I couldn't ask for a better one than mine. I hadn't always appreciated them, but that was rapidly changing with Erica in my life.

My mother glanced between the two of us, up and down, giving us the full assessment. "Erica, you look better than I've ever seen you. Truly. All that travel must have been good for your soul."

Erica glanced up at me. "I think it was."

My mother smiled, her eyes wrinkling in the corners. She was an attractive woman, full of a contagious kind of energy, even more so with my father at her side. My father joined us, wearing his favorite apron. He wore the house chef title proudly since retiring. I used to see my parents and take their easy manner together for granted. Now I saw a familiar version of Erica and me. I saw forever with a woman I wanted to grow old with.

Dad slapped my arm and hugged Erica. "How are the lovebirds?"

"We're great, Dad."

He nodded toward the dining room, where my sister, Fiona, sat next to an unfamiliar man. "You came back just in time to meet the new guy."

"Oh! Yes, you have to meet Parker." A second later, Catherine was pulling us into the room and introducing us to the apparent guest of honor.

He stood. "Blake, pleasure to meet you."

"Likewise."

We shook hands, and Erica and I sat down across from the couple. I sized up the man whose arm was draped around the back of my sister's chair. Parker appeared to be my age, maybe slightly younger. Dark blond hair stylishly cut. He was dressed casually, in jeans and a button-down. He didn't look particularly expensive, but like he'd put an appropriate amount of time into his appearance.

His and Fiona's fingers hooked loosely together as my mother served up Dad's famous homemade meatloaf. I would have been a little more excited about a home-cooked meal and catching up with everyone, but found myself distracted by Parker. He turned and murmured something in Fiona's ear. She grinned and leaned into his touch.

I cleared my throat loudly, interrupting their moment. "So how did you two meet?"

Fiona's eyes widened. The question had come out with less finesse than I'd intended, but I was eager to know more about this stranger who meant enough to her to introduce to the family. I was also hoping to get him to stop nuzzling her at the table.

"Um," she started.

"We met at your wife's bachelorette party," Parker said, never taking his eyes off Fiona.

"Is that so?" I hadn't been wild about Erica going out on the town in the very tight, very short dress she wore that night, but naively I hadn't really considered Fiona being approached. My jaw tightened, a reflex to the unwelcome thought of Parker or anyone else getting physical with her after she'd been drinking.

"He was bartending, and he got my number before we left," Fiona said, her voice sweet and light.

I relaxed a little, her words having amended the vision my mind had conjured. Fiona was my sister first, but she had also been a good business partner, always focused and on point when she was dealing with my properties. I wasn't used to seeing her distracted, and while I'd always protect her as her big brother, she hadn't given me too many opportunities to. Perhaps because our brother Heath had required so much attention for so long. Now her new love interest was sitting across from me, not nearly as uncomfortable as I wanted him to be considering he was very likely fucking my sister.

"So that's what you do? Bartend?" I'd never been an elitist, but for some reason I couldn't resist the temptation to knock him down a peg.

"Blake..." Fiona's voice lowered.

"I'm in grad school," he continued, leveling a steady stare my way. "I bartend to make ends meet. My parents aren't putting me through school, so I'm paying my own way."

My father chimed in then. "That's very commendable, Parker. There's nothing quite like owning your successes. We're not strangers to hard work, are we, Blake?"

"I'm certainly not," I replied. "I can't speak for Heath, of course."

Heath smiled and made an offensive gesture, which thankfully our mother didn't notice. We chuckled, and the tension was broken for the time being. Dad had made his point. My wealth had changed our circumstances, but we'd come from a blue-collar family. Maybe I'd give Parker the benefit of the doubt, but not until I knew more about him.

"Erica, will you tell us about the new project you all are working on?" my mother asked. "Greg and I have been wanting to hear about it."

Apparently I was the only one interested in grilling the new guy, so I let Erica and Alli take over the conversation and talk about their work.

As dinner progressed, Parker made small talk with my parents and the others. If he'd been put off by my interrogation, he made no sign of it. By my side, Erica had barely touched her food. Her fork trailed through her potatoes.

"You okay, baby?"

She glanced up at me with a small smile. "I'm fine. I think I'm just exhausted. It was a long first day back."

Her words reminded me of my own fatigue. We'd hit the ground running as soon as we got back, which I was regretting about now. "Do you want to go rest?"

Eyes closed, she exhaled heavily. "I think so. I'm sorry, Greg. Dinner was amazing. Can I take some home with me?"

My mother got up from her chair. "Of course! Let me make you a plate."

Erica moved to leave, and I rose with her.

"I'll walk you home," I said.

"You don't have to."

I tucked a strand of hair behind her ear, grazing her cheek with the backs of my fingers. "I'd feel better if I did."

She placed a hand on my chest and smiled. "I'm fine. Enjoy time with your family. I'll see you when you get back. You don't have to rush."

I placed my hand over hers, rolling the pads of my fingertips over the diamond bands on her ring finger. Damnit, I hadn't seen her all day, and sharing her with my family tonight wasn't the same. I'd grown addicted to having her all to myself. As much as I'd neglected matters at work this past month, at a few points today I had entertained the idea of taking off with her again as soon as we could.

I relented. "All right, but call me if you need anything."

"I'll be fine." She brushed a kiss against my lips and left us for the night.

We finished dinner, and while my parents busied themselves with packing up the leftovers, Heath, Parker, and I had lingered around the table.

"So how's married life treating you?" Heath said, leaning way back in his chair.

"Very well." I reached for my beer, tipping the bottle to my lips. The past month had contained some of the best days of my life, and I was looking forward to many more.

"I still can't fucking believe you're married."

I lifted my hand, examining the thin platinum band I'd chosen. "Believe it."

Parker cleared his throat. "How about you, Heath? Are you and Alli looking to tie the knot?"

Heath lifted his eyebrows and let out a short laugh. "Not sure that's any of your business just yet."

Parker shrugged. "Just curious. I'm new here. I mean, when you find the right person…" He looked past us, to where Alli and Fiona sat chatting together in the living room.

I straightened in my seat, my muscles flinching under my sleeves, preparing to knock Parker into next week. "You've been seeing my sister all of a month."

He took a swig of his beer. "Closer to three, but who's counting?"

Heath shook his head with a laugh. "Can't argue with that, Blake. You locked Erica down with a ring after a few months."

"She's different," I muttered.

Parker cocked an eyebrow. "How so?"

"She doesn't have any big brothers, for one," I said, the threat in my voice unmistakable.

He pursed his lips with a nod. "Fair enough. Do you have some hoops you want me to jump through? Bank statements or something?"

I smiled. He had no idea, but I'd know more about his life than any employer would in a few hours. Bank statements would be the least of my findings. I shook my head. "Not necessary. If I have a problem with you, you'll know it. In the meantime, be good to her. *Very* good. She probably won't tell one of us if you break her heart, but I'll make a point to find out if you do."

"And what makes you think I'm going to break her heart?"

"Grabbing girls' phone numbers at nightclubs isn't a great testimonial."

He relaxed back in his chair. "Why do I get the feeling I'm going to be guilty until proven innocent when it comes to you?"

Parker's cool demeanor reminded me too much of my own. I wasn't sure if I liked that about him, or if Fiona should be running for the fucking hills. Either way, I wasn't going to waste any time scrounging up every last shred of information I could on him.

"Dessert, boys!" my mother called out from the kitchen.

"Thank Christ," Heath muttered.

I smiled inwardly, all too aware of Heath's general disinterest in dealing with conflict. He was the fun-loving one. He'd have better luck getting information out of Parker over drinks and a game of pool. Unfortunately, Parker would probably get more out of Heath, walk away with an ally, and then I'd have two skulls to crack. Such was my life as the eldest child and one I'd grown to accept.

I entertained a flurry of questions from Alli about the trip over dessert and took the first chance to excuse myself. The sky had grown dark. Erica was probably sleeping, but I didn't want to be away from her any longer than I had to. We'd spent nearly every minute together for the past month, and as much as I'd craved her presence before the honeymoon, I was downright dependent on it now.

I crept into our bedroom. The lamp at her bedside table cast a warm glow across her features, peaceful in sleep. My mother was right. Erica looked better, a thousand times better, than when we'd left. She never seemed to attach any great importance to her beauty, but that didn't diminish it. She took my breath away. In simple moments like this, wearing nothing but one of my T-shirts, she was a goddess, made just for me. Her chest moved with her steady breaths. I wanted to touch her, kiss her breathless, and make her mine.

Instead I switched off the light and left the room without a sound.

CHAPTER FOUR

ERICA

I poked at my eggs and toast, no less exhausted than I'd been the night before. I wanted to blame the time difference for my restless sleep, but my thoughts had been a jumble all day and likely had carried over into the night.

I'd wanted to talk to Blake about Max's sentencing, but a part of me was still coming to terms with it on my own. With all the money and influence behind the Pope family, I should have been grateful that he would serve any time at all. Men like him usually got a slap on the wrist for having their way with unwilling pretty girls. Mark hadn't been any different. A young man of privilege who had skirted past consequence for years.

Max too had grown up in the lap of luxury, with an incredibly successful family behind him. Now he'd be spending every day behind bars in the company of criminals. Would his hatred for Blake and me only amplify in that time? Or could he possibly change for the better? It was all too much to comprehend.

Blake stood silently in front of the coffeemaker, mug in hand, while the pot filled.

"Eager, are we?"

He made an unintelligible sound and rubbed his forehead.

"Were you up late?"

"Later than I expected." Unwilling to wait any longer, he filled his mug, placing the pot back in the cradle with a sizzle.

"Catching up with Heath?"

He turned toward me, his eyes tired. "No, something else."

"What did you think of Parker? You were giving him the third degree."

He sighed and slid a hand through his disheveled hair. "Yeah. I don't know. Something about him put me on edge, I guess. But he checked out fine."

I frowned. "What do you mean?"

Before he could answer, a loud knock startled me.

"I'll get it." He set his mug down and moved for the door. Beyond the threshold stood a man dressed in a brown suit.

"Blake Landon?"

Blake's stance in front of the stranger was wide and defensive. "That's me. Who the hell are you?"

The man narrowed his eyes at Blake, and my stomach burst into a flurry of nerves. Blake's cockiness had no bounds at times.

"I'm Agent Evans. I'm with the FBI." He flipped open his wallet, revealing his ID. "Can I come in?"

"No, but you can tell me what the fuck you're here for."

"Blake," I hissed.

He ignored me, staring the man down in the way he so often did when it came to people he didn't care for.

"I'm here to discuss the very curious results of the Massachusetts governor's election."

"What business is that of the FBI?"

The detective paused, a tight smile pulling at his lips. "When the results indicate voter machine tampering, it becomes the FBI's business. We'd appreciate your cooperation."

Blake's jaw locked, resulting in a twitch. He glowered a moment, and my heart dropped into my stomach, threatening the meager amount of breakfast I'd managed this morning.

The man's stare passed between us. "Mind if I come in?"

Blake didn't respond, but stood away from the door enough for the other man to enter. Evans looked to be in his early forties. He was taller than I was, but short next to Blake. His eyes were shrewdly narrow as he scanned our yet-to-be decorated home.

"Can I get you coffee?" I twisted my fingers together, unable to hide my anxiety about his presence. Voter tampering? What the hell had Daniel gotten himself into now?

Evans offered a smile that did little to ease my nerves. "That'd be great. You're Erica Hathaway?"

"Erica Landon," Blake corrected. "She's my wife."

"Right. Congratulations."

"Can we cut the shit? Why are you here?"

Evans casually tucked his hands into his pockets. "Is there a reason why you're being so contentious, Mr. Landon? I'm simply here to ask questions."

"I haven't had overwhelmingly positive experiences with the FBI."

"I'm aware." Evans's tone was low and full of meaning.

Blake cocked his head. "Are you?"

"I wouldn't be here otherwise, and I think you know that."

Blake exhaled. "So much for sealing the records."

"Your reputation precedes you."

"All I know is that you're in my house, and you still haven't given me a good reason why."

"Do you mind if I sit?"

Again, Blake didn't reply, and Evans made his way to the couch. I brought him his coffee and perched at the edge of the adjacent chair.

He took a sip from his cup and looked over at me. "I understand you just returned from your honeymoon. I assume you are aware of the election results?"

"Fitzgerald won...by a landslide," I said.

"That's true."

"What's so curious about the results?" I asked.

"Well...up until a few hours before the polling places closed, he was falling behind."

"That's not especially unusual," Blake said.

"It is when his votes in several districts exceeded the number of registered voters in those areas and pushed the election in his favor."

"Why would he do that?" The words fell out of my mouth, my disbelief obliterating any filter I should have had around this man who clearly wasn't here to make friends.

Evans shifted his stony stare from Blake to me, warming slightly. "That's what we're trying to find out. What's clear is that if Fitzgerald is behind this, he most certainly had help. Expert help."

He glanced up at Blake, the look in his eye communicating something that perhaps only he and Blake knew now. No doubt it had to do with Blake's rumored history as a computer hacker. He'd gotten into hot water years ago. But why would Evans be bringing this to him? Did he think Blake helped Daniel pull off election fraud?

My stomach roiled. I gripped the edge of the couch cushion as the blood drained from my face.

"Are you okay, Mrs. Landon? You don't look well."

I stood weakly. "I'm fine."

"You should go." Blake took a quick step toward Evans.

Evans rose on cue. "Sure. But you'll be coming with me. Mrs. Landon, you as well."

"Like hell. You can leave her out of this," Blake shot back, anger brewing behind his eyes.

Evans took a step toward him. "Mr. Landon, you're suspected of rigging the governor's election to tip in the favor of your wife's estranged father. We have questions, and we'd appreciate your cooperation."

Oh my God, no. I couldn't breathe. Bile rose in my throat. This wasn't happening. This couldn't possibly be happening...

"On what grounds?"

"You have motive. You have the resources to pull this off. And last, but certainly not least, you have the skills to do so."

Blake folded his arms across his chest. "You're going to need more than that to bring me in."

"And chances are we'll find it. We have a search warrant for your office downtown. They're confiscating your machines this morning."

"What the—" Blake took a menacing step toward Evans.

Evans brought his hand under his blazer to where his

firearm was holstered. I moved quickly, standing between the two men.

"Blake, please. Let's just go talk to them and clear this up."

I rested my hand on Blake's chest. His heart thundered under my touch. An intense energy rolled off him.

Evans sidestepped us and moved toward the door. "Let's do this the easy way. It's just questions. Let's get on with it."

★ ★ ★

ERICA

I waited for a long time in the interrogation room, staring down at the cold brushed metal of the table. I was cold too. From my fingers down to my toes, but that wasn't why I felt so numb. The initial panic had worn off on the drive into the city, and now a fog had settled over my thoughts, making everything slow and surreal. How could this be happening?

A sick feeling brewed in me. If the feds linked Blake to the voting fraud... I couldn't even fathom it. This wasn't a brush with the law like when he had pummeled the hell out of Max. He could be facing real time behind bars, for something he didn't do. My head fell into my hands.

The door opened, and through it walked Detective Carmody, a man whose face I wished I didn't know. He closed the door, shutting out the noisy office outside. He wasn't striking, but he wasn't a bad-looking man either. His eyes were tired.

He folded his thin frame into the chair across from me. "Erica. We meet again."

The first time we'd spoken, he'd asked about Mark's death. The case was closed now, but he was one of the first people to learn that I was Daniel's illegitimate daughter—a fact I'd failed to volunteer at the time. He already knew far more about me than I wanted him to.

"You know why we're here?"

"Blake didn't do this." As I said it, I was willing it to be true. I knew Blake. He wouldn't do this to me.

Carmody responded with an almost sympathetic smile. "How can you know that?"

"I just know. He'd never do anything to hurt me, and ruining Daniel's chances of winning would hurt me."

"By that measure, ensuring that Daniel won the race would be doing a service to you."

"It was obviously rigged. How does that serve anyone?"

Carmody sat back in his chair and paused. "How well do you know your husband, Erica?"

"A lot better than you do."

He nodded, a ghost of smile on his lips. "He has a past, you know."

"Are you saying that you're singling him out because of something he did when he was a kid?"

He leaned in. "Has Landon ever spoken to you about accessing information illegally?"

Before I could tell him to shove it, a middle-aged man pushed open the door and strode into the room. His nearly black hair was slicked back neatly and matched a simple black suit. His skin was pale, almost translucent, in stark contrast to his suit and hair. He regarded me with an impassive look before shifting his focus to Carmody.

"I'm Dean Gove, Blake's attorney. You were supposed to wait until I arrived to question her."

"We were just chatting," Carmody replied, his tone matter-of-fact. He rose. "I'm Detective Carmody."

The two men shook hands.

Gove frowned. "You're with the Boston police? I understood this was an FBI matter."

"There seems to be some question as to whose juris-diction this falls under. Clearly state laws have been bro-ken, so for now, we're all looking for answers."

So much for presenting a united front. I could only hope that any rift between his department and Evans worked in our favor.

Not bothering with introductions beyond a brief nod, Gove sat down beside me and pulled out a notebook and an expensive-looking pen. "All right. Tell us why we're here."

Carmody kept his attention on me.

"Let's start with Daniel Fitzgerald's campaign. His campaign manager confirmed that you were involved intermittently over the past several months. Is that correct?"

That sick feeling swept over me again. Goddamn Daniel. "Yes, that's true."

"Can you elaborate on that?"

"I've been running my own startup, so I didn't really have time to invest all my efforts into his campaign when he asked me to. I agreed to consult as needed with his mar-keting team to increase his social reach."

"You were previously estranged until this year, correct?"

I closed my eyes a moment. "Yes."

"Why would you participate in his campaign if you barely knew him?"

Good question. Blake would want to know that answer too.

"He's my father. When I found that out, I wanted to help."

He glanced down at his notes, scribbling something. "Okay. So you helped with marketing. Anything else?"

"No."

"What about Blake? He has even more resources than you do. How was he involved?"

I sent a tired look in his direction. I knew what he was doing, and I was sick over it. "He wasn't involved at all. He didn't even want me involved."

Carmody lifted an eyebrow. "Really. Why is that?"

Gove cleared his throat. "I think we're getting off topic here. Let's stick to the facts. Mr. Landon's feelings toward her involvement in the campaign have no bearing in this meeting."

"I'm not sure about that."

"Then you can take it up with him. Erica, you don't need to answer that. Move on, Detective."

Carmody scribbled more in his notebook. "Were you involved with the campaign work leading up to election day?"

"I just got back from my honeymoon. We've been out of the country for a month, so no."

"What about Blake? What was he working on?"

Nothing was the answer on the tip of my tongue. He wouldn't do this. He couldn't do this to me.

"Nothing that I know of. We agreed to unplug and pick up with work when we got back home."

"Are you certain of that?"

Was I certain? *No.*

"I'm certain," I lied. "We were together all day every day. If he was working on something, I would have known it."

Carmody stared at me. His eyes were an odd color. Dark blue with amber around the irises. My heartbeat quickened. I didn't know what any of this could mean, but at least to the FBI, it pointed to Blake's suspected guilt. Something inside told me that Carmody knew I was lying. But I'd lie all day long for Blake, if it kept him out of harm's way. There wasn't anything I wouldn't do for him now.

"When was the last time you spoke with your father?"

"It's been a couple months."

"Any reason for the gap in communications?"

I released a heavy sigh. I'd never feel comfortable discussing my relationship with Daniel with the authorities after what he'd done. This situation was no different.

"He didn't want to see me anymore."

"Why is that?"

I closed my eyes, remembering the last time we'd spoken.

You're my daughter. My only child. I love you, but it's time for me to go now.

My heart broke when he'd said the words. The same

empty kind of pain seared through me now as it had then. Pain that I'd kept under the surface, believing it didn't deserve oxygen. But everything about his rejection still hurt.

"After I was shot... he thought it would be better if he kept a distance."

"He shot the man who tried to kill you."

I nodded. "I know."

"How does that make you feel?"

Gove cleared his throat. "Is this all you have, Carmody? We didn't come here to discuss Erica's feelings about her father."

Carmody finally turned to acknowledge Gove. "Seems relevant to me."

"It might be, if you had any evidence against my clients, which you apparently don't." Gove tucked his notebook away and stood. "Where's Mr. Landon now?"

"He's speaking with Agent Evans."

Gove pointed at him with a glare. "If this was a ploy to get him alone with the FBI, I'm going to have your ass."

Carmody winced. "I'm not working with Evans."

Gove cursed under his breath. "What a fucking circus. Show me to Landon, and let's move on."

The detective's jaw tightened and he rubbed the stubble on his jaw. "Fine. You're free to go, Erica."

I stood, no less numb than I'd been moments ago. The fog had only thickened. I was sinking under the weight of everything being said. Gove caught my elbow and led me out of the room, through a few hallways, until we were in the busy lobby of the police station.

"I can wait here," I said.

"You should go home. Blake let me know Clay would take you. I'll swing Blake back home as soon as we're done here."

I glanced past him, as if I'd see Blake at any moment. I didn't want to be here, but I didn't want to leave him here either. "I'd rather wait."

Gove's eyes softened. "This could be a while, Erica. He wants you to go home."

My heart fell. "You take orders from him too, huh?"

He laughed softly. "For what he pays me, you're absolutely right."

"It'll be a small price if you can get him out of this mess."

"That's what I'm here for. Don't worry, all right? We're taking care of this." He nodded toward the automatic doors opening and closing in front of me, bringing gusts of crisp air into the lobby.

"Fine, but please have him call me as soon as he can."

"I'll give him the message. We won't be here a minute longer than we need to be. I need to get back there before they try to pull any stunts with him though."

Reluctantly I made for the doors. I caught sight of the black Escalade at the end of the block. Clay would take me back home, where I'd wait and wonder. I wanted more answers than I had, and I wouldn't know any more until they let Blake leave.

I pulled out my phone, went to my contacts, and pulled up Daniel's number. We hadn't spoken in ages, but if anyone could shine some light on this shit storm it might be him. After a minute, the ringing switched over to his voicemail. I hung up and sent off a short text, hoping somehow he'd help me get closer to the truth.

E: We need to talk. Please call me.

If Daniel had made arrangements to tip the votes in his favor, after everything he'd done to try to win, I wouldn't be surprised. If the loss of his stepson had once made him sympathetic to voters, an advantage he'd been well aware of when he'd put the hit out on Mark, I'd put nothing past him now.

But if Daniel didn't rig it…who did? The police clearly thought they had their man.

A few seconds later my phone chimed with a text.

D: Don't call. Don't text. Stay far away from all of this.

I cursed under my breath. He'd seen my call and ignored it. Bastard.

E: The FBI is talking to Blake. I need answers.

When he didn't respond, a truly hopeless feeling washed over me. Suddenly, more than anything, I needed Blake's reassurance that we were going to find our way out of this, but he was at the center of it, and I had no idea how long they'd keep him.

I'd started toward Clay when I heard my name. Something about the male voice that uttered it sent a shiver down my spine. I turned and my heart seized.

We were face-to-face, inches apart. Not yards, which is what the restraining order had dictated after he'd attacked me. This close, Max looked haggard. His usually cropped blond hair was unkempt and stubble lined his jaw. Always clean-cut, he was as worn down as I'd ever seen him.

A sickening mix of panic and revulsion spread through me. What was he doing here? The question caught in my throat but never passed my lips. I swallowed hard and took an unsteady step back.

"You're supposed to be—"

"The judge gave me some time to get my business affairs in order. I'm being processed today." He shook his head, and his lips drew back in a bitter smile. "Can you imagine it, Erica? Having your freedom ticking down by the minute?"

My adrenaline surged. We were in public, but it didn't make me feel any safer. My lips trembled as I found my voice. "I have a restraining order. You can't be here," I insisted, praying he'd turn around and leave.

He took a step toward me, regaining the distance between us. "Won't matter soon."

I took another step back, blood thundering in my ears. "I have to go." I had to get the hell out of here, and fast.

"Wait." He caught my arm, keeping me from fleeing.

I struggled for air, fear shooting through my veins. "Let me go!"

He grimaced and tightened his hold, painfully pinching my skin. "He'll ruin you. All of you." He spoke the words through gritted teeth.

I twisted away and stumbled backward, nearly falling to the pavement. I caught myself when he let me go. As I put a few steps between us, he stood stock-still, his eyes devoid of emotion.

"He'll ruin you . . . the same way he ruined me." There was something final and hopeless in his tone.

In a flash, Clay was between us, obscuring Max's figure with his broad frame. "Sir, back away."

"We were just talking."

"I'm not going to have any choice but to physically move you if you don't start walking in the other direction right now."

"She'll never see me again. Trust me."

Clay stood his ground and Max turned. Hands stuffed in his pockets, eyes cast to the ground, he climbed the stairs to the police station and disappeared into the building I'd just left.

"Are you okay?" Clay turned to me.

"I'm fine . . . I'm fine." But other than the violent tremors coursing through me, somehow I was frozen in place, unable to take the next steps toward the car that would take me home.

"Mrs. Landon?"

Worry filled Clay's eyes. My own brimmed with a rush of tears that spilled down my cheeks. Without thinking, I reached for him. I felt like a child hugging an oversize stuffed animal. Clay's enormous arms enveloped me with an embrace that seemed too gentle for his strength. I buried my face in his T-shirt and sobbed. He hushed me, and after several moments, I caught my breath.

"I'm sorry." I wiped at my tears feebly.

"It's okay. You're upset."

"I . . . I guess I wasn't expecting to come home to all of this."

"I understand."

I released an uneven breath. If anyone understood, maybe Clay did. He was paid to be on alert, to protect us from all those who would try to hurt us. Maybe he could fathom a fraction of what I now felt. "Thank you, Clay. For everything."

"You never need to thank me for doing my job."

"I know, but I want to."

He rested his palm on my shoulder. "Let's take you home."

"I want to wait for Blake." Oh, how I wished they would let him go. I hated knowing that he was in that building, and that I had to walk away from him right now.

"He'll be home soon. And I'll stay there as long as either of you need me."

I stood firm, unwilling to leave. His countenance was pinched. "You should rest, Erica."

Hearing him say my name almost threatened to unleash another wave of tears. Another minute passed and my shoulders sagged.

"Okay," I finally said, and let him take me home.

CHAPTER FIVE

BLAKE

The interrogation room was cold, lit by harsh fluorescents. Nothing about it was designed to make a person feel comfortable, yet I was decidedly far from seeking comfort, unless it was in the form of physically removing the smug look from Evans's face. I hadn't liked him the moment I saw him. Instinct immediately warned that he was going to cause me nothing but trouble. Rarely were my instincts far off, and now we were several hours into him giving me trouble.

Dean Gove—my attorney and, for all intents and purposes, my longtime friend—sat beside me, looking both bored and unsettled. We hadn't had a chance to speak freely yet, but nothing substantial had materialized in the time I'd been here. At Evans's request, I'd detailed the timeline of the honeymoon and travel schedule. I had nothing to hide there. We discussed business, mine and Erica's. That was straightforward enough. We discussed my history with Fitzgerald, which was carefully edited to omit the laundry list of felonies I knew he'd committed, not the least of which was homicide. For all Evans knew, Daniel was simply the biological father of my wife, though no doubt Evans suspected more. I was hoping he would steer the conversation toward the actual election soon, the details of which would explain why we were having this conversation at all.

After a brief break, Evans returned with two Styrofoam cups of coffee and a manila envelope tucked under his arm. He set one cup in front of me. Out of sheer boredom, I accepted it. The dark liquid was scalding hot and tasted like it had been on the burner for hours. I set it back down with a grimace.

"This isn't your first brush with computer fraud, is it, Blake?"

Dean leaned in. "Don't answer that."

No shit. I glared into Evans's small eyes. He already knew about my past, I had little doubt.

I'd been nabbed for hacking as a teenager. Back then when the feds brought me in, I'd cooperated. The charges were dropped, and the records were sealed because I was a minor. Rumors lingered, though, especially when a year later I produced the most sophisticated banking software on the market, thanks to my extensive experience in compromising what was already out there at the time.

Whatever Evans knew had to be the result of the FBI's desire to come back and get their pound of flesh. I'd gotten away with my freedom, while others had lost so much more. Still, he wasn't supposed to know about any of it, and I certainly wasn't going to offer it up.

"Fuck you," I said.

He laughed, shaking his head. He spun the folder on the table in front of him. My curiosity piqued, but the folder couldn't contain any actual evidence against me. He was taunting me.

"Let's try this again. You wrote the earliest software created for Banksoft, right?"

I paused. "Yes."

"Correct me if I'm wrong, but you had what one would call 'specialized knowledge' of banking software at that point, isn't that right?"

The asshole was persistent, but I was willing to bet only one person in the room had a genius IQ. "Get to the point."

"Interestingly enough, there is shared code between certain types of banking software and the software that's used to run voting machines."

"I'm well aware of that." Any programmer worth his salt knew that. Evans was clearly enjoying this foray into technical jargon, but I was quickly becoming bored with it and hoped he'd get to the fucking point.

He smirked. "I'm sure you are."

I willed my fists not to clench under the table.

"Blake, we've been looking at the binaries that were installed onto the voting machines, and we found something interesting. The encryption routine used is the same one you designed ten years ago . . . for Banksoft."

That would certainly explain why I was here.

"Show me the rest of it," I said in a controlled tone.

He drummed his fingers on the envelope, glancing down at it. "It's being carefully reviewed by our team."

I ground my teeth down and registered the twitch in my jaw as I did. Something about the past few minutes had become all too familiar. Assumptions made, accusations thrown, and a bunch of men in suits trying their damnedest to back me into a corner. Fear knotted in my stomach. But I wasn't a kid anymore, and I wasn't going to be intimidated into a bad situation, especially for something I had no part in.

Evans spun the folder methodically and waited, as if he was expecting me to crack.

I leaned in, increasingly pissed now that he was withholding information that would clear this up for me. "Listen to me. It's a small miracle your team was able to identify the encryption and match it to my code. Let me see the rest of it, and I'll show you what you're not finding."

Evans bared his teeth with a sneer. "Wouldn't that be convenient?"

"For both of us, it would seem." I stifled a growl. I wanted to wring this guy's neck.

"How about you tell me who rigged the machines?"

I sat back and let out a short laugh.

"Did you have help?"

"I have no fucking idea what you're even asking right now."

Evans's expression grew less mocking and more serious. "It's pretty simple. If you didn't do this, who did?"

I had a few ideas. Someone who did sloppy work and had retribution on the mind. Someone who'd love to know I was sitting here, getting grilled by the FBI. But still, I couldn't be sure.

I couldn't take credit for the skewed election results, but I hadn't always been so innocent. And Evans wasn't the only one who knew it.

I'd been a troubled adolescent—aimless, angry, and too intellectual for my own good. When I'd joined the hacker group M89, the few members in its ranks had been wreaking havoc on small websites with minimal impact. Brian Cooper was the group's leader, and together we came up with a plan that I had the expertise to put into action. A group of Wall Street executives were trying to ruin the whistle-blowers threatening to expose their Ponzi scheme. It was a small story in the news, buried under hundreds of other stories of injustice in the world, and together we'd decided to do something about it . . . something big.

The code I'd ultimately write would deplete the bank accounts of those executives and fund our group to do more, to punish the people who deserved to lose everything they'd stolen. Except weeks before we were ready to act, the plan changed. Brian wanted to broaden the net and use the code to skim small amounts from other accounts, accounts held by people who hadn't done anything wrong other than trust those execs with their retirement money.

I was young and bent on a misguided kind of justice, but what Brian wanted wasn't justice. I refused to go through with it, so we parted ways. When Brian released the code, the feds caught us both. Scared as I'd been, I'd told the truth, and when they turned to Brian for answers, he didn't last long. He'd taken his own life days after we were taken into custody, an outcome that I'd spent too many hours since wondering if I could have prevented.

Trevor was Brian's younger brother. Not unlike Brian, he'd turned into an amateur miscreant, fueled more by vengeance than skill. He'd dedicated his life to ruining me because of Brian's death. His stunts aimed at fucking with my businesses, or Erica's, had grown in scope over time, but this might be beyond even him.

"Show me the code, Evans, and I can probably figure it out for you."

He was still a moment and finally stood, his chair screaming along the concrete floor. "We've got you on this, Blake. One way or the other, you're going down. You should figure out now how you want to play it. Let me know when you want to talk."

"If you had anything on me, I'd be in handcuffs."

"You're one of the only people with access to the original source code."

"Banksoft has more than ten thousand employees. I'm sure a few of them have access. Why don't you start there?"

He bent and placed his hands on the table. "Because they don't have a motive. An election is rigged right in your backyard, guaranteeing your father-in-law the governor's seat. All signs point to you, a known hacker."

"Rumored," I clarified. "And you're overlooking one minor detail. I wasn't in the fucking country when it happened."

"You have a whole team working for you, trained by you, paid to do your bidding. I wouldn't be surprised if a man of your means decided not to handle a matter of this nature personally."

He was dead wrong there. If I had done it, I sure as hell would have taken care of it personally. But I hadn't, and the fact that they could turn their focus on any of the people who worked for me only spiked my growing irritation.

"If you're so convinced I'm behind this, prove it. Open up that little envelope of yours and let's see it."

Picking up the envelope, he straightened. "Trust me,

I plan to prove beyond a shadow of a doubt that you're behind this."

Dean rose beside me. "Sounds like you haven't yet, so I think we're finished here."

★ ★ ★

The drive home from the station was long, but somehow not long enough. Not enough road to settle the thoughts blasting through my brain. Dean drove me home in silence. I had no desire to talk after hours of questioning.

My first impression of Agent Evans had proven accurate. He was a pissant of a human, and cocky to boot. He thought a shiny badge and a cheap suit gave him authority. He wielded whatever information he had with nauseating swagger, his only real power built on a foundation of inefficient bureaucracy and a sliver of information that he shouldn't even have access to. He'd damned me before he'd stepped through the front door.

I remembered men like him, droves of them who'd been brought in to intimidate me and the others in the original M89 group. Now they were demanding that I supply them with a lie that would damn myself. I'd harnessed every ounce of willpower I possessed not to give him an answer that would physically shut him up.

If not for Dean's reassurances and the fact that I trusted him more than I trusted almost anyone, I would have told Evans to fuck himself, gone home to Erica, and waited for my name to clear on its own.

"They'll want to talk to your family tomorrow to establish a timeline."

Dean broke my internal tirade as I stared out the window. They'd involved Erica, and now the rest of my family would be subjected to this goddamn odyssey.

"They'll cooperate."

"I figured as much. I'm more concerned with what the feds are going to find on your machines at the office."

I stared at the man beside me. He was older than me, but had a youthful look about him. It was almost disarming, until you learned firsthand how shrewd he could be.

"Is this time for my confession?"

He let out a short laugh. "Might be a good time for it, so I can be prepared for whatever they throw at us. I would have liked to have talked to you before Evans pounced, but you did well in there. They definitely don't have anything on you yet, which is promising. He seems determined, however."

"They're not going to find anything. I'm always careful."

We never discussed it at length, but Dean understood. I'd even helped him through a few tough cases by accessing files that he'd never have been able to uncover on his own—legally, anyway. I paid him well, but he owed me. Whatever went down here, he wouldn't sleep until it was resolved. That much I knew.

"They won't just be looking for a tie to the voting machines, Blake. They'll be looking for anything. Any instance of wrongdoing to hold you. Do you understand that?"

I fisted my hand on my lap. Fucking FBI. Even though I'd been creative with my fact-finding on occasion, I'd never truly believed that I would have to face them again. Not like this.

"I guess they'll find what they find then."

Dean slowed to a stop behind the Escalade already parked in the driveway. "I need to know if they're going to find anything that we need to take care of."

"I'm careful, Dean, all right? I've been doing this all my life, and I know how to cover my tracks. Whatever they find will be bullshit. Easy to brush away."

"I hope you're right, because if they find a pinch of evidence, they're going to turn it into a lot more than you might expect."

I clamped my jaw tight. What a fucking mess this could turn into...and for what? Someone who either wanted Daniel to win, or to ultimately lose over all of this.

"What is Fitzgerald saying?" I asked.

"I'll find out soon. I'm guessing he had a long day at the station too. I plan to get more information from his camp tomorrow and gauge his position. Do you think he'll try to implicate you?"

"If it saves his ass, he would." I'd have liked to think he wouldn't for Erica's sake, but the man had no soul. I couldn't take anything for granted.

"I guess we'll find out in the morning. Let's meet at my office early and start running through everything."

I sighed and stepped out of the car, eager for a breath of fresh air. Hours in a cage with a steady diet of subpar coffee. I was edgy and needed to get away from all of it. Before I shut the door, Dean called out.

"Blake?"

I leaned down and peered into the car. "What?"

"Don't lose any sleep over this, okay? You know me. I'm just trying to be thorough. We'll figure it out."

CHAPTER SIX

BLAKE

Inside the silence was broken only by the low rumble of the waves crashing against the seawall. A storm was coming in. Upstairs I found Erica sleeping in our bed. I went into the adjoining bathroom and turned on the shower, wanting to wash away the shittiest day on recent record.

Under the water, I tried to take Dean's parting advice and let everything go, at least for tonight. But there was no way. Evans's questions and his condescending fucking face filled up my thoughts. Every contingency plan spun through my head. I replayed every hack I'd executed that could possibly trace back to me. Sure, a part of me took for granted that I was good enough never to get caught again. But here I was...under the microscope of the authorities...again.

The feds had come after me and Brian Cooper years ago, and when it was all said and done, he had taken his own life. Ours had been a friendship gone wrong, and the day he died, everything changed. I changed.

When the FBI let me go all those years ago, I didn't register relief. Only guilt, frustration, and, eventually, renewed determination. I hadn't sworn off hacking, but I'd sworn I'd never get caught again. And I'd sworn no one would ever meet the same fate Brian had because of me.

When I meddled, I worked alone, and when it came to the business, my team played it straight with no exceptions.

My reputation had already been tainted, so I held myself to a different standard. Some might call what I did cheating, but I wasn't above circumventing the systems that society put in place to keep the truth beyond reach. It wasn't my fault the people building the systems weren't smart enough to keep them from being vulnerable.

When I met Michael Pope, he took that philosophy and turned it into purpose. He'd seen an opportunity that someone with my particular talents could take advantage of. I didn't care about his money, and he knew it. I'd had no interest in spending my life building software for corporations, but he made me realize that doing it once, the right way, would give me freedom…the kind of freedom I'd been thirsting for. Now, out of nowhere, my freedom was in question again. And I had a hell of a lot more to lose.

I toweled off and returned to the bedroom. I had no chance for sleep, but seeing Erica curled up in our bed reminded me that even a few seconds beside her might bring me down. I slid behind her quietly, breathing her in. A mix of shampoo and her natural scent. I wasn't sure what it was about the way she smelled, but as soon as she was in my lungs, something in my muscles released. I held her closer, wanting more of that magic only she could wield over me. She moaned quietly, a sound that went directly to my groin.

She turned to me with tired eyes. "Blake." Her voice was hoarse from sleep.

She was stretched out on her back, wearing only a

black tank and a pair of black lace panties that I wanted to peel off with my teeth.

"You're back." She slid her hand up my bare chest.

I brushed a soft kiss against her lips. "I'm back."

"Is everything okay? What happened?" Her eyes were wider now, more alert.

The concern in her voice was evident, and as much I wanted to calm my own fears, I wanted to obliterate hers.

"Everything's fine. Go back to sleep, baby. We can talk tomorrow."

I skimmed down her bare arms, unsuccessful in my attempts not to take in every curve. God, she was beautiful. More than that, she was my salvation.

"I missed you," she whispered.

She guided me back down to her lips, which I fully welcomed. I want to let her rest, but my body wasn't going to allow it. She wasn't making it easy either, sliding the tip of her silky tongue over my bottom lip before biting it gently. I groaned and took her mouth in a long and hard kiss, channeling all the day's frustrations into our connection.

Fuck. I was hard as stone against her. There was no hiding how badly I wanted her. She lifted her leg over my hip, arching into me, transforming my longing into a rock solid need.

"Erica... I'm not going to be able to stop myself if you keep doing that."

"I don't want you to..." she murmured.

I inched my hand between her legs and cupped her firmly, as if I were staking a flag that told the world she was mine, and the warm heaven under my palm was also mine. She whimpered, lifting into my touch.

Maneuvering past the barrier of her panties, I dipped into her wet heat. I groaned and kissed her neck, inhaling the musk of her skin. A fragrance heaven made just for me. I resisted the urge to take my tongue all over her body right now—a journey I'd made many times, every time more delicious than the last.

I withdrew my hand, sucking the flavor of her from the tip of each finger. I craved her more than she'd ever know. My heartbeat raced and my mind ran rampant with all the devious things I could do to her. If her scent bewitched me, the taste of her body—the salty sweetness of her skin, the honey between her thighs—made me downright feral.

I couldn't make love to her tonight. I had to have her my way.

Her lips parted as she grabbed at me, caressing and tugging us closer. I rocked into her, adding the pressure of my thigh between her legs. She whimpered.

I tasted her lips, sucking and nibbling. "I can't be gentle. Not tonight." It was a warning, and a promise.

Her gaze flickered to mine, a silent understanding in the darkness. "Then don't be." She softened beneath me. "I've been waiting for you..."

That's all I needed. I silenced her with another fierce kiss. All-consuming, all taste and need. She was so fucking sweet. The line of her torso moved like a wave against me, enflaming my skin everywhere we touched. She loved me, I knew, but I never tired of the evidence that no matter where her mind was, with very few exceptions, her body wanted what I wanted. I could only hope that tonight I could walk that fine line and give us what we both needed.

She made a small sound of protest when I finally tore myself away.

"Come here," I said, standing beside the bed. My stance was wide, every muscle coiled tight. My cock throbbed for the touch I'd be demanding soon.

She slid across the sheets and stood before me wordlessly, a hair's breadth away. Close enough that I could feel her heat and smell her arousal. Finding the edge of her tank top, I guided it up slowly, prolonging the moment until I'd see all of her. I tossed the garment aside and withdrew my touch, a small torture in itself. She swayed toward me, but I caught her wrists, holding her safely away.

Something came over me then—a calm reassurance that didn't diminish but only quieted the fierce longing raging through my veins. The promise of controlling her pleasure now, of drawing out every last second of it, leashed the animal inside me that wanted to gorge on every inch of flesh before me.

"Panties off. And then I want you on your knees." My tone was sharp and unforgiving.

In an instant, I could sense her heat multiply. Her breathing turned shallow. The rapid beat of her heart drummed at her wrists where I held her. Without a word, she slipped from my grasp and slid her panties down. Lowered to her knees, she gazed up at me, smoke and fire in her eyes. Lust powered through me, and the line of desire shooting straight to my cock threatened my plan. I stepped away to grab a few items from a nearby drawer. Returning, I crouched in front of her, binding her wrists together with a pair of leather cuffs she knew well.

"You know your safe word."

She swallowed. "Yes."

Whenever I mentioned the safe word, I had the feeling it gave her equal measures of anxiety and reassurance. I imagined the fighter in her never wanted to have to use it. The irony was that between the two of us, I was the only one who had.

I lifted to my feet, anticipation rattling through me. The sight of Erica bound before me, peering up at me, was almost more than I could handle. Reaching down to her, I traced her lower lip, over the curve of her cheek and along her jaw, until I sifted my fingers in her hair. She gasped at the firm tug, her eyes going liquid. I grasped my cock with my other hand, stroking from root to tip.

"I want to taste you...please." She licked her lips as she spoke.

She clasped and released her fingers in her lap. Her fear, it seemed, had transformed into desire, and I reveled in the transformation every time. Blood surged to my cock. My thighs bunched with renewed restraint. I drew in a steeling breath, one that would hopefully keep me from losing all my resolve and coming the second she wrapped her sweet lips around me. I teased the tip of my cock against her lips.

"Slow," I ordered. I was going to draw this out until we were both mad with the need to fuck.

She sighed, a sound full of relief and wanting, and lifted on her heels. Flicking her tongue lightly over the crown, she claimed her ground, a centimeter at a time. I would have closed my eyes, but I didn't want to miss a second of her submission. I cursed inwardly at the painstaking pace I'd demanded. My instinct was to control her, tighten my grip on her hair, and move her over me in a series of firm thrusts that would take me over the edge. Fighting it, I loosened my hold and let her set the pace—one that was slowly driving me insane as I disappeared inside her warm, welcoming mouth.

Fuck. If it was possible to show tenderness this way, she was, with every tantalizing stroke of her tongue. Then she took me to the back of her throat, a blunt pause between the careful sheathing of my cock into her mouth. The sensation was electric, dizzying, and ignited a change in my own need—the need for something far from tender. Unable to hold back anymore, I gripped her hair, angling her, opening her farther so I could thrust. She moaned and I went deeper, quicker, until I was close. Too close for what I wanted tonight.

Today wouldn't be erased this way. Simple release would only leave me hungry. I wanted to shatter her and let her tight little body shatter me too. Maybe somewhere in this fucked-up dance we could find some peace and sleep dreamless through the night. I needed to take her over the edge...with me...together.

I withdrew from her mouth. Her lips glistened, full and swollen. Her eyes were misty and heavy-lidded. Suddenly I was lost. Lost in the perfection of the woman before me. She was everything to me. Then a new and unwelcome thought began to haunt me.

God...what if they find a way to take me from her?
No—fuck no.

"Stand up," I ordered softly.

She rose and I walked her to the bedpost at the foot of the bed.

"Lift your arms...higher."

I helped her, hooking the small length of leather strap between her wrists to an obscured piece of hardware hidden at the top of the bedpost disguised as decoration. We were face-to-face, a breath apart. She lifted to her toes, her body stretched out beautifully in front me. I molded my palm to the ample curve of her breast. I skimmed down her rib cage, over her hip, and down her thigh. Admiring. Craving.

"It's like someone carved your body out of my dreams. These..." Lowering my head, I took her nipple between my lips, flicking over the hard rosy tip with my tongue. I released her with a pop. "These are divine."

With a breathy sigh, she bowed into the intimate kiss as much as her bonds would allow. I took more, sucking her harder, massaging the other until her sighs turned to moans. The hook that bound her above clanked. My little fighter...I loved her fight. Almost as much I loved breaking her down. Looping my arm around her waist, I drew her to me tightly. My teeth came down around her nipple while I twisted my fingertips firmly around the other.

She let out a small yelp, pressing her hips forward. The tortured groan that followed was an intoxicating mix. Pleasure and pain. I'd give her both tonight.

"I'm going to punish you now, sweetheart."

She widened her eyes, her breathing growing rapid again. Her anxiety came in a flush of red across her cheeks.

"Not because you deserve it." I paused, wondering how I could explain it—this game between us and what it really meant for me. I reached around her to the bed, picked up the blindfold I'd retrieved earlier, and positioned it over her eyes. "I can't explain why, except that I need it."

"Blake, it's okay..."

She trapped her trembling lip between her teeth. My heart sped up at the sight. My sweetest gift, always so ready to accept this darkness inside me, to shine light on it until it became something different, something that was only ours. I thumbed her lip loose, covering her mouth with mine, taking her next breath for my own.

"How could I ever live without you?" I whispered against her.

"Blake." Her voice was unsteady.

I squeezed my eyes shut, grateful she couldn't see the pain inside me then. Fuck, I was losing control. That quickly, she'd brought the dominant in me to heel. Her willingness, her love.

I swallowed hard, backing away before I took her right then. Spinning her to face the post, I pulled her hard against me. She lifted, rubbing her ass against my cock. The smallest of touches made me crazy for her. I stifled a groan and returned to the drawer. Decisions had to be made, and I was hardly in a state to make a good one. Impulsively, I grabbed a flogger. The tails of this one were long and moderately heavy, designed to give her the pressure she'd been used to, which had never been especially light. We hadn't toyed with this one yet, but I knew she could take it.

Standing behind her, I admired the writhing body before me, bound and alive with want for the pleasure I was going to give her.

I whirled it once, so the tails struck her thighs and ass. Once more across her shoulders and upper back.

She sucked in a breath and shivered, the muscles in her shoulders tensing before releasing again. I waited, a silent question.

Faint pink lines formed on her skin where the tails had struck. I repeated the motion. A figure eight of measured contact, across her shoulders, ass, and thighs.

She flinched, and then hummed softly. I could almost see the adrenaline sliding through her veins, the endorphins taking over, making this so much more than pain.

By some miracle, she loved taking it as much as I loved giving it. I wanted to feel guilty for making her this way, but she'd begged for it. She'd demanded that I take her to the darkest, dirtiest places of my mind, and I wasn't strong enough to say no.

With a flick of my wrist, the flogger made contact again. Back and forth, up and down; careful to avoid the middle of her torso, I painted her the loveliest shade of pink.

Her small cries and gasps turned into moans. Slowly she gave up her fight. Fists loose, she let her head rest against her arm. My own desire became nearly unbearable. My head buzzed with it. My cock ached for it.

I let the leather handle slip from my grasp and went to her, winding my arm around her front. She trembled in my arms, her skin slick with sweat. Electricity rolled off her in waves. On the edge, she was exactly where I wanted her.

"You still with me, baby?"

"I can take more." Her voice was raw with emotion and adrenaline.

I hushed her. "No, sweetheart. You've had enough. You were so beautiful...so willing. I can't tell you..."

The words caught in my throat. I rested my forehead

against her shoulder, the heat of her punished skin matching the searing heat of my body. "Let me show you what it means to me."

"Kiss me. Touch me," she begged.

I skimmed over her shoulder, following the trails of pink with my mouth. Down her back, over the round curves of her ass, I rained kisses on her tender flesh. A thousand tiny apologies for the satisfaction it had given me to test her this way. I rose and made my way to her neck, flicking my tongue against her racing pulse.

"I love you, Erica. You're everything. Goddamn, you undo me."

She mewled, a quick lift of her toes creating more friction between us. I slid my hand to her front to the apex between her thighs. She cried out, shaking. She was drenched, and so close.

I withdrew and turned her slowly to face me. Her skin was flushed as much from her excitement as her punishment. I resisted the urge to kiss her everywhere, to feel every inch of her energy under my lips. This was exactly where we needed to be.

She tugged feebly at her bonds. "I can't see you."

I clenched my jaw, already feeling more vulnerable than I wanted to. "Not tonight. I want you to feel me, and you're about to feel all of me. Now wrap your legs around me."

I caught her by the knee, helping her. The swift motion opened her to me, revealing the moisture of her arousal slick down her inner thigh.

"Christ." The sight robbed me of the last shred of control. If she weren't so primed, I'd worry about beating her to the orgasm we both hungered for now. I took her other leg and wrapped her around me. Easing the tension in her arms still stretched high, I positioned myself inside her by the tip.

I growled, parting with my last ounce of restraint. Then I speared into her, joining us suddenly and completely. Her body gave no resistance, as if we were always meant to be this way.

"Blake!"

The wail that came from her lips shattered me. Heat licked down my spine as her inner walls tightened around me. The furious need to fuck took over, and instinct spurred me into a rapid string of thrusts. Her cries came unfettered, unfiltered, between her breathless gasps. I was unhinged. Nothing could slow me down. The slap of skin and the creak of the bed sustaining the pressure as I pounded into her echoed through the air. She rolled toward her orgasm, her pussy pulsing tightly around my cock. Her cries became deeper and louder.

"Wait for me, Erica."

Pulling against her restraints, she cried out again. "I can't."

"You can. Wait. I need to be there with you." I fucked her harder, losing myself inside of her. The race for release my only aim. The tension of her body, clinging to me everywhere in every way, consumed me. She became every thought, the single point in a sea of things that didn't matter. And for all the thrills of waiting, of drawing out her desire, I couldn't stop now.

"Fuck...Erica, come now for me."

A current of energy shot down my spine, drawing my balls up painfully.

"Now!"

She screamed, every muscle in her body binding hers to mine for a few breathless moments. I burst inside of her, thrusting through the waves of pleasure crashing over me. Empty...complete. I held her tightly, weakened and reeling. My fingers ached when I loosened my hold on her thighs and lowered her back to the floor. She'd wear my marks by the morning.

I unbound her hands, my own unsteady. Immediately she tore off the blindfold and wrapped her arms around me. Her small frame, slick from our heat, crashed into me.

My knees buckled, and I brought us to the bed before I took us both down. She held me so tightly, as if she'd never let go. The longer we lay that way, the more I believed that nothing could ever tear us apart. Raw emotion hit my heart. I drew in a shaky breath and held her close.

She whispered my name, pulling away enough to look me in the eyes. I blinked, bringing her into focus through the blur. Caressing her palm down my cheek, she kissed me.

"Are you okay?" she whispered.

Was I?

"I'm here with you. That's all I need."

She took a small breath, relaxing against me. "We'll get through this. I promise."

I closed my eyes, wanting to believe her.

"I know," I lied.

CHAPTER SEVEN

ERICA

I blinked away sleep, assuring myself that last night hadn't been a dream. That the whole damn day hadn't been one surreal, heart-wrenching, earth-shattering dream. I lifted to my elbows and eyed the clothes strewn across the floor. The black leather flogger tossed on top of them was proof that I hadn't imagined any of it.

I sat up and swung my legs over the edge of the bed, wincing at the ache in my muscles. Most of our best nights came at a price, with physical discomforts that I'd feel after. Yet last night I'd needed Blake's intensity in a way I couldn't completely explain.

Even in my half-awake state, nothing could have kept me from him when he came home. I'd drifted off to sleep early, haunted by nightmares that he was never coming back to me. That when I'd walked away from the station, it was the last time I'd ever see him. Having him back home, in the flesh, made me want to possess him as passionately as he wanted to possess me.

I closed my eyes and remembered the sting of the leather. A new sensation that bit my skin. The shock of it, and then the heat. The electricity that brought everything alive in a new way. A thousand tiny points of contact, each screaming with the pain I felt...the pain between us that had no other place to go.

I rose and assessed myself in the mirror. Twisting to examine my backside, I was surprised that the punishments of the night hadn't produced any evidence. Not that I minded the marks. I tended to relish them, cherish them as tiny memories of some of our most unforgettable encounters.

I fingered the small bruises decorating my thighs from where Blake had held me too tightly. A flush of pink worked its way from my cheeks to my chest. I'd felt none of it in the heat of the moment, yet the evidence of his passion had the ability to warm me through.

I'd never be able to make sense of it, but somehow Blake had completely taken over my mind, overwritten any preconceptions I'd had about sex and pain, and brought me to heights no one had ever come close to. We'd found peace with it. We'd made an island between the two of us. Our bodies, our love, and the fierce way we came together made sense when the rest of the world failed us.

If only we could live on that island and never have to leave...

Reality quickly tempered the fantasy when the low hum of the television downstairs reminded me that Blake was home. He hadn't told me yet about how the interrogation with Evans went.

Showered and dressed casually for work, I meandered downstairs. Blake sat on one of the linen-covered couches, his focus trained on the morning news. Daniel's face flashed across the screen. Recent footage showed him sidestepping reporters as he left the same police station Blake and I had visited yesterday. Daniel's stolid expression reminded me of the darker side I knew, the side that was revealed only when he'd been wronged and thirsted for revenge at any cost. Was it aimed at Blake?

I reached for the remote and turned down the sound. Blake's focus was unflinching.

I sat beside him and tugged gently at the hem of his collared shirt, hoping to break him out of his trace. "Blake."

His chest expanded with a deep breath and he glanced over at me. His eyes were distant, as if he was deep in thought.

"Are you okay?" he asked.

I frowned. "Of course."

"Clay told me that Max approached you."

I exhaled a breath and nestled against his side. "Alli told me he was sentenced when I got back. He was on his way to the station to get booked."

"What did he say to you?" Tension laced his words.

"Nothing," I lied.

"Erica."

"Nothing important."

Max was gone now. A closed chapter. At least until they let him go again. I couldn't think about that, though. He'd promised Clay he'd never see me again. I could only hope that might be true.

Blake was silent, yet somehow I could hear him demanding that I give him what he wanted. His muscles tensed beside me.

I sighed. "He said, 'He'll ruin you.'"

"Me?"

I drew circles over his jeans where the muscles in his legs bunched. "Assuming he meant you, yeah."

I lifted my head to gauge his reaction and try to read his thoughts. He closed his eyes and looked away, effectively blocking me out.

"Talk to me, Blake," I pleaded.

"What do you want to talk about?"

There was an edge to his voice that gave me pause.

"How about we start with yesterday? What happened?"

"The FBI and the police took turns interrogating me for nine hours. That's what happened."

I hesitated over what I wanted to ask. He seemed wound tight already, and we'd barely spent five minutes together. But I needed to clear the air. Above all, I needed to get him talking so we could get to the bottom of this.

"What did you tell them?"

"I told them whatever I felt they needed to know."

I didn't like the ambiguity in his tone. We'd been incredibly close last night, and now we felt a million miles apart again. Was he hiding something from me? I twisted the diamond bands on my finger, contemplating all the things he might not be telling me.

"Is there anything you didn't tell them that you want to tell me?"

Then our gazes locked. I searched his eyes but found nothing.

"What are you talking about, Erica?"

"I mean . . . What happened with the election?"

He laughed lightly but there was no humor in his voice. "Are you asking me if I did it?"

I left the warmth of his side and stood. I paced a small

circle in the room, suddenly needing some space. I swallowed over my next words, not wanting to admit that's what had been burning in the back of my mind ever since he walked out of sight with Evans yesterday. "I guess I am."

He leaned forward, resting his elbows on his knees. "You think I took time away from a month-long honeymoon with my bride to rig Daniel's election, ruin his career, and risk mine? No. The answer is no. I did not do that."

My shoulders softened, tension releasing. "I'm sorry, Blake, I—"

"Me too, Erica. I thought that would go without saying, but maybe I haven't given you enough reason to give me the benefit of the doubt."

"It's not like it's beyond your capabilities."

He grimaced. "So everyone keeps reminding me."

"I just thought—"

"I would never hurt you, Erica. I fucking *hate* Daniel." His jaw tightened, as if he were biting down on a thousand things he wanted to say. "I won't deny that I despise the man, and I'll be the first to admit that I relish the thought of ruining him. But I don't hate him enough to put you and me in harm's way again."

A few minutes passed between us. He sat back into the couch, arms crossed, his gaze landing everywhere but on me.

"What did the police say? They couldn't have found anything linking you to it, right?"

"They consider my connection to you motive."

According to Carmody, that could play out against us either way, depending on whether Blake intended to hurt or help Daniel. But the way Gove shut down that line of questioning assured me that it wasn't nearly enough to hold Blake on.

"That's not enough."

He was silent, yet somehow the silence told me there was more.

"What else do they have?"

"The voting machines were rigged using my code."

Ice hit my veins. I stilled my aimless pacing. "What code?"

"Code I wrote years ago when I was developing the banking software. There are unique encryption routines that were used, and the feds have spent the past two weeks studying them, linking them to me."

"You can't be the only one who could have done that."

"It's banking, Erica. With billions of dollars on the line, there are only a few people with access to the source code."

The wheels in my head spun, and gradually I began piecing together the possibilities. "Okay. So who has it?"

"Me, of course. Michael Pope, and a select few at the company we sold it to."

"Why aren't the police talking to them?"

He sighed heavily. "I'm assuming they are, but all of this is so close to me that they aren't looking much further. I'm their best bet. Beyond that, it seems like Evans is on some sort of mission. Wants to nail me for what I did a decade ago with some fresh charges."

I'd gotten the same impression from my brief time around Evans. Carmody didn't inspire trust either, but between the two of them, Carmody didn't act like he already knew the absolute truth. He was still looking for it, and it remained to be seen what either of them would find in an effort to paint Blake as the guilty party.

My mind spun over this new information. Banksoft was a multibillion-dollar company. That they'd have a leak, one with any interest in the Massachusetts governor's election, seemed unlikely. If Blake was telling the truth, and I believed he was, the breach had to be rooted from Michael's copy. Michael would never hurt Blake, but his son Max certainly would.

"Do you think Max could have given Trevor access to it?"

Blake nodded slowly. "I'm assuming that's the case."

"Did you tell the police that?"

"No." The simple answer was clipped.

"Why?"

"Because fuck them."

I gasped. "Fuck them? They're trying to send you to prison, Blake. You're not even going to try to point them in the right direction?"

"They have nothing on me, Erica. I was out of the country. They're going to waste weeks looking for some shred of actual evidence linking me to the election, and they won't find it, because I didn't goddamn do it."

My breath was ragged in my chest. All of this new information had my adrenaline spiking. "That's it? You're going to wait for *them* to clear your name?"

"What do you want me to do?" He threw his hands up.

I walked closer, my hands fisted tightly by my sides. "I want you to work with them to get to the bottom of this.

You and I both know this wasn't random. Trevor has targeted both of us. He's been trying to infiltrate your work for years, but this is different. This is your freedom we're talking about, not some website that we're working on."

"They aren't going to work with me. I don't have access to the code. If I did, I could find what they aren't finding."

"Then let's find it. You know how to get information."

"I'm under a fucking microscope. They're going through my computers with a fine-tooth comb. You think they aren't going to be watching what I do like a hawk now?"

He looked away, his gaze fixed on some point on the distant horizon. I didn't know where he was, but I needed him back with me. We needed to get to the bottom of this, and quickly.

"Why do I feel like you don't want to fight back even if you could?" I sat down beside him and took his hand. "It's because of what happened to Brian, isn't it?"

Silence filled the room as he held his ground. Finally he turned, his eyes tired and devoid of the fierce determination that I had grown to love about him.

"This has nothing to do with Brian."

"I think you're wrong. I think it has everything to do with him. Whatever happened between you two back then, the guilt has stayed with you. You haven't let it go, and neither has Trevor. And now history is repeating itself, and that's exactly what Trevor wants. He wants to see you suffer for what happened to his brother. And while you're getting interrogated and our lives are being ripped apart, he's out there somewhere planning his next move. He'll never stop until he takes you down."

"Enough!"

I startled at the tone.

He rose quickly. Cursing under his breath, he grabbed his jacket and moved for the door.

I hurried after him, unwilling to accept him leaving again so soon. "Where are you going?"

"I have to meet with the attorney and figure out a game plan. We need to be ready for whatever they come at us with."

"Does he know about Trevor?"

He turned to face me. "Let it go, Erica. I'm taking care of this. It's going to blow over. Trust me."

"How is that you 'taking care of it'?"

"Just . . . trust me, okay?"

"No."

His eyes widened. "No?"

"Not until you tell me how you're going to find Trevor."

His jaw tightened as he shrugged into his jacket. "Fucking drop it, Erica."

Anger rushed in over the tears that threatened. "I'm not going to stand by and watch you ruin your life."

"I'm not ruining my life," he muttered.

"No, you're ruining *our* life. Remember every decision we make affects the other. Or does that only apply to me when I don't do what you want?"

He winced and reached for the door handle. "This conversation is over."

Before I could find a way to make him stay, he was out the door.

Emotion burned thick in my throat. I wouldn't let him give up this time. Every time Trevor threatened us, Blake had turned the other cheek. Not this time. Never again.

Blake's Tesla sped down the street, and I retreated into the empty house. I sat at the island in the kitchen contemplating what to do next. I couldn't shift gears and focus on work right now. I was too angry. Too scared that contrary to what Blake said, this situation would *not* simply blow over.

"Damnit." I slammed my hand on the counter, curling my fingers around the pain. My throat tightened and tears burned behind my eyes, but something in me refused to let go. Crying right now felt like somehow I would be giving up. I wouldn't—I couldn't. Instead, that sick feeling came over me again. Except this time it didn't pass. I ran to the bathroom and emptied my stomach into the toilet.

A fever rushed over me, and then my damp skin cooled. I stood shakily and wiped my mouth. The person I saw in the mirror didn't look so good, but after several minutes, my wan complexion finally gave way to some color.

My clothes hugged my body. I'd gained weight on the trip. Weight that had replaced what I'd lost after the shooting. I traced the band of my jeans and the soft skin above.

A flicker of hope lit inside of me. An irrational and ill-timed hope.

It wasn't possible . . .

I brushed my teeth. I tried to push the thought away,

but a hundred possibilities swarmed my mind. Our love, this life we were building, Blake's freedom, and maybe more was at stake. If he wasn't going to protect it, who would?

Suddenly the chaos of my thoughts stilled, and I knew what I needed to do. I went upstairs into the closet and found my suitcase, ignoring the tangle of sheets and the reminder of our night of passion. Then I started to pack.

CHAPTER EIGHT

BLAKE

I'd spent the day at Dean's office. Fitzgerald's people were claiming ignorance about the whole affair, which might have been true. We ran through the timeline of the honeymoon in more detail. According to the time stamps the FBI supplied, I would have had to rig the elections on the flight from Cape Town to Malé, which would have been completely impossible since the code had been loaded by USB to the various machines, and I was thousands of miles away from those.

Beyond that, Erica had been the center of my world for weeks. Nothing had broken my focus on making the trip a memorable one for the both of us.

My mind wandered back to that simpler time. So much had changed in the space of a few days. This was anything but paradise. The honeymoon was over, and our life had begun. I refused to believe this was the beginning our future together.

Perhaps they'd turn the attention to Fitzgerald, but if he went down, he wouldn't go alone. He'd implicate me just to spite me. He'd always believe I was behind it until someone told him otherwise.

And then there was Trevor.

If I'd ever had a desire to bring justice to his door—wherever that might be—I would have told Dean about him in the years past. But I hadn't. And today wouldn't be the day to bring it to light. Dean had spent a lot of time today explaining away any of my suspected guilt. Good practice for him, but I could see the wheels turning, the question burning in his mind. If I didn't do it, who did?

I could hear Erica's voice in my head, telling me to do the right thing. *Tell him.* Put them on the right path. But something inside me hesitated, and I stayed true to the path I'd always walked. No need to complicate matters anyway. Pointing fingers would probably only further convince Evans of my guilt. He didn't strike me as the type of person who'd go on a hunt for someone like Trevor to save someone like me. Waste of time.

Dean searched for possible scenarios, and we agreed that the use of my code alone wasn't a smoking gun for the case. Too many other people had access to it. Even if all signs pointed to me, it simply wasn't enough. We had to wait to see if they could come up with anything more. That was the looming question mark. What would they find, if anything? And how long would we have to wait until all this went away?

The day was coming to a close and I scrolled through the email on my phone, eager for anything to take my mind off this mess.

"You should go home." Dean circled his desk and tossed my coat on my lap.

"You're kicking me out?"

"It's been a long day. Go home and be with Erica. I'm sure she's still pretty rattled over this."

"You'd be right," I muttered.

"She didn't want to leave the station until they were done with you yesterday. I tried to put her mind at ease, but I knew she wasn't having it."

"Doesn't surprise me."

I worked my jaw, battling with my empathy and the person in me who'd never bent on this matter. I'd go home to Erica and we'd pick up where we left off this morning, which wasn't a moment I was exactly proud of. Leaving her before we could talk things through. She'd cornered me, stood up to me. Not that any of that surprised me. She'd always had her own mind. I had seen that fire in her when she walked into my boardroom months ago. I never wanted to put out that flame. I wanted her to burn for me, fight for us, and that's exactly what she was doing.

Dean dropped back down into his chair and cocked his head. "I have to say, I was curious to finally meet the woman who meant enough to you to skip the pre-nup, despite all my best advice. I only wish it had been under different circumstances."

"Me too."

Dean's half joke reminded me that I'd agreed to share everything with Erica. I'd demanded it, despite her misgivings. Not just the wealth, but the joys and burdens too. A voice of reason reminded me that as much as we tried to battle our demons in private, it never worked out that way in the end. As determined as I was to go to war with Evans on my own, Erica and I had bound ourselves too tightly for that.

With our earlier argument still weighing on me, I left Dean's office and made my way down to the street. The sun had gone down. The days were shorter, the nights colder. Except my nights were never cold when Erica was with me. God, I couldn't get her out of my head. We were on two sides of a line and she kept calling me over. I wanted to relent, but something held me back. I walked the streets of downtown Boston until I was in front of my office. The windows were dark.

I pushed through the doors and let myself into the empty bullpen. I flipped on the lights, revealing the wasteland of our office. Every desk was a mess. Wires had been pulled and were strewn around the floor. Cady had called earlier, confirming that the authorities had confiscated all the machines in our office. But somehow seeing it in person stirred up a new kind of rage. Toward Evans. Toward all those faces I'd grown to hate when I was a teenager. It hadn't seemed fair then and it sure as hell didn't feel fair now, when I hadn't done a goddamn thing to warrant it.

"You okay?"

I turned, and James was standing in the doorway.

"What the fuck do you think?"

He shook his head and backed away. "Sorry, man. I'll leave you alone."

I released the tension in my fists. "It's all right. It's just been a rough day. Sorry."

He nodded and took a step closer, surveying the damage. "Alli told us what went down. It's fucked up." He hesitated, his focus landing on me. "You look like you could use a drink."

That much was true. Though it wouldn't get me any closer to resolution on the matters at hand. "Thanks, but

I should get back home. It's getting late. Erica's probably wondering where I've been."

He frowned.

"What?"

"Well...she left this afternoon," he said.

"What do you mean?"

"She came in this morning with a bag, she and Alli met in her office for a bit, and then they took off for the airport together. Alli said they'd be back in a day or two. Said to email if anything came up with work."

I balled my hands into tight fists again. This day just kept getting better. "Do you have any idea where they went?"

His eyes were wide then. "No idea. She didn't stick around long enough for me to ask her about it."

"Fuck." My vision turned white with anger.

"Have you called her?"

"I have to go," I said, pushing past him.

I sped home, calling her phone repeatedly only to hear her voicemail time after time. I barreled through the front door, half expecting to find Erica there. But the house was quiet and dark. I went to the kitchen, explored every room on the first floor, and then went to our bedroom. She was gone. The bed was how we'd left it, except for a piece of paper on my pillow.

I picked it up, adrenaline racing through me as I read it.

You promised you would always deserve my trust...my happiness...my love.

★ ★ ★

ERICA

I promised him I'd never run away from him again, but he'd broken promises too. And right now, I was doing what I needed to do. I was doing what he wouldn't.

Alli and I stepped off the plane and into the warm Texas air. Twenty minutes later, we'd arrived at our hotel in the heart of Dallas. The bellhop dropped our bags inside the room. I tipped him and walked to where Alli was gazing out the big picture window overlooking the sprawling city's skyline.

I'd never been to Dallas, and I wished I had a better reason for coming now. I didn't relish the idea of going anywhere without Blake, but after this morning's fight, I knew that I couldn't rely on him right now.

"Pretty," Alli said, before dropping into a nearby lounge chair. Her purse vibrated at her feet. "It's Heath." She glanced up at me without bothering to retrieve her phone.

"Not yet," I said.

She rolled her eyes. "I feel like a freaking fugitive, Erica. If I don't talk to him soon, he's likely to file a missing-person's report."

"I don't want anyone knowing where I am right now. Not until I have a chance to talk to Michael alone."

"I can't imagine what kind of hell Blake is going to put Heath through when he finds out I'm with you."

Blake was so far away, and he didn't even know it. I regretted leaving him the way I had. But I was angry too.

Angry that he wouldn't fight for us. That after everything we'd been through together, he could still shut me down so quickly.

"You said you'd help me, Alli. I'm meeting with Michael first thing in the morning. You can talk to Heath then."

I'd explained the situation to her at the office, ready to take off on my own if I had to. But I'd gone on enough wild goose chases to know that it was always better to have company. Danger had a way of finding me, and I was more than a little shell-shocked from the consequences. But I couldn't get to the bottom of this from the safety of our home.

"I wanted to come with you, Erica, but I don't like keeping secrets from Heath. It's something we don't do anymore, under any circumstances, and you're asking me to go against that."

"Whatever you tell Heath will go right to Blake, and you know it. Blake won't have it any other way. I'm positive that Max gave Trevor access to Blake's code, and this is the only chance I have of making that connection. Michael isn't the type to have a heart-to-heart with me over the phone, and I don't want Blake getting in the way."

Alli hesitated a moment before speaking. "Do you really think you're going to win him over? Michael Pope...shipping magnate, billionaire, and arguably one of the most intelligent and successful businessmen in the world?"

When she said it like that, I had my doubts. But even with my doubts, he was the best chance I had. "I don't know. He seems to like me. I know he cares a lot about

Blake. I mean, he disowned Max after what he did to me. If I can make Michael realize what's at stake, maybe he'll help me." I sat down in the chair opposite her. "This is important, Alli. If Blake won't act to clear his name, I will. I won't lose him. I can't."

Her phone vibrated again with an incoming call. She shot me a pleading look. "He hasn't stopped calling since we landed. What do you want me to do?"

I sighed. "Fine. Just don't tell him where we are."

She answered quickly and put the phone to her ear. "Hey, baby... Yeah, sorry. Last minute girls' trip." She stood and walked around the room. "Everything is fine. There's something Erica needs to take care of and she wanted me with her... Heath, please, just don't ask questions right now. It's complicated. But we're fine. I promise." She cast a sideways glance at me. "Yeah, something like that. I'll talk to you later, okay, when things settle down... Love you too."

She hung up and shot me a pointed stare. "You owe me."

"I know. Thank you."

She rested a hand on her hip. "I don't know about you, but I'm starving. Let's change and grab some dinner."

I forced myself up, pushing through the fatigue that had settled into my bones over the course of the long, emotionally taxing day. I could have gone to bed and slept for days, but Alli was right. We needed food, even though my stomach hadn't stopped turning since this morning.

I opened my bag to look for something comfortable to change into.

"What is this?"

Alli gasped as she picked up a pink box that I'd shoved into my bag at the last minute. In it were two pregnancy tests that I'd picked up earlier, convincing myself that I was completely insane for doing so.

I resisted the urge to snatch them back from her.

"What does it look like?" I tried to sound nonchalant, but I was already on edge that she'd discovered them.

Her eyes were wide. "Are you pregnant?"

I drew in an uneven breath. "I have no idea." Was I completely foolish for even suspecting it?

"Are you kidding? You think you might be, but you haven't taken a test yet?" Her voice had risen at least four octaves.

"I haven't gotten around to it." That was mostly true.

"Well, for God's sake, go take it. I'm freaking out here!"

Glowing with anticipation, she started to open one end of the box. I grabbed it from her, my anxiety ratcheting to new levels. I cursed myself for not hiding the box better.

"I thought we were getting dinner," I said in a desperate attempt to veer her off topic.

"As if I could eat knowing you might be knocked up. Don't be crazy."

"Alli, stop," I snapped.

She leveled an incredulous stare at me.

My heart thumped wildly in my chest. I wasn't ready for whatever reality came after the test. I couldn't... "I can't do this right now."

"Jesus, why?"

I tossed the box back into the bag and walked toward the window. The sun had set, and Dallas was lit up with a million city lights. How could I do this now? I was in the middle of a tornado. No way could the sun shine through this storm.

"I'm not sure I'm ready to know, either way."

Alli came closer and stood by my side. "Have you been trying?"

I closed my eyes and thought of Blake.

"Kind of." My voice was barely a whisper.

"Okay, stupid question. You're off birth control and you've been honeymooning for a month. Of course you have been. When was your last period?"

"I stopped keeping track after the shooting. It's been erratic ever since. I don't know. If it's positive, I'm going to freak out and worry. I'll worry if it's even going to be viable. And if it's negative, I'm not sure I want to know that after all that time together…after trying the way we have been, that it still couldn't happen."

"Erica, people try for years and can have success. Give yourself a chance. If it's meant to be, it'll happen. But not knowing either way can't be anything but torture. At least for me. I can't imagine it's any different for you."

True, the status of my uterus was a persistent thought in my mind. Imagining that I was pregnant was a happy thought, if a little terrifying. But imagining that I wasn't and that I'd just dreamed up the possibility was the real torture. Having that play out in real life would be even worse.

"I don't know if I can handle it right now with everything else that's happening," I finally admitted.

Alli went back to the box and brought it to me, holding out one of the tests. "I'm not going to be able to even function until I know. Call it a favor for me going on this crazy mission with you. And whatever it is, we'll deal with it. I'm here for you, either way. I promise."

I shook my head slightly, but she stood firm, her jaw set with a determined look I knew well.

"I'm not taking no for an answer. Seriously, go in there and take it."

After a long moment, I plucked the test from her hand and went into the bathroom. I shut the door, sat down on the lid of the toilet, and stared at the unopened package.

This wasn't happening. I can't do this. I don't even want to know. I cycled through the mantra until Alli spoke up.

"Are you doing it?"

I heard the question clearly enough to know that she was directly outside the door.

"Not yet."

"Do it," she ordered.

I opened the package and inspected the test. Seemed straight forward enough.

"Erica!"

I paused, knowing she didn't really want to hear what I had to say. *Not right now. Maybe tomorrow. It can wait.* No... none of that would be acceptable.

"Damnit it, Erica. I'm your best friend, and I'm demanding you pee on the stick."

I rolled my eyes. I wondered how low long it would take before she barreled through the door.

"I'm getting to it. Give me a minute for shit's sake."

I cursed again under my breath. I didn't bother with

directions and carried on with it. The little windows of the test darkened and I waited.

I waited and waited, my mind a whirlwind of what ifs. Would I even tell Blake if it was negative? That all that trying, all that love and faith between us, had been for nothing?

I stood up and busied myself in the mirror, trying to fluff my flattened hair, needing anything to occupy my mind right now. As the test did its work, I convinced myself that it was negative. That all hope was lost. When I let myself believe it, the devastation hit my gut, right where the nausea had been twisting for the past two days.

That was a sign, right? The way I'd been feeling...

What if I *was* pregnant? What if we were actually going to have a baby?

I struggled for a breath when I imagined what that might feel like. Then panic gripped me when I thought of Blake and what he'd say. But that's what we wanted, right? We'd danced around it, maybe because neither of us was entirely sure it was possible. But we'd tried...We'd flown into the possibility with the blind determination we brought to any other endeavor, yet here I was doubting and scared.

Memories of our last night in the Maldives flitted through my mind. Blake making love to me under the stars. The curtains around the cabana billowing in the wind, the only barrier between us and the night. The sliver of the moon and a thousand tiny pinpricks of light shining through as we came together with one purpose in mind.

My hand rested over my belly, the scar that I'd traced more times now than I could count. My wound...and now, maybe a life. My breath rushed out of me at that overwhelming thought.

"What does it say?" The tone of Alli's voice bordered on hysterical.

I was about to yell something back at her when I glanced at the test again. I blinked twice at the extra line that had formed.

Seconds passed, rushing by with the quickened beat of my heart. *Oh my God. Oh shit. Wow. Oh my God.*

"I'm coming in there. I don't care if you're decent."

She barged in and took the test out of my hands. "What does it say?"

"I think it says I'm pregnant."

CHAPTER NINE

BLAKE

"Where the fuck is she?"

Heath groaned, stretching under his duvet. "Man, I told you last night, I don't know."

"Like hell you don't. Alli's with her, isn't she?"

"Yeah, but she won't tell me where they are. I talked to her again late last night, and she said everything's fine. She said not to worry."

The lack of sleep combined with a new rush of adrenaline spiking my blood had me wild with frustration. "Not to worry? Are you fucking kidding me? My wife has disappeared into thin air and no one's telling me anything. I think you know me well enough to know that I'm more than fucking worried."

Heath scratched his head and rose from the bed. "Dude, you need to breathe. I'm going to take a piss, and when I come back, we'll talk. Do some yoga while I'm gone."

I left the bedroom, slamming the door behind me. I sank back against the smooth dark leather of the living-room couch. The coffee table was covered with bridal magazines, which sent visions of my own wedding through my mind. Erica smiling, happier than I'd ever seen her.

I closed my eyes, letting some of my anger ebb away.

Suddenly I wanted a way to go back to that day, one of the best days of my life.

Steps away from our home, we'd said our vows. As content as I would have been to share them in private, saying them in front of our friends and family in that moment had meant more to me than I'd expected. I'd written mine the night before. Finding the words to express what she meant to me had been difficult, but somehow I'd found them and committed them to memory. And when she walked down the aisle toward me, I was lost. Speechless.

I couldn't tear my eyes away from her. She was a vision—hair done up but some strands loose around her face, light makeup making her blue eyes glow as they peered into mine. Her dress, made of soft white lace, fit perfectly to her body. The justice spoke, but the only words I heard were hers as she began to say her vows. Her voice was soft but strong as she locked me in with her eyes.

"When I imagined this day, I could never have imagined how deeply and completely I would love the person standing here with me. I thought love like ours happened only in books. I thought men like you lived only in fairy tales. But here you are, my dream come true, my happily ever after. And every day we've been together has been a gift, bringing me closer to you. For that, I'll always be grateful. I promise to love you, stand by you, and cherish all of our days together." She swallowed, her blue eyes shimmering with emotion. "Blake, you'll always have my heart. You'll always have my trust."

The autumn ocean breeze whispered between us, seeming to steal the air from my lungs.

"Erica," I whispered. I brushed my hand over her flawless cheek.

She gazed up at me through her dark lashes and leaned into my gentle touch. I fought the urge to kiss her. Not yet, a little voice reminded me.

My grand speech had flown out the window, into the wind somewhere. Suddenly nothing had ever been as important as the words I was about to say to her. They had to be real. From the deepest place in my heart, they had to speak directly to hers.

"I promise to be deserving of your love and your trust. You'll never want for love or comfort or happiness. I promise that you'll always have a safe place in my arms and in our home. I'll love you completely, with every ounce of my being, every day, for the rest of my life."

The justice began to speak. As soon as I heard the word kiss, *I beat him to the finish and brought her to me. She came willingly, her arms like silk winding at my nape, as if she'd been waiting too. I brushed my lips over hers and kissed her tenderly.*

"You want some coffee?" Heath asked when he came into the room, tearing me from the memory.

My eye twitched. I'd already had enough coffee to fuel a college campus. All it had done was make me edgier. "You have anything stronger?"

He paused. "It's nine in the morning, and you know I'm done with the strong stuff."

I sighed. "I know. Sorry. I wasn't thinking."

You'll always have my trust.

I leaned forward, burying my face in my hands. Her words were a tattoo on my heart, indelible in my mind. We'd made promises. Were those simply the words of a couple hopelessly in love on day one of marriage? Was her trust in me so easily shaken? Maybe other people slacked on their vows from time to time, but she sure as hell wasn't letting me forget mine.

Had she given up on me so soon? Had I given her a good reason to?

If she'd only come home...

Where was she? We'd fought, and I was being a stubborn bastard, but I figured she was used to that by now. I thought her days of running away were over too. We were married now. We had to fight our way through these things—together. She couldn't just walk out on me. Not like this. Not when everything else was falling apart.

Something cold tapped my shoulder. I opened my eyes to Heath holding out a beer. I took it, grateful. He sat on the opposite couch, still in his boxers, holding a cup of coffee.

"You look like shit you know," he said, peering at me over the rim of the cup.

I ran a hand over the coarse hair on my chin. I'd pulled on the closest thing within reach this morning, which was the wrinkled shirt I'd worn yesterday. With Erica gone, the last thing I cared about were my looks. I leveled a desperate look at my brother. "Where is she?"

He shook his head, his eyes tentative. "Alli said there was something Erica had to do. She wouldn't tell me anything else, except that I shouldn't worry."

Un-fucking-acceptable my mind shouted, but I forced myself to stay calm. "Did you ask about her?"

"Of course I did."

"And?"

Heath looked past me, working his tense jaw.

I gripped my fingers around the bottle I held. "Heath. Talk to me, or I swear to God…"

"She's upset, Blake. She's your wife, so I figure you knew that already. What happened before she left?"

"We fought."

"About?"

I lifted the bottle to my lips and took a deep swallow. "She wants me to track down Trevor, or at least let the feds know who they should be looking for."

"And you won't?"

"He's not worth our time. Hers or mine. He's—"

"He's what, exactly?"

"Not the answer. The authorities can't pin this on me. Sending them after him is a waste of time."

Heath set his coffee down on the table and clasped his hands together. "You know I'm not big on confrontation, but this fucker has been after you for years. Maybe I've been too busy making a mess out of my own life to speak up about it until now. But he needs to be stopped. The fact that someone as smart you hasn't put an end to it is ridiculous."

I didn't respond for a moment, tempering the verbal lashing I wanted to dole out. Maybe he was right. Maybe he and Erica both were. I cursed under my breath. I rubbed my eyes to soothe the stinging from lack of sleep.

"Erica thinks it's because I feel guilty about Brian."

"Do you?"

I swallowed down more of my beer. "Maybe," I confessed, almost too quietly to be heard.

"You were young. And this kid isn't Brian. He's just as fucked up, but he's never been a friend. You don't owe him anything."

"I know that."

"Do you? Because sometimes it really doesn't seem that way."

I'd never met Trevor face-to-face, but somehow he was always Brian in my mind. I'd never admit it, but I couldn't separate the two. He was a shadow, a ghost no one could catch. But to me, he was a ghost who carried around the blackest memory I had. Brian had been as misguided as me, but he'd taken things too far. I'd devised the whole plan with him, but he was the one who had followed through, far beyond the original intent. Because he'd taken the fall, I was free.

The threat of prison had been lifted, but the guilt that he'd taken his own life haunted me. For months. When I started working for Michael, I thought I'd moved past it. But maybe I hadn't.

"I can't change what happened."

"None of us can. But you can stop letting this...menace...vandalize your life. If you don't stop him, the feds are going to put you away, Blake. You don't need me to tell you, but you're not a minor anymore. This is a fucking felony. You've got a wife, a family who cares about you, hundreds of people who rely on you. And you're going to mail it in because you can't stomach turning the tables and making sure Trevor lands his ass in jail for all of this?"

"He's not doing anything that I don't do."

"Maybe that's true, but you do a lot more than he does. You've built dozens of companies that are putting good things into the world. You've helped Mom and Dad. You've helped me, when I've given you no good reason to. You're Erica's rock, and right now you're failing her by being too blind to see the difference. Why won't you face him?"

"If he ever showed his goddamn face, I would," I snapped.

"You know what I mean."

"I'm not going to be bullied by a shadow."

"Well, that's what is happening."

I stood and paced around the room, Heath's words rattling through my brain.

"Facing off...I guess it makes Brian real again. Trevor wants to draw me back into this nightmare. That's what this is all about. He wants to turn me into the person the FBI already thinks I am."

"You're not that person. You're so far from the kid you were, Blake. You're an adult. You've had a million experiences. You're married. You have people who need you and give you purpose."

"Exactly. I don't want my purpose to be giving him ammunition."

"All you have to do is draw breath and you're giving him all the ammunition he needs to keep coming back at you. Protect the life you've built. That should be your purpose. And if that means taking this little fucker out of the picture, that's what you need to do."

I leaned against the couch and let out a tired breath. "When did you get so fucking focused?"

"I have only you to blame for that. Alli had to fall in love with a completely different guy after I cleaned up."

I nodded. "You're lucky."

"So are you. You just need to realize that you've got

this all wrong, and that's why Erica's not here. Work it out in your head, and she'll come back. I have no doubt about that."

I shot him an imploring look. "Sounds like you have inside information that I don't."

He shook his head. "Nah, just a gut feeling. If Alli left me without a word, I can guarantee I'd be looking long and hard at what the fuck I did wrong. And no amount of pride would keep me from trying to make it right so I could get her back."

"You're starting to sound like the older brother."

He smirked. "You've saved my ass enough. I owe you a few."

★ ★ ★

ERICA

When I woke up the next morning, the reality that I was pregnant didn't seem any less surreal. A part of me wanted to run back home to Blake and bask in the news, but another part of me was glad for our distance now. Life had thrown me some hard lessons, and I needed a chance to temper this wave of excitement until I could make sense of it. So much was uncertain.

My first priority was getting Michael's help. I rose early and took a cab to his office while Alli stayed at the hotel. The driver pulled up to an impressive high rise situated in the heart of the city, and I took the elevator to the top floor. I'd reached out to his assistant the day before, letting him know that Blake was going to be in town and wanted to meet with him. She'd put it in his calendar without hesitation. When I arrived, after a little explaining that I was Blake's wife and I intended to meet with Michael regardless, his receptionist showed me into his office.

Michael sat at a large desk in the middle of an enormous room. For a man who had the world at his fingertips, he seemed to have nothing around him. The surface of his desk was almost entirely free of clutter, save a notebook, laptop, and pen. Every surface gleamed. Every decoration was perfectly positioned.

Michael came to his feet. His eyes regarded me almost cautiously as I walked toward him. "Erica. I wasn't expecting you."

"I know. I'm sorry for that. It was important."

"Of course. Have a seat." He showed me to the sitting area in what appeared to be the west wing of his spacious office. He took a chair opposite a matching sleek black leather couch where I sat. "What brings you to Dallas?"

"I wanted to talk to you about Blake. I imagine you already know about the trouble he's in."

He nodded slowly. "Yes, the police came to me, so I know some of the details. I haven't spoken to Blake about it, though."

I was reassured that the police were at least doing their due diligence with Michael, even if their first suspect was Blake.

"They asked you about the Banksoft source code?"

"Yes."

"What did you tell them?"

He eyed me for a moment, his lips an unmoving line.

"I told them that to my knowledge, outside of a very select few trusted staff members, no one else had access to my copy of it."

"Is that the truth?"

"Erica, I'm not one for games. What are you getting at?"

I steeled myself to say what I'd flown halfway across the country to say. "I want to know if Max had access to it."

Michael smiled tightly and clasped his hands together. "It's feasible. Max has been involved in many of my business dealings."

"I believe he gave the code to a man named Trevor Cooper. He's a hacker—"

"I know who he is."

I was stunned silent a moment. "You do?"

"He's a programmer who'd been working for Max for a while, helping him with some side projects. We funded his work through one of the investment companies that Max and I once jointly held."

"All that money was used to try to take down several of Blake's ventures, my company among them."

Michael held my gaze steadily. "If that's true, I'm very sorry to hear it. As you may already know, Max and I no longer have financial ties. And when we did, he was rarely involved in my daily business activities. I helped fund several of his projects, if only to keep him from wanting to be too involved with mine. I knew Trevor in name only because the company had cut checks to him."

"Do you know where Trevor is now?"

"No. The investment company was dissolved and all its accounts were closed shortly after your engagement party. I don't know what became of Trevor."

Damnit. I felt like I was climbing a mountain and the top of it kept eluding me.

"Michael, I need you to help me find him. He used Blake's Banksoft code to rig the governor's election knowing that it would implicate Blake. If anyone wants to see Blake suffer more than Max, it's Trevor. He's held a grudge against him since before you took Blake into the fold."

"I'm not sure how I could possibly help."

"Reach out to him. Draw him out. Or tell the FBI what you really know. That Max very likely gave him the code. If the FBI knew it, they would at least start looking for the right person and stop investigating Blake for a crime he didn't commit."

"You're asking me to implicate my own son, Erica."

"I'm asking you to help me bring Trevor in. Whether you like it or not, Max was a part of this, and he's been systematically trying to take Blake out of the game for years. I thought you cared about Blake. Are you willing to watch him go to prison for this?"

His countenance was tight, betraying his discomfort. This was why I hadn't called. Face-to-face he couldn't deny the truth. And the truth was that his son, his flesh and blood, had a hand in this.

"There has to be another way," he finally said, casting his gaze to the floor.

"There *is* no other way. Michael, please, I'm begging you. Help me find him. I can't—" *I can't do this alone.* I struggled for words. I tried to push down the overwhelming emotions bubbling to the surface. Maybe I could explain to Michael just how desperate I was, but I didn't want to lose his respect by breaking down the way I wanted to right now.

Before I could find the right words, he moved to sit beside me. He took my hand in his. His hand was warm and dry, tanned by the sun. His eyes were soft and almost sad.

"Erica, I know this is hard for you. And I know that what you went through when Max attacked you must have been tremendously difficult. No one deserves to go through something like that. I'm ashamed of him, more than I ever have been in my life. But when you have children of your own, you'll learn that no matter how they fail you, no matter how they hurt you and shame you, they will always be your children. I love Blake like a son...but he's not my son. Max is my flesh and blood. I will do whatever I can to help Blake, but not at Max's expense. I've never stood between them, and I won't start now."

A single tear escaped, sliding down my cheek.

He squeezed my hand. "Erica, you just have to find a different way. Blake's smart—one of the smartest people I know. That's why he's not here, because he knows how I feel."

I ripped my hand away from his touch that now felt more condescending than anything. "He's not here because he won't defend himself."

I stood and moved for the door. I curved my hand around the doorknob and hesitated. Across the room, Michael stood. His stance was casual, his face lined with appropriate concern. I'd always thought of him as different, because Blake seemed to think he was. Had I been so wrong?

"Sometimes I think about the men in my life. I think about how so many of them march around like gods, wielding their power and ego like a weapon with no regard for who they hurt or whose lives they destroy. And the rest of us are left picking up the pieces. For some reason, I always thought you were different. I guess I was wrong."

His silence confirmed the hard truth of it. I left his office and hailed a cab back to the hotel, resigned in my defeat.

For the first time since I'd landed in Dallas, I turned on my phone. I waited, preparing myself for the deluge of communications that I must have missed. A dozen texts came through at once, one from James and the rest from Blake. All wanting to know where I was, if I was safe, to call soon.

One voicemail message waited for me. I began to listen to it, bracing myself for whatever Blake had to say. I didn't expect it to be even-toned.

"Erica, it's me."

My heart twisted at the first sound of his voice.

"I don't know where you are, and it's killing me. I'm not saying I don't deserve this, but... please, just call me so I can hear your voice and know that you're okay. I know Alli is with you, but I can't help but worry about you. I want to be with you wherever you are, to protect you from whatever trouble you're getting into. And I already know what you're thinking right now. That I won't protect myself, so how can I protect you? And you're right. I'm too stubborn for my own good, and you shouldn't have to put up with me. You promised you would, though. Please... just call me."

The sadness in his voice gutted me. I missed him more than I'd let myself believe.

I walked into the hotel room and found Alli working on her laptop.

"How did it go?"

I simply shook my head, and her shoulders sagged with the defeat I felt.

"He won't help?"

"Not if it means implicating Max." I slumped onto the bed beside her.

"I'm sorry." She hooked an arm around my shoulders. "What do we do now, *chica*?"

I leaned against her, willing myself to believe that I could find another way to the truth. But I was tired, and all I wanted right now was the comfort of Blake's arms. If I could get him to change his mind and fight for us, maybe there was still hope.

I closed my eyes with a sigh. "I want to go home."

CHAPTER TEN

BLAKE

I must have called her a hundred times. No answer, every time. I'd called Heath a dozen more times. No updates. All I knew was that she was gone, and I had no idea when she'd be back or if she would be at all.

I sat at the dining-room table, lost in my own thoughts. The last swallow of scotch slid down my throat. Nothing could numb the pain of knowing she wasn't with me though. She'd chosen to leave, and maybe I'd given her every good reason to.

I rubbed my eyes. One sleepless night had turned into two. I'd dozed off a few times, but woke in a panic. I'd go through the house again, check my phone and email. Call Heath with no regard for his own need to sleep. I'd realize she was gone all over again and worry until my eyelids wouldn't stay open any longer.

I heard the front door click shut. Clay had been checking in on me. If he hadn't worked for me, I had a feeling he would have been more vocal about how terrible I must have looked. How insane I was being. But nothing anyone could say would fix this. Nothing would be right until she was home. If she gave me a chance to explain myself, I'd make it right.

Then she was there.

Standing at the edge of the table, in jeans and a loose sweater, looking tentative. She was closer than she'd been in days, but somehow she felt a million miles away from me. I pushed out of my chair and went to her. She took a step back like she was scared.

I stopped short in front of her. Clenching my fists to keep from touching her, I tried to pull myself together, but the look in her clear blue eyes was ripping my heart out.

"Baby, I'm not going to hurt you."

She swallowed, her lips parting slightly. "Aren't you angry with me?"

"No. I'm— God, just come here."

I hauled her to me, lifting her off her feet as soon as I could get my arms around her. I nuzzled her neck and breathed her in. She was more potent than any drink. I said her name, over and over. She was home. And safe. Thank God.

I sought her mouth, gliding my lips over hers reverently. The kiss reminded me of the one that had sealed us as husband and wife. Until her tongue touched mine. Tender at first, and then seeking more. I groaned when she slid her fingers through my hair, gripping by the roots. I caught a breath and pulled away enough to see the new fire gleaming in her eyes. She wrapped her legs around me, and I walked us into the living room.

I laid her down on the couch and covered her body with mine. The feeling of her warm little body under me was like heaven. Desire prickled my skin, but simply having her with me again overwhelmed me. I didn't have words for it. I caressed her cheek, thumbing over her parted lips.

"God, I missed you."

Something like sadness passed behind her eyes. Before she could explain why, I kissed her again. I swallowed all the things I knew she wanted to tell me. I kissed her, deeply and passionately, until she broke the contact. I wanted to make love to her and forget the past two days had happened. I wanted to start over, but I knew it wouldn't be that easy. Reluctantly, I lifted my body from her, enough to look into her eyes.

"We need to talk," she said breathlessly.

My muscles coiled with tension. I wasn't going to let her leave me. Maybe she'd be better off with someone who was less fucked in the head, but I didn't care. Selfishly, I'd fight like hell to keep her any way I could.

Mentally preparing myself for the deluge of thoughts that she'd no doubt collected over the past two days, I gradually moved to a sitting position. She did the same, lifting her knees onto the couch on the far end from me.

"Do we have to talk this far apart?"

"I can't—I can't think straight when you're touching me, Blake. And I need you to hear me."

My mouth went dry, but I wanted to know right away. I didn't want the torture of hearing her dance around it.

"Are you going to leave me?"

Her eyes misted. "Blake . . ."

An unseen force punched me in the gut. I rubbed my hands against my knees, preparing myself to do whatever I needed to do in this moment. "You were right. I made you a promise and I broke it. I'm not perfect, and I know that's not an excuse, but you have to believe that I love you,

Erica. More than anything, and I'll do whatever I need to do to keep you—"

"You don't have to worry about keeping me, Blake, but..."

A glimmer of hope took the edge off my fear. But... "But what?"

"Blake..."

Her lip trembled and she tugged anxiously at the rip in her jeans. I started to worry again that something was terribly wrong. I wanted to have her close again, to assure her that whatever it was we could get through. We'd been through enough hell together already.

"Blake, I'm pregnant."

All the air left the room. Everything went black and white, blurry around the edges, except for the woman sitting beside me. Erica. My wife. In color, in focus, the words that she'd just spoken echoing clear as a bell.

Pregnant.

Several empty seconds passed as I tried to wrap my head around what she'd just told me. I sucked in a breath that brought much-needed air to my lungs and oxygen to my stuttering brain.

"How long have you known?"

"I just found out. I took a pregnancy test when I was in Texas. Well, Alli made me take a few, but they were all positive."

I shook my head, hoping to shake some clarity into it. "Wait, Texas?"

New sadness met her eyes. "I went to talk to Michael. I was hoping that he would help us."

Inwardly, I cursed myself up and down for making her believe she had to do that. "Baby...why would you do that?"

"Because I knew you wouldn't."

I closed my eyes. She was right, but none of that mattered now. I opened them and pulled her to me. We didn't need this distance. She came willingly, straddling my lap.

I touched her cheek and held her, dragging my mouth from hers, along the curve of her jaw, to her pulse rushing under my lips. I wanted to touch her everywhere, as if somehow that would make this all seem real. This crazy thing that we couldn't see. Nothing was different on the outside, but the words she'd uttered had suddenly changed everything. *Everything.*

"You're really pregnant?"

I needed to hear the words again. She worried her lip until I thumbed it loose.

"I wanted to wait to tell you..."

"Why?"

She glanced down, fidgeting with the collar of my shirt. "I don't know. Just in case, you know, it didn't last. I figured it would be better if you didn't have to go through that too."

My determination flared, and I shoved the possibility of a failed pregnancy out of my mind. The fact that she was pregnant was too new, too amazing, to dim with those fears. I tipped her chin, lifting her gaze to mine.

"Everything is going to be okay. I promise. And whatever happens, I'm here. I want to feel all of it right beside you."

Her lip started trembling vigorously again. "I need you

with me, Blake. That's what you don't understand. I can't do this alone. I don't want to raise a child alone, without a father. I know what it's like to have that piece of your life missing, and I won't sit by and let them take you from us."

The way she said *us* sent my heart speeding.

"I won't let that happen. We're going to be a family." The words were foreign in my mouth, but instinctively I knew they were true. In the blink of an eye, our future meant more than it ever had.

"We can't leave this to chance. We have to find Trevor and end this. Promise me."

"I promise." I said it before I could think twice. The fact that I'd ever fought Erica over this suddenly seemed absurd. What the fuck was I doing?

Her eyes lit up, glowing with the tears that glistened. "Do you mean it?"

"I've never meant anything more."

"Then how do we find him? If Michael can't help us, I don't know who else we can go to."

Even though I'd had no intention of following through with the plan, I'd already mapped one out. "I need the code that was used to the rig the machines. Trevor does shoddy work. He's bound to have left something behind, something that points back to him."

"Don't you think the feds would have found something by now if he did?"

"Not necessarily. It's my code. It's been a decade, but I know it inside and out. And they're the good guys. They're not looking for tricky shit the way I will. Trevor is a hacker. Takes one to know one, I guess."

"How can we get it?"

I rubbed my hands up and down her legs, wishing I had the power to do more. "They've all got eyes on me, Erica. Otherwise I have no doubt I could get it."

"What about Sid?"

I shrugged. "Maybe. Depends on whether that's a risk he would take."

"He's done some creative research for me before."

I smiled, the sensation oddly strange. Had it been so long since I'd smiled? It had been days since she'd left. "Creative research? Is that what we're calling it now?"

"I don't judge you for what you do, Blake. I may not always agree with it, but I know that your heart is in the right place. Sid's is too. His ethical baseline is probably a little more in line with what I'm comfortable with, though."

"Okay. We'll see what he says." I took a lock of her blond hair and rolled the silky strands between my fingers. Would our baby have blond hair? Blue eyes that mesmerized me like hers did every day?

"Does Gove know about Trevor?"

I shook my head, torn from happier musings. Guilt settled over me all over again.

"Will you at least tell him and see what he thinks? Evans may not believe you, but it could be enough to get him to back off a little."

That tightness in my stomach returned, but faded just as quickly. I wasn't positive, but I was pretty sure that was the feeling of learning my lesson.

"I'll talk to him tomorrow."

Her lips curved into a smile and the worry in the endless oceans of her eyes lifted. "I missed you," she whispered, kissing me softly.

I circled my arms around her torso and held her to me as if she might disappear. Her tongue slipped past my lips, delving and teasing. She was sweet. So soft. I met her passion, reveling in the singular pleasure that was her taste, her touch, her exquisite aroma in my lungs.

I could tell from her body language and the sensual way she moved over me that she was waiting. Waiting for me to take what was mine—her body, her pleasure. God, did I want to, but something held me back. The woman I held in my arms wasn't the same.

★ ★ ★

ERICA

The sound of the shower door closing stirred me from my nap. I twisted in the sheets. The fatigue from earlier lifted gradually as I got my bearings. The clock read 10:00, which meant I'd crashed for only a few hours. I lay back on the pillow and stared at the ceiling. More importantly, Blake had finally come to his senses, and for the first time in days, I felt relief.

I was grateful to be home too. Back in the bed we shared and back in Blake's arms. Except that's all Blake had allowed. Ever since I'd told him about the pregnancy, he'd seemed guarded, like I might break if he let the slightest bit of passion slip into his touch.

Maybe the hormones had taken hold. Maybe I simply wanted that closeness with my husband, no differently than I ever had. Maybe the way I loved Blake had transformed, knowing that I was carrying our child, knowing that we'd made a life between us. Whatever it was, I wanted him badly, and I wasn't going to let him deprive himself, or me.

The water stopped and a second later Blake emerged, a towel around his waist. His chest was gloriously bare, save the tiny lines of water trailing down from his still wet hair. The man had the body of a god. The fact was doing little to tame my now raging libido. I lifted up on my elbows to boldly drink him in.

"Did I wake you up?"

I shook my head, lifting the corner of my mouth in a suggestive smile. "Come to bed."

"You've been traveling all day. You should rest."

"I'm all rested up. Come here." I bent my knee. The friction between my thighs and the vision of him creating more of it there sent my temperature rising.

His tongue passed slowly over his lower lip. "I will in a bit. I'm going to do some work."

Bullshit.

I rose from the bed and walked to him. I didn't wait for an invitation. I slowed in front of him, gazing up into his beautiful eyes, now a heart-melting shade of green.

I glided my hands down the broad planes of his chest. "I love you."

"I love you too." His eyes were shadowed with emotion. "I wish words were enough to show you how I feel, Erica. I've said it a hundred times, but every day I love you more, and the words stay the same."

Something in my heart twisted. I hated that he'd been hurting so badly. He was clean and shaven now, fresh and alert, but he'd been a wreck when I came home. I'd never seen him so devastated.

I shouldn't have left him so coldly. I knew he'd forgiven me, but a part of me wanted to atone for it. I wanted us together. I ached for our bodies together.

"I shouldn't have left you the way I did. I was angry and so scared."

"I know," he said quietly.

After leaving Blake with a reminder of the commitments we'd made, I'd thought a lot about our vows and what they meant—their symbolism and the words themselves. They were promises to build on, not laws waiting to be broken. We were human. Imperfect. Still young in many ways even though we'd been well acquainted with the ways of the world.

We'd hurt each other. We'd landed some powerful blows and somehow found our way back to understanding and love. We'd changed. We'd grown. And every hard lesson had woven us closer together through the journey.

Nothing could shake my love for Blake, and tonight my vow was to fight for that love. I tangled my fingers in his hair with one hand and drew a line down his chiseled jaw with the other. My beautiful lover.

"Even if we fight and fuck up, we'll always find a way through things. I promise."

"You have no idea how badly I wanted to believe that was true." He tucked my hair behind my ear. "It would have been easier to believe if you'd returned my calls though."

I closed my eyes. "I'm sorry."

His hurt echoed inside me.

I'd said the words, but now I needed to show him. And the magnitude of what I felt couldn't be said with a gentle touch. Love and lust were two highly combustible ingredients, stoking the small inferno already burning inside me.

I pressed my lips to his chest. Tracing my fingers down over the hard ridges of his abs, I found the knot of his towel and tugged.

"Erica..."

I hushed him and let the towel fall to the floor. I flicked my tongue over the silky disk of his nipple until it pebbled under a puff of air. I gave the other the same treatment. I kissed my way along his collarbone. Then his neck, where I sucked him boldly until he let out a tortured groan. He palmed my ass, forcing us tightly together. His arousal was unmistakable, hot against my skin.

Pure female satisfaction roared through me. I wanted to please him. I wanted to give him everything tonight.

I tugged off my shirt and he reached for me, caressing me until I shivered. Gazing into his eyes, I slowly lowered to my knees.

I slid my hands down his firm legs, worshipping the lines of his impressively toned body. From his etched lips to his feet, he was a remarkable physical specimen. Lucky for me that his heart was just as beautiful as every other part of him.

I dropped my hands to my thighs. I closed my eyes and leaned forward, letting my forehead rest against him. I sighed, never so content to be here, now. Outside of the thrill and the pleasure that always followed, a part of me had always riled a little bit in this pose. But something was different tonight.

I never believed that I was naturally submissive, despite what Blake might have wanted or needed me to be for him. I would always be there when there was a fight worth fighting.

I wasn't submissive...but I was in love. Deeply and irrevocably in love. And I was Blake's now in a way I never had been before. And he was mine. I had no doubt of that.

Now all I wanted was the strength of his hands on me, his strong body giving me the pleasure that only he could. I wanted to feel the dominance in his touch, and with my submission, to give him what he needed and what I craved.

"Not tonight, Erica."

I lifted my head, peering up at him. "I put you through hell, remember?"

He dropped down, his knees hitting the floor in front of me. His gaze riveted to mine. "It doesn't matter. I've already forgiven you. You deserved more than me walking away from you the other day." He kissed me tenderly. "Forgive me."

"Only if you make love to me," I whispered.

CHAPTER ELEVEN

BLAKE

Goddamn, I wanted her. I wanted everything she was offering to me. I claimed her mouth now with deep strokes, the way I wanted to claim the depths of her body, so unapologetically deep she'd feel me there tomorrow. Our hands roamed. Our mouths melded hotly together. I rose to my feet and carried her to the bed. Taking the space between her thighs, I climbed over her.

Our limbs wove around each other, holding and demanding. I closed my eyes and felt her all around me. Her soft touch became impatient. My hips snapped bluntly against hers at the sensation of her nails dragging down my back.

"Fucking hell." I dropped my forehead to the pillow beside her.

"What's wrong?"

What the hell was wrong? I couldn't get the fact that she was pregnant out of my head. That's what was wrong. Visually nothing had changed, but knowing she was pregnant, carrying what might be our only chance for a child together, brought all my fervent desires to a screeching halt. Suddenly nothing was as important as that, and fucking her like a feral beast wasn't something I was going to risk if it could hurt her in any way.

She stared at me expectantly. "What is it?"

"I'm afraid I'm going to hurt you," I finally admitted.

She winced. "Hurt me?"

"Fuck you too hard. I don't know...hurt the baby, I guess."

She smiled. "You're well-endowed, Blake, and it's glorious, but I promise, you're not going to hurt the baby."

I stared down at her, wishing I could believe it. "I take nothing for granted."

"You've been making love to me for weeks, and I've been fine."

"I can't control myself. You know that as well as I do."

My thoughts wandered as I skimmed down her chest, around the curve of her breast. When I imagined wrapping my teeth around that tight rosy nub, a rush of blood surged to my already throbbing cock.

She pressured me to my back and straddled me. As appealing as the vantage was, I still wasn't in the right headspace. My focus and hands went to her luscious tits. If only I could take her the way I wanted to...

She swiveled her hips over me, dragging the damp cotton of her panties over me. A frustrated groan escaped me. The panties had to go...

"That's seriously not helping." All I wanted to do was slam her down on my dick.

Her eyes twinkled as her lower lip disappeared into her mouth. "Why do I get the feeling you want to fuck me like a wild animal right now?"

Those were tame words for what I wanted to do her. I wanted to bend her over my knee and slap her ass until she screamed. I wanted to drag my teeth over her skin and feel her shudder under the edge of pain. I wanted to spread her wide and fuck her deep. Her mouth, her sweet little pussy, and anyplace else she'd let me in. Wild animals weren't nearly as depraved as I was.

"That's exactly the problem. I don't trust myself, and you shouldn't either."

She lowered over me, bringing us chest to chest. Soft, sweet, heavenly skin.

"I trust you to give me exactly what I need. You know my heart and my body better than anyone else. That's what makes you my husband and not some wild beast."

I held my breath, repeating what she'd said in my mind. Blood thundered loudly in my ears, firing heat and desire straight from my heart down every limb.

She laced our fingers together and brushed her lips against mine. "I like you a little wild too. I know what you need, Blake. Now, give me what I want."

I'd wanted to make love to her the second I saw her again. Damn, this was a hopeless fight.

Without another thought, I flipped her to her back again and didn't waste a second tugging her panties down. I focused on the tuft of curls above her smooth pussy. My mouth watered, and I imagined running my tongue all over that soft skin, delving into the luscious honey just beyond. As much as I wanted that...

My hungry gaze flickered to hers. Her chest rose under labored breaths. She moved restlessly, and I knew exactly what she wanted.

I caught her hip and positioned her beneath me. I couldn't wait to be inside her. I pressed my cock against the mouth of her pussy and sank into her.

She dug her fingernails into my forearm and arched with a gasp. I clenched my jaw tightly. A far away voice told me to be gentle when I wanted to slam her up the bed. I obeyed, determined to treasure her tonight and lock up the animal that wanted things hard and rough. I'd let him loose another day.

When she came back down, I captured her lips.

"Perfect," I whispered against her.

She trembled slightly, her eyes hazy and liquid. I loved the abandon that swept her features when the last barriers between us disappeared—when I was a part of her, and when she'd taken hold of me. I withdrew only to reclaim her, slowly, taking my time, dragging my cock over the sensitive bundle of nerves just inside. The firm way her body clutched me told me she'd been right. I knew her body. I knew all its secrets.

I loved her that way, inch by inch. Thrust by thrust. So steady and measured, I nearly lost my damn mind.

Our hands clasped tightly. She clung to me, holding on through the orgasm that I could feel building with every helpless whimper, every shuddery clench. Flushed skin, my name on her lips…she was close. I could have gone with her, but somehow through the blur of my desire, I held back. I wanted to give her a night of pleasure, not a quick high.

I lifted her hips, meeting her movements, hitting that hidden spot inside her over and over. Her pussy rippled with spasms that matched her cries.

"Let go, Erica," I said, so intent on her climb that I nearly forgot about my own.

"I want to come with you."

My chest constricted and my aching cock reminded

me how badly I wanted to let go too. Too much time had passed between us. Too many emotions had ripped through me in her absence that suddenly everything was barreling down on me.

"Erica."

I strained to rein in the nearly violent need to ram her hard and fast. I could almost taste the promise of release.

Her walls came down around me. Her nails scored down my chest. Everything went red and the sound that tore from me echoed off the walls, punctuated by Erica's thready, broken cry.

★ ★ ★

ERICA

I woke to Blake's warmth all around me. I stretched, curving against the line of his body. I turned to find him already dressed. The scent of coffee lingered on him.

"Good morning," he said.

I smiled. He looked better. And I sure as hell felt better. I toyed with his hair, rumpling it just the way I liked.

"Last night was amazing."

A concerned wrinkle formed between his brows. "How do you feel?"

I mentally cataloged my body's physical feedback. Every day seemed to be a little different, and now that I knew I was pregnant, I understood why.

"Other than being epically tired, which seems to be my new reality, I feel great."

He rested his hand on my ribs, grazing his fingertips

down over my navel. He couldn't have broadcast his thoughts any more clearly. I stilled his hand.

"Blake, seriously. I'm fine."

"I'm just asking."

His tone was innocent but I knew better.

"Am I going to have to tie you down every time I want to have my wicked way with you?"

He flashed me a dark look. "I'm sure that won't be necessary."

I smirked, a tiny idea forming in my mind.

"I don't know. If you're so worried about hurting me, maybe the only choice is to let me take the reins until you aren't."

"Funny," he muttered dryly.

"I wasn't trying to be funny." I pretended to be serious, but he was doing so well for the both of us.

"I think you know I can't do that." His tone was deceivingly calm, the words unmistakably clear.

"You can't or you won't," I challenged.

He lifted an eyebrow. "Both. I'm pretty sure we've established that restraints are a hard limit for me."

I rolled to my side and slid my hand under his shirt, appreciating the toned ridges that led to a slight bulge in his jeans. "Being dominated isn't so bad, Blake. It could be fun, in small doses."

"All my instincts scream 'no' when you say things like that. Sounds like a recipe for disaster."

I smiled, clucking my tongue teasingly. "Whatever are we going to do with you, Blake?"

He pursed his lips and hoisted me on top of him possessively. "I could think of a few things."

I warmed under his heated gaze. "Me too. Now it's just a matter of convincing you." I peppered tiny kisses along his jaw, tugging his earlobe into my mouth with a soft bite. He groaned, lifting his hips so his growing erection connected with my clit just so. I was still bare and extremely sensitive. If he wasn't careful, he'd need a new pair of jeans.

Heat bloomed across my skin, and memories of last night slowly seduced me. Maybe convincing him he didn't need to hold back wouldn't be so difficult. We were already seconds from tearing each other's clothes off.

Except the last time I'd gotten bold in the bedroom, Blake had undeniably been rattled. Then again, he hadn't expected me to tie him up in the middle of night.

"I blindsided you last time. Give me another chance."

He dismissed me with a short laugh, which only made me want to make my case stronger.

"Listen, you're always controlling my pleasure."

"And you love it," he said bluntly.

"I do. But I'd be lying if I said I didn't think about giving that to you too. It's not all about being on a power trip, you know. The things we do...You give more than you take."

"So what? Are you saying you want to switch?"

I sat straighter and shrugged. "Maybe."

The directness of his question sent heat to my cheeks. I liked the sound of taking control more than I'd expected to.

"And what would this...domination...entail?" He brought his arms behind his head with a disarming smile.

A little thrill fluttered through me. "Well, you're not

exactly what I would call obedient. So we'd have to undergo some vigorous training for you to learn your place."

"And where is that?" His tone was low, his voice vibrating through me.

I hummed and lowered over him again. "Under me." I whispered against his lips, sliding my hand over his now very hard cock. "Unless I want you someplace else, that is."

He groaned and lifted his hips into my eager grasp. "I'm under you right now. Seems like a reward is in order."

"Don't be greedy."

I smiled to myself, knowing how many times he'd accused me of the same thing. He was patient only when it came to teasing me. When his own desire was on the line, his position might very well change.

He narrowed his eyes. "I've created a monster."

"You can call me *Master*," I joked with a coy smile.

He laughed again. "I think Mistress is more appropriate in these matters."

"I might like the ring of that."

A part of me couldn't believe we were having this conversation, even if he was only humoring me. Then again, I'd been home less than twenty-four hours after my hormone-fueled mission to speak to Michael and teach Blake what would become a painful lesson. Who knew what he was really thinking right now?

His wandering gaze betrayed him though. "I'm intrigued. When's the first lesson?"

"Maybe tonight, but only if you're on your best behavior," I said in a light voice. I had no idea what I was doing, but this could be fun if he let it go anywhere.

He released his hands and stroked up and then down to my thighs lazily. "You mean you're going to send me to work with visions in my head of you riding me all night?"

I frowned. "You're working today?"

We'd had a successful track record of keeping the weekends for ourselves. Especially after the insane week we'd had, I figured we deserved some downtime now more than ever.

"I was going to meet with Gove and discuss the Trevor situation."

"Oh," I said quietly. I couldn't argue with that. Any lingering stress started to melt off when I felt like we were moving in the right direction. Finally.

Reluctantly, I lifted off Blake and got ready for my day. We meandered downstairs, and I started to make myself a cup of tea. Blake came up behind me and kissed my neck before taking over the task.

"I've got this. Go sit."

"You're spoiling me," I muttered and took a seat at the island.

"You should get used to that. What do you want for breakfast?"

I wrinkled my nose. My stomach was still on the fritz. "Not hungry."

He pressed his lips together in a way that told me he wasn't thrilled with that answer.

He cleared his throat, went through the fridge, and pulled out some already diced fruit and a tub of yogurt. "While you were sleeping, I scheduled a doctor's appointment for you."

"You picked a doctor without me?"

"Dr. Henneman is the best obstetrician in the city, and you'll have only the best when it comes to this. There'll be no arguing that."

Any vulnerability I'd seen in his eyes before had been swiftly replaced. I wasn't quite sure when the shift in power had occurred, but it definitely had.

I rolled my eyes. "I see you're right back in the driver's seat."

"When it comes to your health, I always will be. With everything your body has been through, I want you and the baby to have the best care."

The baby. The way he said it sounded so certain. With the odds stacked against us, I'd had a hard time convincing myself that somehow in nine months, I'd have a baby in my arms. Still, I reached for that faith I'd promised Blake back on the islands. I'd believe it, until someone told us otherwise.

"Okay."

"The appointment is Monday. I had her after-hours staff call her to confirm it."

I took a sip of my tea. "Are you coming with me?"

"I'm going to be with you every step of the way. I promise you that." He placed a small bowl of sliced berries and melon topped with a dollop of yogurt in front of me. "Now try to eat a little, please."

CHAPTER TWELVE

ERICA

I was contemplating how I would spend the morning without Blake when Alli called.

"Hey. I wanted to check in and make sure everything was okay."

I smiled. "Yeah, we're good."

She released a sigh. "Thank goodness. I can't handle it when you two are on the outs."

I registered renewed guilt now that I was on the other side of it and had seen how upset Blake was. I can't imagine what he put Heath through not knowing where I was.

"I'm sorry, Alli. I shouldn't have pulled you into it."

"It's okay. You needed my support, and that's what I'm here for. I'm just glad that things worked out."

"They did. We're better."

"Good. Well, I'll let you get back to your making up."

"Actually Blake's in the city meeting with the attorney. I'm just killing time."

She hummed. "Are you up for a little retail therapy? I need to replenish my closet now that it's getting chilly."

"Sure," I said, liking the sound of that.

An hour later I was on Newbury Street, perusing the shops with Alli. We talked and laughed, consulting each other on what to buy when we couldn't decide between two things. I bought more than I expected to, considering we'd gone out to replenish Alli's wardrobe, not mine. But after a month abroad with Blake sparing no expense along the way, I was slowly acclimating to Blake's much higher standard of living. Knowing that I was spending my own money and not Blake's helped in my current situation, however. The payoff from the Clozpin sale afforded me as much financial freedom as I could hope for without dipping into our joint account for anything outside of necessities. Blake could argue about it, but I'd argue right back. I still valued my financial independence and the fact that I'd earned it.

After Alli and I had wasted a few hours shopping, we ducked into a little Mediterranean restaurant for lunch. My earlier queasiness had subsided and now my appetite was back with a vengeance. We tore through a couple appetizers that took the edge off.

Alli sipped her wine. The light danced off the liquid and caught on a sparkling red gem that dangled from the short thick chain around her neck.

"That's pretty. Is it new?"

She feathered her fingertips over it. "Thanks. Heath gave it to me a little while ago. I feel like it's too fancy to wear to work though, which is why you probably haven't seen it before."

Good taste, I thought, but then wondered if he'd given it to her to make up for anything else. Their relationship hadn't always been on solid ground, but since he'd returned from rehab they'd been incredibly solid. They'd been inseparable at the wedding. I couldn't mistake the stars in her eyes when they danced, and a little part of me hoped that the magic of our day might inspire Heath to want to take the next step with Alli. I knew she was ready. Maybe he was too.

"How have things been between you two?"

"We're good. Things were a little rocky after you and I left Clozpin, but we're good now. Better than ever."

I looked down at my napkin and wondered if Sophia had anything to do with that. I'd been the one to tip Alli off that Heath had a possibly not-so-innocent history with Sophia. I genuinely hoped that hadn't caused a rift between them, but after everything Sophia had put us both through, I thought she should know the truth—at least to the extent that I did. Only Heath and Sophia knew the whole truth.

"Did you two ever talk about Sophia?"

She nodded, taking a bite of her salad in silence.

I immediately felt like a jerk for voicing my thoughts out loud. "Sorry, Alli. I didn't mean to pry. It's between you two."

She shrugged. "It's okay. I'm not trying to keep it from you really. It's just . . . If Blake knew, I think it would make things uncomfortable between them. I don't want that any more than you do."

I was angry at Sophia then, for Alli's sake. Not only had she lost her job to that evil witch, but she very likely had to face the truth that she'd slept with Heath. If Alli felt anything the way I felt knowing that Sophia had loved Blake, and likely still did, I knew that it hurt like hell.

"You don't have to tell me anything you don't want to, but you can trust that I'm done letting Sophia fuck with our lives. She's caused enough damage. Somehow she always finds a way to get to me, but I'm done letting her. I swore it the day we left Clozpin for the last time."

Alli let out a heavy sigh. "Well, the truth is after she booted me from the business, I confronted Heath about her. I hinted—well, maybe I did more than hint—that I knew there might have been more than friendship between them. I told him I wanted to know the truth, even if it would hurt to hear it." Her brows drew closer as she stared out the window.

"What did he say?"

She turned back and met my gaze. "He didn't deny it. I have to give him credit for that."

"They slept together?"

She nodded, unable to mask the disgust. "Once. They'd been partying with their mutual friends at the time. High, of course. Blake was traveling so he never knew."

Suddenly, I hated Sophia all over again. "For all her claiming to love him…"

"Supposedly their relationship was on the rocks. One thing led to another. Drugs and alcohol. Bad decisions ensued. He never admitted it to Blake because he didn't want to hurt him, especially after everything Blake had done for him. I guess he always felt like Sophia used their friendship to stay close to Blake."

"I wouldn't put it past her. She'd stop at nothing to have Blake back." She'd proven as much with her despicable behavior toward me.

"Even at his lowest, Heath has a tender heart. I think he was too nice to call her on it. But of course he hasn't heard from her since Blake severed ties from her business. No love lost, I suppose."

Thankfully Sophia had been mercifully absent from our lives for months. I could only hope she'd given up trying to get him back. Blake and I were married, with a baby on the way now. I hated that she owned a part of his past, but at least I had his future. Of that I was certain.

Alli fidgeted with her necklace absently.

"Do you wish you didn't know?" I asked.

"At first I wished I didn't. I was upset of course. We've been through enough. I didn't want to think about him with other women, especially the one who abruptly fired me. I was furious and just as devastated as you were. But that's life. There's no point living in the past when we have an amazing future to look forward to."

I agreed, and a warm feeling floated over me. Their happiness always had that effect on me. Her cheeks flushed and she stared past me.

"What?"

"Nothing," she said.

A few seconds passed and the secretive smile never left her lips.

"Alli, what the hell. Spill it."

She shook her head. "God, I can't believe I'm telling you this." She drew in a deep breath and exhaled in a rush. "We've been talking about eloping."

My jaw fell. "Are you serious?"

"I haven't exactly been making my marriage dreams a secret, you know. We've been talking about taking the next step, and that's kind of how we're leaning."

"I figured you'd talked about it, but I had no idea that you'd take off and do it without telling anyone. That's crazy!"

She shrugged with a smile. "I don't know. The more I thought about it, the more romantic I imagined it would be. Plus I sort of got a lot of my wedding planning out of my system with yours. You were so easygoing, I ended up using half my ideas on you."

I pouted a little. "Oh, I'm sorry."

She laughed. "Don't be. I had an incredible time. It was a beautiful wedding. I'll never forget it and I have absolutely no regrets. You deserved an amazing day, and I was thrilled to be a part of it any way I could."

She smiled warmly, and I knew that she was being genuine. Blake and I had toyed with the idea of eloping too, but I knew his family wanted the wedding and would be sad to miss it. And when the day came, I was glad for our choice too. Alli and Fiona had done an impressive job planning everything while I was on the mend. No detail was missed, and the day was filled with a hundred special moments and thoughtful touches thanks to them. For all my bemoaning the prospect of a big family wedding in the months prior, a little part of me wanted that for Alli now too. But, ultimately, I wanted what she wanted. My job as her best friend was to support her the same way she supported me, whatever she decided to do.

"Is Heath really on board with this too?"

"Yeah. I mean, he's so easygoing about everything. Eloping is so much more his style. At first I was kind of upset when he brought up the idea. I wanted him to propose, you know? I wanted the surprise, the fancy diamond, the white dress, and the big reception. All those little things I'd dreamed about forever." She shook her head. "I don't know. I think I finally realized that life doesn't always have to go in order. I spent half my life planning the perfect wedding around a person I hadn't met yet. It's a little silly to think that we'd automatically want the same things."

"I'm sure he'd give you the big white wedding if that's what you wanted."

"I know he would. But, honestly, the more I think about it, the more it feels right to have it just be us."

Any doubts I had about their possible elopement swiftly melted. They loved each other, hopefully with the same singular passion that Blake and I shared. Suddenly nothing seemed more romantic than binding that love between them, with only them, the two most important people in the room.

"Sounds really romantic. Alli. Selfishly, I'll be sad to miss it, but I know it'll be wonderful."

She smiled. "We'll take pictures. Lots of pictures."

I caught her hand across the table, all the more grateful to have her in my life. When she'd left for New York months ago, I worried that our friendship would wane with distance. Circumstances brought us back together, and now falling in love would keep us in each other's lives forever. "We'll be sisters. Can you believe that?"

She squeezed my hand, light in her eyes. "You've always felt like a sister to me, so I can only say that having it official will be an added bonus."

"You've always been my family, Alli. Even when I haven't made it so easy for you."

She pursed her lips. "You *are* very temperamental, but I kind of love you for it."

I sat back and contemplated that assessment. Was I temperamental? I preferred *strong-willed*, but maybe the hormones taking over my body had shortened my fuse and altered my decision-making. I wasn't entirely convinced, but I was certain Blake would probably have a lot to say about that, in light of recent events.

"I'm sure Blake would agree, but thankfully he's as forgiving as you are."

Her soft expression became more serious. "How did things go when you got home?"

I thought back to the night before. I'd known that coming home and explaining my absence to Blake wasn't going to be easy, but I'd missed him terribly. We had so much to talk about, so much to work through. My heart broke when I saw him sitting alone at the table. Listless, staring into nothing. Then suddenly he'd come back to life when I came into his view. Remembering him so hurt and tired made my chest ache all over again, and I rubbed at the hurt there.

"Things were intense, as usual. Sometimes it's not always easy for us to get on the same page, especially when it comes to matters that we both feel strongly about. He's very stubborn, and, frankly, so am I."

"Well I'm sure you figured it out, one way or the other. You look like you barely slept." She winked.

A smile hinted at my lips. "We're better. We talked the way we should have before I'd left. We...made up."

"And?" She lifted an eyebrow.

I'd never really talked to Alli about my sex life with Blake, especially after she'd started hooking up with his brother. It seemed...weird. We'd discussed flings in the past, but I'd always been too swept up in my relationship with Blake to really get into the details. Not to mention a lot of the details were probably illegal in some states. I couldn't take for granted that half the things we did in the bedroom wouldn't completely terrify my best friend. Maybe today was a day for confidences though.

"I think the whole pregnancy thing has him unnerved. He doesn't know what to do with me," I said, hoping to keep it simple.

She hummed and tapped her lips. Mischief sparkled in her eyes. "Maybe he needs motivation."

"Call me crazy, but you look inspired." I couldn't imagine what she was thinking.

"I could be. I think we have a few more stores to hit."

★ ★ ★

BLAKE

I walked into the sports bar a few blocks outside of Fenway and looked around. Dean was at the bar, staring up at the televisions. He'd dressed casually, in jeans and a jersey. A well-worn baseball cap shaded his eyes. I took the stool beside him.

"No suit?"

He glanced over at me. "Casual Saturday. Plus, I'm heading to a game this afternoon with the kids."

"Sorry. I didn't mean to cut into your family time." For probably the first time in my life, I meant it. I'd been notoriously work-driven, especially with any matters that required the expertise of an attorney. But in a few short months, I'd be spending every spare minute with our new little family.

That reality hit me hard. Everything was going to change.

Dean cleared his throat, derailing my thoughts. "I know I'm one of your favorite people and all, but to what do I owe this pleasure?"

I stared up at the televisions broadcasting another game. I wasn't ready to dive right into the confession I'd kept from him for the past several years. It seemed strange to think, but Dean was one of the closest friends I had. Though we almost never interacted outside of business-related matters, he knew me better than most. Circumstances had demanded it.

"You know something funny? Every time I see you, it's because something has gone haywire in my life. You're lucky I don't hold it against you."

He laughed. "You're the one always getting into trouble. Not me."

"Not this time."

He glanced down at the bar and spun his coaster in a small circle. "So what's up? What's gone haywire now?"

"Is there anything new with Evans?"

I cared about the answer, but I was still buying some time. I hadn't heard from Dean during Erica's excursion, not that I would have cared about anything he had to say.

"Not that I can tell. Hopefully between him and the police, they're stalling out with whatever they've found. The Election Commission did a recount though. The governorship is going to Fitzgerald's opponent. Fitzgerald didn't make any statements on Friday after they announced it, though. We'll see what he has to say, if anything, next week."

Satisfaction coursed through me. I knew Erica would have mixed emotions about the news, but nothing was mixed about my wanting Daniel to feel the weight of that loss. I wanted him to feel it completely and for as long as possible. He didn't strike me as someone who handled failure well, not unlike myself.

"Probably could use the weekend to let that news settle in," I finally said.

"No doubt. I'm sure it's turning his world upside down. Hopefully that doesn't complicate things for us."

I couldn't imagine what Daniel's next move would be after such an extremely public letdown, but Dean was right to wonder if it would bleed into my current situation.

"I wanted to talk to you about the election actually."

He responded with a short nod, waiting for another kind of confession, no doubt.

"I know who tampered with the voting machines."

He shot me a stony look. "Say that again?"

"I can't exactly prove it's him, and that's why I never mentioned it to you earlier."

He spun on his stool and glowered. "You know the actual person who's behind this and you never fucking mentioned it?"

I bypassed his reaction and proceeded to detail all of it. From my first brush with the authorities as a kid, most of which he already knew or had heard, through the years of Trevor's persistent bullshit stunts, to his all-around damaging partnership with Max.

Dean's expression had turned from agitated to skeptical, a quality I valued and paid him well for.

"Sounds like he has a steady track record of meddling with your software ventures. You really think this kid rigged a state election?"

"When he got bored of messing around with my sites and Erica's, he partnered up with Max and one of Erica's former colleagues to create a competing site. Shoddy work, of course. I took it down pretty easily and then he disappeared again. Off the map. Until now. He's upped his game, it would seem, and he's making it damn hard for me to look too hard for him because now the feds have their eyes on me."

"So you've been dealing with him for years, for nearly as long as I've known you, and you never told me?"

When I'd laid it all out, I couldn't believe how long I'd really let this go on. Heath was right. Erica too. Trevor needed to be stopped, one way or the other.

"I guess it wasn't worth the fight until now."

"Damnit." He lifted his cap and scrubbed his forehead. "All right. So how do we find him and get Evans off your scent?"

"First I need to prove he did it. Second, I need to find him. He's anonymous, in every sense of the word."

"What does that mean? Everyone has a trail."

"For all intents and purposes, he's untraceable. Erica found him once, and then he disappeared again."

His eyebrows lifted. "*Erica* found him?"

I rolled my eyes. "I wasn't looking for him. She was. I'm sure if I'd given it a little more effort, I could have tracked him down."

He did a poor job of masking a smirk. "Sure. Anyway, how did she do it?"

"She found out his mother was living in the area. She

confronted him—without my permission, I might add—and things got heated. She left, and next thing we know Trevor and his mother up and move with no forwarding address."

"If we know her identity, that's something. A start anyway."

"True. I just need to do some digging."

Dean's eyes went wide. "*No.* No digging, Blake."

"I have people who might be willing to help. It won't trace back to me."

"It better fucking not." He shook his head. "Christ, you're going to give me an ulcer."

"If you don't already have one, you're not working hard enough."

He let out a short laugh, his anxiety fading a bit. "Thrilled to hear my quality of life means that much to you, after a decade of being at your beck and call." He grabbed his phone and typed in a few notes. "All right. Do your digging, very *very* carefully. I'll do mine as well. Let me know what you find, and we can decide how to approach Evans with it. I don't think that throwing out the name of a virtually unknown assailant is going to do anything more than grind his gears."

"My thoughts exactly."

My phone dinged with a text.

E: When can I expect you?
B: Finishing up now. Be home in about an hour.
E: Wait for me in the living room.

I hesitated, spinning over what she could possibly be cooking up for tonight. I hadn't taken this morning's teasing banter too seriously. Erica had a reputation for wanting to take charge until I had her begging to be dominated again.

But maybe there was more than play behind her proposition. Maybe she shared my concerns. Maybe she was right to. I was uneasy and aroused all at once.

B: Should I be worried?

I hovered over the send button a minute, not sure if I wanted her to answer that. Finally I sent it. By the time Dean had finished his beer, her reply had come in.

E: Terrified.

Little fucking minx.

CHAPTER THIRTEEN

ERICA

Blake's voice echoed through the large foyer. "I'm home!"

My heart beat a dizzying pace. I stretched the second black stocking up my thigh and stepped into my favorite black heels. I fluffed my hair, spread a deep shade of red over my lips, and made a popping sound. Hands on my slanted hips, I assessed my look in the mirror.

Alli had helped me pick out the perfect corset—after she'd chosen another for herself, which should have shocked me until I realized that Heath was likely just as capable as Blake was in the kink department.

The corset's shiny black leather molded perfectly to my torso, pushing the upper swells of my breasts out of the already low-cut garment that barely covered my nipples. A few popped buttons would bare all, and I was already fantasizing about the ways Blake could do that. I paired the garment with a pair of tiny black panties and sheer black thigh-highs.

As usual, I had no idea what I was doing, but chances were good that I looked the part. Blake would either laugh me out of the room or try to devour me. I picked up the tiny crop that I'd chosen earlier for that very scenario. I felt much better going into this dominant situation with a weapon to reinforce my position.

Heat suffused my cheeks, matching them to the deep red on my lips. I'd known Blake long enough and engaged in all manner of debauchery with him. He knew my body intimately, every part of it. Why this suddenly embarrassed me I couldn't understand. I took a deep breath and called out to him.

"Coming!"

If all went to plan, I would be... soon.

The first floor of the house was growing dark. Candles that I'd lit earlier flickered from several small tables surrounding the couches. Blake was sprawled out on one, his focus on some invisible point on the ceiling.

"Welcome home." I sashayed into the room, hoping I sounded more sultry than silly. I was one part insecure, two parts raging with hormone-fueled desire.

Our gazes met in the dusky light. His tracked me as I came closer. I slowed in front of him. My heart raced with anticipation and my head swam with a thousand wild thoughts, but it was the hunger glowing in his eyes that stole my breath.

"You're taking this dominant thing pretty seriously." His voice was a dangerously low murmur.

"Would you rather I go change... maybe into something a little more... demure?" I canted my head, taunting him.

"Not a chance." He reached for me. "Come here."

Oh, I wanted to, but a little voice spoke up and a surge of courage took over. "I'm in charge tonight, Blake." I took the edge of the crop to the hem of his T-shirt and lifted. "Take this off."

A devilish smile crept over his lips. He sat up and

removed his shirt slowly. He tossed it to the floor before resting back into his casual pose on the couch. "And I'm supposed to be able to play nice like this for nine months?"

Feeling a little more empowered, I took the space between his knees. "Being in control all the time is hard work. You deserve a break."

He lifted an eyebrow, trailing a lazy caress along the inside of my thigh. "Is that right?"

My breath caught when the back of his hand came closer to the very tiny patch of fabric covering my sex. I was already wet and envisioning all the amazing ways he could make me feel if the tables were turned. I hoped he wouldn't notice, but the predatory look in his eye promised that he wasn't missing any of the signals my body was sending right now. He journeyed higher, tracing the hem of my panties.

I moved his hand and traced the crop along the outline of the insistent erection pressing against his jeans. "I think these need to go, too."

He stood slowly, inches from me. He shucked his jeans, revealing his tented boxer briefs. I licked my lips. What I wouldn't do to drop to my knees and paint him red with this ridiculous lipstick. My fingers itched to touch him, tease him. I'd do that later.

I grazed the tip of the crop against the head of his cock through the briefs. "These too."

"Seems a little one-sided," he said. Pushing them down, he sprang free.

My gaze was transfixed there. "As it should be."

He hooked a finger under the thin strap of my panties. "These, I think, we could do without."

"No touching," I ordered, not sounding nearly as confident as I should have.

"That's no fun." He smirked and released the strap with a snap.

"Your hands can't be trusted. You can use your mouth, but only when I tell you."

Dark desire shaded his eyes. "Interesting game."

I shoved him back down on the couch and waited a moment before straddling his lap. His thick cock was already straining north, all too ready for me. I lowered and brushed my sex against it. A rush of desire arrowed straight to my clit, making me dizzy with want. If my panties went anywhere, he'd be inside me in seconds, and I knew he wasn't opposed to tearing them off either. Before I convinced myself that was entirely okay, a desirable outcome even, I harnessed my derailed thoughts.

I reached for the top snap that held the corset tight over my breasts and popped it open. My chest swelled against the leather, creating pressure I was eager to relieve. I wanted the girls free as much as I wanted Blake's mouth on them.

"Open your mouth," I said.

He smirked. "Only if you promise to put something delicious in it."

"You talk too much."

I lifted on my knees and held out the open flap of the corset. He licked his lips before taking the shiny leather with his teeth. He gazed up at me, and I swore in that moment something in his eyes told me I was going to pay for this later. My breasts heaved under uneven breaths. Yeah...I was in way over my head.

"Pull."

Without a moment's delay, he twisted and yanked, releasing five snaps at once. Relief and desire met when he leaned in, licking the soft skin between my breasts. I sighed and resisted the urge to lower and grind against his erection. That wouldn't do much for anyone's willpower.

"Blake...stop."

Instead he planted his lips on the inside of my breast, licked and nibbled. I grabbed him by the hair and pushed him back. His eyes went molten. His hands strained in tight fists on either side of us.

"Can we get to the part where I use my tongue, sweetheart...before I tear this corset clean off your body?" He spoke through gritted teeth.

A little too thrilled with his growing frustration, I released him and went for my snaps, freeing them one by one, until I was all but revealed. His focus riveted there.

I smiled and let the garment fall, baring me to him completely.

"You can use your tongue now. Gentl—"

He didn't waste another second claiming my nipple with an open-mouthed kiss. I whimpered when he drew my peak into his mouth with an ardent suck. The sensation was both pleasure and a bite of a pain.

"Careful, Blake. They're tender."

"Sorry," he rasped, easing up just enough. "Mmm, swollen too. They had me seduced from across the room."

He pulled my nipple into his mouth. His tongue was like velvet over the hardened tip. I never felt his teeth. Instead he began to tease the skin around my nipple with hard sucks, decorating my breasts with a dozen tiny pink marks. Jolts of intense pleasure shot through me.

I sifted my hands through his dark brown locks, gentler than before, guiding him to the other breast, which he lavished with the same dedicated attention as he'd given the first. Fire burned under my skin where we touched and everywhere I wanted to be touched. I was soaked. And needy. I threw my head back, giving myself over to the electric sensation of his mouth so wonderfully tormenting me.

His willpower must have crumbled as quickly as mine. His hands crept from his sides to cup my ass, shoving me tightly against his erection. I moaned, and my hips seemed to move on their own accord. He roved over my hipbones, testing the thin black straps again.

"No touching," I admonished gently, gripping his forearm to still his wandering hand.

"But it's mine," he ground out, sliding past the boundary of panties and deep into my wetness.

"Ahh," I whimpered. He massaged my clit, trailing magical circles around it before delving deeper, breaching my pussy with his fingertips. I clenched around him, wanting that...needing that.

Yet as wonderful as that felt, a little voice reminded me of the rules I meant to enforce. I was already losing control when I'd been so determined to keep it.

Without thinking it through, I flicked the tip of the crop against his upper chest. A flash of irritation quickly replaced the hazy lust that had regarded me seconds ago. His mood now seemed as red as the tiny trail I'd left on his pectoral. I dropped my jaw, an apology working its way from my lips when...

"Fuck that," he growled. Curling his fingers, he removed my panties with an unapologetic snap.

I gasped. In a second he had me on my back. My legs spread around his unyielding frame. His hands locked my wrists tightly to my sides.

"Blake!" I groaned in protest.

His gaze traveled the length of me, his jaw tense. I squirmed beneath him to no avail. He was in charge. I was like someone whose firearm had been turned against him in a moment of weakness or confusion. My heart sped up at the thought of the crop being used on me, smarting my skin. I wasn't sure if I wanted that. I was as sensitive as I was wanton.

Shit. This plan had been shot all to hell. While I wrestled with my inability to keep Blake's controlling tendencies in check, his mouth came over my breast again. He delivered a gentle stroke with more painstaking restraint than I would have expected, considering the significant shift in his mood. He moved to the other, and then trailed his tongue down my belly, dipping briefly into my navel. He paused to kiss my scar, as he was now prone to do every chance he got. Then he was positioned between my legs, kissing and nibbling my inner thigh just above where the stocking ended.

I closed my eyes. Oh, I loved that...

I exhaled with a sigh.

"I'm going to fuck you with my mouth, Erica. And you're either going to tell me exactly how you want it, or you're going to be begging for me make you come any way I see fit."

"This was not the plan, Blake."

"You made the rules. I'm just bending them a little bit." He drew my clit into his mouth, flicking his tongue mercilessly over the sensitive nub. He retreated enough to blow a puff of cool air against my sensitive flesh.

Molten heat shot through me. I tensed and struggled against his hold.

"Tell me what to do, boss."

I shifted my hips, frustrated but wanting relief. "Goddamnit."

"That's not too descriptive. I'm waiting for my orders."

I lifted my head enough to glare. "Fuck you."

He grinned deviously and placed the lightest kiss over the flesh that throbbed for more pressure. "We'll get to that. How about we start with what you want me to do with my tongue."

I dropped my head back with an exhale. "I'm not going to beg."

"If you want it badly enough, you'll need to at least ask for it. Say the words, and my mouth is yours to wield." He punctuated his statement with a lick up the seam of my pussy.

I twisted helplessly and arched to get closer, but he pulled back. "Trust me, I can't fucking wait to bury my face in your sweet little cunt. Talk to me, baby."

Fucking hell.

"Lick me."

"Hmm, that's a start," he murmured. Then he obliged,

bathing my most intimate parts in the warmth of his talented mouth. Blood pounded through my veins. At my wrists, where he held me. In my belly, where desire gnawed and grew. My thighs tightened around him, need pulsing in all the places where our skin met. Except his touch wasn't keeping up with my need. I bucked my hips, a silent request for more.

"Blake, just do it," I begged. Was I begging? *Goddamn.* "Do what?"

I threw my head to the side. "Harder."

He came at me with more pressure, taking me right to the edge of where I most wanted to be. But I needed just a little more.

"Blake!"

"You've got a vocabulary worthy of an Ivy League education. Fucking use it."

A tortured groan left me. "Touch me with your fingers."

He released one of my hands to drag his thumb over my clit. Pleasure slid like molasses through my veins when he repeated the journey with his tongue.

"Inside. Push inside me."

"Like this?" The low hum of his words vibrated against my sex as he slid two fingers deep into my sensitive tissues.

"Ahh," I cried. I arched into his touch, stars forming on the edges of my vision. "Deeper," I said breathily.

Deeper he went, over and over, massaging the sensitive spot inside. All the while, eating me like I was his last meal. I began to tremble uncontrollably. Tensing and trying to draw him to me tighter, my whole body begged for more.

"Oh, God...just like that."

His taunting brand of pleasure had given way to an all-consuming onslaught of sensations. For that I praised everything holy with the cry that tore from my lips. I struggled against his hold, but he was firm, keeping up the restraint that would only bring me higher.

"Don't stop." I couldn't hide the desperation in my voice as he coaxed me closer.

Then I flew. Vibrant colors danced behind my eyes. Every thought channeled to the erotic way he touched me. Overcome by the blinding sensations, I came with a sharp cry. Every muscle tensed, and my body quaked beneath his ministrations.

Breathless and shuddering from the powerful release, I tried to regain some control over my brain. Blake never moved. Instead, he continued to lap at me. A series of soft, reverent licks sent tiny shockwaves through me. With my free hand, I put pressure on his shoulder, a silent plea for relief.

He glanced up at me. The wicked look in his eyes matched his devilishly handsome mouth, now glistening with evidence of the mind-bending pleasure only he could deliver.

"I could feast on you for hours. If I didn't want to fuck you so badly, I probably would. But I'm selfish and want to come in your tight little cunt now. Would you like that?"

"Yes," I breathed, wondering how I ended up married to such a dirty-mouthed sex god.

He released me and slid up my body. The brush of his skin against mine sent my nerve endings dancing again. All that talk of wanting him under me had been hogwash. Nothing in the world felt as divine as the press of him over me, his powerful frame pushing me down or up against whatever surface—hard or soft—that he was determined to screw me on.

"Tell me how you want it."

The low timbre of his request vibrated through me. I tossed my head to the side, swallowing hard. I couldn't think. I wasn't sure I wanted to.

"Behind you?" he asked. "It's deeper that way, if you can handle it."

I blinked, piecing together the possibilities, all of them promising a handful of earth-shattering orgasms.

"Or do you want to ride me, my tasty little Dominatrix?" He licked along my collarbone, nipping along the slope of my shoulder.

With a breathy sigh, I melted into the couch like the worn-out rag doll I'd become. My head was still buzzing from the delicious orgasm he'd coaxed out of me.

I heard him chuckle. "Damn, baby. Are you giving up already? You had me all twisted up with your Dom gear."

"Shut up before I get my second wind," I muttered, turning my focus back to his gorgeous face.

"Hmm, let's see if we can revive you."

He came down and took my mouth. I tasted myself on the intimate kiss that left me tingling all over again. When he broke away, the haze of my desire lifted slightly at the sight before me. I grinned, rubbing my thumb under his lower lip.

"Your lips are all red."

He responded with a broad smile. "I can handle that. Unless you want me to go out like this. I'm not into public humiliation."

I wrinkled my brow, confused.

"Never mind. I should stop giving you ideas. Now, if you've found that second wind you were looking for, turn over and put that lovely ass in the air."

Inside I railed at the command. Just enough to say, "No."

He regarded me for a moment. "I can't tell if you're being a good Dom or a bad sub."

"The feeling is mutual."

He laughed, a lighthearted sound that quickly morphed into a gasp when I took his cock in my hand. I stroked him to the tip, down to the base, and back again. I cupped his sac with my other hand, grazing my nails lightly over the smooth skin.

His eyes closed, vulnerability sweeping his taut features. "I need to be inside you, Erica. Right fucking now."

"I'm not going to have to spell it all out for you, am I?" I slid my grasp all the way up, milking a tiny bead of moisture from the head of his cock. I swept my thumb over the slit and brought the taste of him to my lips with a lazy lick. The breathy moan that left me wasn't all show. Having proof of his desire on my tongue inspired all sorts of new ideas on how to tease out his pleasure. "That could really draw this whole thing out."

His jaw fell open a fraction. "You're a real piece of work, you know that?"

I licked my lips, imagining the soft crown of his cock between them. "Takes one to know one."

"You still looking for high ground, sweetheart?"

"Oh, I'm on it," I countered, feeling empowered. His erection thickened and flinched in my grasp.

All well and good, except the dangerous look in his eyes had my heart racing.

"Not for long," he said huskily.

Without another word, he grabbed my wrist mid-stroke, circled my torso, and flipped me to my stomach. He nudged me higher, so my elbows rested on the arm of the couch.

His calves were on either side of mine, the rough hair tickling my skin. And, as previously requested, my back-side was high and available for whatever he had planned. He skated his palm over the curve of my ass. He gave it a squeeze before coming down on me with a quick slap.

"I want to tie you up tight and spank you raw for that little show."

Fever prickled my skin when I imagined him following through on that threat. I moaned and pushed back against him. Now that I'd been stripped of my power, I wouldn't mind a little more of that. After all, I had been a *very* bad girl.

He pressed his body against me, bringing his mouth to my neck.

"But I won't. I'll just watch you come undone around me."

His hot breath sent a violent shiver over me. Empty promises, I thought vaguely. Then everything tensed when I felt his fingers and then his cock pushing into me. He was careful but reached the deepest part of me in a matter of seconds.

The pleasure cut through me, razor-sharp. "Oh, fuck."

He gripped me firmly, withdrew, and sank deep again. "I think I will."

With that, he began to fuck, tearing me apart one thrust at a time. I dug my nails into the fabric of the couch, hanging on through the storm brewing inside.

Nothing was dominant about my position now. I was exposed, held firm by his strength, trapped by the craving of our bodies coming together this way. Every cell was more alive. Every nerve ending seemed to reach for more delicious stimulation.

My thighs were pressed together. I rubbed one stocking-covered foot over the other. My toes tingled and curled. I felt powerless to do anything but take his fierce drives.

And the more he gave, the more I wanted.

"Oh God, it's so good."

"You feel fucking incredible." His hold on my hips tightened, and he pumped faster.

I was right at the edge, ready to fly off the cliff, when he suddenly withdrew. He tossed me to my back again. I was panting, trembling with need.

"Blake!" If this was his last play in an effort to tease me to tears, I was going to...

His mouth crashing to mine robbed me of that angry thought. I opened to him, wanting his taste on my tongue like I wanted my next breath. He settled between my thighs, hiked my thigh over his hip, and swiftly joined us again. I whimpered with relief and pleasure.

When I connected with his hooded gaze, my chest tightened.

"I want to see your eyes when you come," he whispered.

There it was. He'd taken me from lightheartedness to lust, to a soul-branding kind of intimacy that brought everything higher. His reach went beyond the body and straight to my heart. The carnal fever ripping through me became something more potent still.

I anchored his mouth to mine, and we kissed until we were both breathless. Every passionate thrust was a proclamation. Every possessive touch was a promise. Waves of rapture crashed over me, one after the next, until I was boneless and trembling.

The muscles of his shoulders bunched under my touch. He lengthened, hitting me someplace even deeper. The orgasm that I thought impossible after the string he'd just given shattered through me.

His hips slammed against me, and my name tore from his lips with a hoarse cry. His body jerked and spasmed as he filled me.

Collapsing over me with his mouth on my shoulder, he worked to catch his breath. "Damn," he muttered.

"Yeah" was the only word I could manage. I melted around him, relishing the contact. Even after being so intimately connected, I didn't want to be far from his touch.

He lifted to his elbows, his chest still heaving. With a satisfied smile, he was the picture of sated. Flushed. Gorgeous. And possibly a little too pleased with himself.

I ran my finger over his etched lips. "Don't look so smug."

He lifted an amused brow. "Smug?"

"You look like you just took home a trophy."

He laughed and I fought my own smile.

"I did. Your orgasms are like trophies. I'm collecting as many as I can."

I rolled my eyes. Another few points for Blake.

He skimmed his hand over my torso, up and down my leg, and snapped the elastic that held the stockings tight to my thighs.

"I love these. Wear that corset again though, and I won't be held responsible for my actions."

I pushed at his chest. "You're a bad sub."

He wrapped his arms around me, pulling me closer. "Yeah, well, so are you."

I failed to mask a pout. I was more than a little annoyed that my attempt to dominate had gone well off course, but undeniably satisfied with the results. "You're not in charge, you know."

Instead of a cocky remark, Blake regarded me silently, brushing a damp strand of hair from my forehead.

"I know," he muttered. "There's something a lot bigger than you and me taking charge right now."

He cradled my cheek, looking deeply into my eyes. Then he settled his touch over my abdomen. His hand splayed there with a light caress.

"Our baby. The crazy way I love you. Everything I feel right now that I couldn't control even if I wanted to."

I closed my eyes, covering his hand with my own. My heart beat stronger at the vision that emerged. My belly, no longer flat, but full and round with our baby. Tiny kicks under our hands, anticipation in our hearts. I wanted that more than anything.

And he was right. Nothing was more important.

CHAPTER FOURTEEN

BLAKE

We'd had an intense weekend of making up and reconnecting after an absence that had rocked us both. But Monday afternoon came quickly. I wasn't the nervous type, but a part of me felt like a fish out of water as we sat in Dr. Henneman's waiting room.

I waited by Erica's side, her hand safe in mine, to be called in for our appointment. I wasn't a fan of waiting, but watching Erica scan the room, wide-eyed with anticipation, was almost worth it. A young mother sat across from us, her belly stretching the material of her maternity top. The weight there limited her range of motion as she tried to keep her small child from distributing the magazines on the table all over the floor. She scolded him gently, shooting apologetic looks our way when he shouted in protest.

I still couldn't wrap my head around it. I'd seen pregnant women in passing all the time—I'd even employed some. I'd just never associated it with anything that I would personally experience, as a father, a husband. But here I was, and if all went well, we could be there too, trying to keep a toddler from destroying everything we owned.

Powerless as I was to control the outcome, I was silently determined to move heaven and earth to make sure Erica had a healthy pregnancy that resulted in the child we both now fervently wanted. I'd be there to support her through everything. Months of pregnancy. Morning sickness and discomfort. Labor...

Before my thoughts could take another spin through the "oh fuck" cycle, Erica's name was called. I rose and followed her into the white examining room where the nurse took her vitals. A few minutes later, the doctor joined us. She was a pretty woman—thin and tall, with pixie-cut white hair.

"Erica?"

Erica took her outstretched hand from the examining table where she sat. "Yes, and this is my husband, Blake."

"Wonderful to meet you, Blake. Congratulations to you both. You must be thrilled."

She smiled warmly, but concern lodged in my gut. I nodded quickly, my jaw tight. All my uneducated fantasies about parenthood were swiftly placed on pause when I remembered the risks, the dangers, and the very real possibility that all those dreams could be crushed by the woman standing in front of me. Erica was legitimately pregnant. Keeping it that way was another matter, and though I'd never voiced my doubt before, Erica's concerns echoed my own.

Life hung in the balance, and my powerlessness over that fact had me instantly uneasy.

"I'm not sure if you've had a chance to review Erica's records—" I began.

The doctor sat on her stool and glanced over at me. "I have actually. They were faxed over this morning."

"So you're aware of the injuries she sustained."

"Yes." Her chipper expression dimmed a bit. Her attention slid to Erica, whose expression mirrored hers. "I imagine what you've been through was nothing short of devastating. I'll be honest. I'm actually quite surprised that you've been able to conceive so quickly."

"So were we," Erica said, her voice quiet.

"But here you are." Dr. Henneman brightened again. "And I can tell you that the labs that came back look great. Your hormone levels are where they should be, so my plan today is to do an ultrasound and hopefully we can get you a due date."

Before I could pepper the doctor with more questions, she had Erica lay back on the table. She dimmed the lights and a couple minutes later, the fuzzy gray screen on the ultrasound machine came to life. I held Erica's hand, sharing the comfort of someone else who was experiencing this for the first time and having no idea what to expect. Math, science, the technical details of anything were always well within my grasp. But there was nothing technical about the little orb on the screen and the tiny flicker at its center.

"That's your baby," the doctor said, pointing to the fuzzy oval.

Erica's hand tightened in mine. I brought it to my lips, kissing it, never taking my eyes from the screen. A torrent of strange emotions swept over me, feelings that had no name, no frame of reference. All I knew was that everything was changing. Right before our eyes, the whole world had taken on new meaning. The doctor carried on with her examination, zeroing in on the tiny heartbeat. My own heart thumped loudly in my ears when she gave the rhythm sound.

After a few more overwhelming minutes, the doctor gave us a due date for early July. Erica was seven weeks along, and I quickly calculated the date of conception back to our wedding night.

Wow. I smiled and silently patted myself on the back. But I still couldn't shake my worry.

The doctor printed out some ultrasound photos and handed them to me while Erica cleaned up.

"Is that it, then?" I hesitated, not sure how to broach any one of the hundred questions running through my head, all surrounding Erica's health and history.

The doctor smiled warmly. "For now, yes. Everything looks great."

"You're optimistic."

She laughed. "Would you rather I not be?"

"I prefer realistic over anything. What happened to Erica was very serious. It's been weighing on us."

She offered a sympathetic smile. "I understand, more than you know. I specialize in high-risk pregnancies, so I meet a lot of parents who are expecting the worst. Your concerns are valid, but Erica is healthy and I'm hopeful."

I paused, brushing my thumb over the edge of the picture. I wanted to believe all of it. I truly did. "Have you treated anyone with comparable . . . issues?"

She nodded. "I have treated couples facing some very discouraging odds when it comes to conception. I've seen many overcome those odds, and I've seen some who haven't been able to. You're very lucky."

"What would you say the chances are that she'll have a normal pregnancy?"

One glance at Erica and I wanted to flog myself for asking when I read the trepidation in her eyes.

I shifted my attention back to the doctor and her expression was no longer sympathetic, but more serious. "Right now, I would say they are one hundred percent until I see something of concern."

Somewhere tension released.

The doctor tilted her head. "Have faith, Blake. Don't fret away this special time with worry. Everything looks wonderful so far. Come see me in a month and I hope to put your concerns to rest all over again. We'll do this every month, and toward the end, every couple weeks. And I will be here every step of the way to answer questions and alleviate any concerns you may have."

I blew out a breath and glanced at Erica, who seemed to share my relief. I should have carried a more confident facade for her sake, but the doctors had the answers in this situation, not me, and Erica was the patient. This was my chance to get as much information as I could, because Googling this shit only horrified me. In this case, my limited access to technology did me no favors.

"And sex is fine, just in case that might be something you were worrying about too."

I lifted my eyebrow. This woman had no idea how I fucked, and I wasn't about to run the details by her.

"Completely fine," she reassured with a wink.

We stood and the doctor helped Erica off the table.

"You have a very protective father-to-be on your hands, Erica."

Erica rolled her eyes with a smile. "Trust me, I know."

★ ★ ★

ERICA

We drove back toward home. Autumn leaves flew across the road in windy gusts, scattering across the grassy yards that were dulling from the vibrant green of summer. The earth was dying, yet I held life, a tiny fragile promise.

I hadn't been sure what to expect from today's appointment, but I couldn't have been happier. I wanted to shout our news off the rooftops but knew that we should wait a little longer. Still, I couldn't believe how incredibly lucky we were.

"You all right?" Blake caught my hand and held it in his lap.

I met his gaze and smiled. "Yeah. Just happy."

"Good." His concern softened into a look full of warmth, full of love that I felt in my heart all the way to my fingertips. "I'm sorry if I freaked you out in there."

"It's okay. You asked a lot of the questions I wanted to. It's hard to feel like I don't fully understand what my own body is capable of."

"If you don't understand, I'm completely in the dark."

I laughed. At least when it came to pregnancy, I suppose that was true. Beyond that, he seemed to know all too well what my body was capable of. Heat flooded my cheeks at the small reminder of that fact.

Hello, hormones. That quickly, I wanted to be home. I wanted to be in his arms. I wanted to celebrate and revel in our good news over and over.

Blake's phone ringing from the Tesla's dashboard broke the fantasies my brain was stitching together. The caller ID read *Remy.* Blake's eyebrows knitted.

"Are you going to answer it?"

Assuming the man calling was the same one who owned and operated the sex club to which I'd very naively gained entrance months ago, my curiosity burned. As far as I knew, Blake wasn't in regular contact with Remy. What could he want to speak to Blake about now?

"Not right now. I'll call him later," Blake said quickly. He released my hand and hovered over the end call button.

"Just talk to him now." Before he could stop me, I accepted the call from the console.

He shot me a glare when Remy's accented voice filled the car.

"Blake, hello. Do you have a minute?"

"I have exactly one minute. What do you want?" The tension in Blake's tone was unmistakable.

"It's about Sophia."

A knot began to form in my stomach, filled with immediate regret and worry. I'd wanted to know Remy's reason for calling, but now suddenly I didn't. I didn't want her presence anywhere near us.

Blake's tension grew, too, evident in the tick in his jaw. "What about her?"

"She's been hurt."

Blake paused, his focus fixed on the road ahead. "What happened?" he asked calmly.

"It was at the club. A patron, he was fairly new. I suppose she and I both underestimated him. But you know how she is. She..." He cleared his throat. "You know her demands. She challenged him, and he took the bait. Unfortunately he took it too far."

"Fucking hell. I could have predicted that. Is she okay?"

"She's at the hospital."

I pretended to look away, as if I could give him any privacy now. Even as I pretended to want to, I watched out of the corner of my eye as Blake's grip tightened on the wheel.

"You should go see her. She'll want to see you. No one will understand. You're the only one she has," Remy said, a touch of pleading in his request.

My mind shouted a string of heartless protests. Maybe this wasn't one of Sophia's dark plans orchestrated to lure Blake back into her life, but that is what she would hope for from it. I knew her well enough to know that.

"I'm not the only one she has. Call her parents."

"They won't understand this, Blake." Remy's voice lowered. "You know that."

"Then maybe she should start talking about it. I couldn't be what she wanted then, and I'm not what she needs now. Going to see her now...that's not the answer. She's a fucking prize-winning masochist, and you knew it. You left her alone with some sick fuck, Remy."

"I don't deny that I failed her. Don't you fail her now too."

Blake took a breath and spoke evenly. "The answer is no. Call her parents."

"I don't know—"

"I'm on the road right now. I'll text you their info when I get home."

Blake ended the call without another word. A sick feeling settled over me with the reminder of how Blake had loved her once. Maybe that couldn't compete with how we felt for each other now, but the reality of it still hurt.

"I'm sorry, baby."

I stared out the window, reaching for the happiness I'd felt before Remy called. "You don't have to be sorry."

"She upsets you, and I swore I wouldn't let her do that to you anymore. Of all days . . . Christ. I'm sorry."

"It's fine," I lied.

I hadn't let Sophia get under my skin for months, but somehow she'd managed to drive herself into our world again, whether she meant to or not. I scolded myself for caring, for cursing the woman who was hurt enough to be in the hospital. For Blake's sake, I tried to feel sorry for her. I couldn't imagine what could have gone wrong though. Within the walls of the club, where the most depraved acts could be acceptable, maybe even commonplace, the possibilities were many.

"What do you think happened to her?" I asked.

"Let's not talk about it, okay?"

"Do you think she's really hurt?"

His shoulders sagged. "It's entirely possible. If the guy beat her badly enough that she landed in the hospital, it's probably not good. The things you and I do . . . it's nothing next to the things that happen at the club, Erica. The threshold for pain and acceptable behavior goes much higher than yours. For someone to take it over the line, to injure her..."

"Maybe you should go see her." I forced the words out. But maybe she needed Blake more than I realized.

He pulled into the driveway, parked, and turned to me. "No."

Relief and the inexplicable need to be sympathetic battled within me.

"It's okay, Blake. I won't deny that I completely despise Sophia, but you loved her once. This is an unusual situation, and I understand if you want to see her."

He lifted his eyebrows. "But I don't."

"If you feel like you should..."

"You're my priority. You're my whole life. You and our baby, and protecting our future...That's the only thing I'm worried about now. Sophia has problems that run deeper than I could ever fix. That's why I left, and if she has any chance of getting better, she needs to face them. Me being there for her now does nothing to help her in the long run. Maybe now she'll come clean with her family."

"What if she doesn't?"

He hesitated. "Remy will be there for her."

"How do you know?"

He rested back into his seat. "Because he's in love with her."

In love? Though my interaction with Remy had been only mere minutes, he had left an impression. The man who owned the sex club Blake used to frequent was both intense and intimidating. But also handsome and charismatic in a way I didn't have words for. Sophia had attended the club with Blake in the past, but somehow associating her with Remy seemed odd. He was a dominant creature, no doubt, perhaps equally or more so than Blake. But I couldn't imagine Blake sharing a woman, even one as awful as Sophia, with anyone.

"How…if you were with Sophia?"

"He was honest with me about his attraction to her. Something about her fascinated him. He wanted to share her, at least physically. Suffice it to say, I don't share. I refused, and he didn't press the issue after that. After she and I split up, I gave him my blessing."

"Were they together?"

Blake's jaw tightened. "A few months later. Sophia made sure to let me know it, too. Last-ditch effort to stir my jealousy and try to get me back, I suppose. But as far as I know, nothing ever materialized between them."

"Because she still wanted you."

"I guess you could say they weren't compatible."

"But he's a Dom."

"Not all Doms are the same, as evidenced by the one who put her in the hospital. Let's just say on the scale of intensity, Remy's proclivities align a little more closely to mine. Anyway, it doesn't matter. I'm sorry she's hurt. I truly am, but I'm not letting her steal another minute of time away from us."

I took his hand and held it in my own. I traced the lines in his palm. I was overwhelmed and grateful that he felt that way. That no matter what, our future meant more to him than a woman who'd done nothing but try to tear us apart. I would have loved him and understood either way, but I felt his fervency and loyalty in the deepest places of my heart.

"Thank you," I murmured.

"I mean it," he said softly, tipping my chin to meet his warm gaze. His tightened expression had relaxed. Love replaced the concern and unease that had swept in over our moment.

"I know, and I'm grateful. I want you to know that if you change your mind—"

"I won't."

I simply nodded, sensing something final in the way he said it.

"You're a better person than I am, Erica. I'm not sure if I could ever let you go to the side of another man who ever had your heart."

I laced our fingers together. "You're the only man who's ever had my heart, Blake."

"Thank God for that." He kissed me. "Come on. Let's go inside."

CHAPTER FIFTEEN

BLAKE

Erica had skipped work for the appointment on Monday, and the day had ended in bed. Just her and me, between the sheets.

I couldn't keep my hands off her, which was par for the course. But Erica was changing. She was fiery and more sensitive at once. Responsive in new ways. Tender in others. Physically, I felt like I was discovering her all over again. There was something magical and terrifying about all of it, but I wouldn't want to be on that roller coaster of emotion with anyone else.

I woke up in the morning entranced by the woman lying beside me. Her light hair was a tangle on the pillow. Her lips parted as she slept soundly.

I'd been with plenty of other women, but all the shameless nights I'd spent at The Perle couldn't measure up to one night with Erica. No one had ever ruled my heart like this. No one.

My thoughts floated to Sophia, the only one I'd confused the word *love* with. I lay back on the bed, trying to ignore the visions my imagination was conjuring of her in the hospital. She was hurt. To what extent, I wasn't sure. I wanted to know and I didn't. I'd cut her out of my life completely, but my conscience nagged me. This morning, my conscience spoke in a voice that was too reminiscent of Sophia's, insisting that she needed me.

Sophia had often walked a dangerous line when it came to the lifestyle. I'd struggled over that line many times. With Sophia. With others. But I'd never battled so hard with it until Erica. Realizing early in our relationship that she'd had a violent sexual past, I made the decision to walk away from anything that could bring her back to those memories. I wasn't sure how successful I would be at the time, but Erica hadn't given me the chance to try. She'd never questioned my basest desires when it came to sex. Even this weekend, her second failed attempt at dominance, was proof of her openness. The fighter in her seemed intent to try those limits and push past boundaries, some of which I wanted her to heed more carefully, for her own sake. Not to mention mine.

But every time, somehow, we found pleasure. We found each other.

Nothing so profound had materialized with my ex. My dominant appetites had tailored to Sophia's submissive tendencies easily, but I soon realized that her needs went far beyond simple submission. She'd beg for pain— the kind that left marks for days, the kind that threatened to scar.

If my desires had grown dark, they'd been inspired by something far darker in her. Despite all her begging to have me back, Sophia didn't want a Master. She wanted a monster, and I couldn't be that for her.

I'd come unhinged only once. I'd flown to New York City on a red-eye from the West Coast, exhausted and ready to see her. What I found instead was her and

Heath passed out in bed, semi-clothed. I didn't bother to ask whether or not they'd fucked. Half a dozen other people I'd never met were in similar states of post-bender undress all over the condo. I'd sent Heath and his cohorts packing.

When I came for her, seeing twelve shades of rage, she'd never flinched. Satisfaction simmered in her eyes, as if she'd orchestrated the whole damn thing to stir my jealousy and bring out a side of me that I'd always regret. Nothing about the punishment she took at the end of my belt had brought me solace, though. The way she always did, she'd begged for more when she'd already taken more than I could stomach. She wanted me to fuck her after, to take what was mine. But she wasn't mine anymore. Something in me always knew that whatever I'd had with her had been tainted. And whatever she and I had was already fucked from the start.

Regardless of whatever lies she'd have liked the people around us to believe, I never slept with her again. Doing so would have been dangerous. Emotionally and physically. Ultimately Sophia had never given me real control. Somewhere deep down I had known, even if the controlling bastard in me never wanted to admit it out loud.

Maybe she did need me now, but I had let her into my head for the last time. I sure as hell wasn't inviting her into any circle of my world that overlapped with Erica's. It was over.

Erica stirred, and I turned to take in her still-sleeping form. Sophia was in the past. So far in the past that one look at Erica rendered her almost invisible to me.

Whatever had been empty became whole again at

the mere sight of her. She was home. Together, we were complete.

Determined to let her rest, I went downstairs to make her a small breakfast for when she woke. Her appetite had been off in the mornings, but having a little bit of food in her stomach seemed to ease the nausea that waned by later in the day. Thank God the morning sickness came in waves, because I wasn't sure how I would keep my hands off her. Then again, this was only the beginning. I had no idea what to expect over the next eight months. I made a mental note to hit the bookstore this week and study up on everything I didn't know, which I was guessing was a hell of a lot.

A loud knock on the door broke the quiet of the morning. My parents had kept their promise of not dropping by unexpectedly, but I still expected my mom on the other side of the door when I opened it.

Instead I came face to face with Agent Evans and Detective Carmody.

"What are you doing here?"

Carmody gave me a quick once-over. "Better go get dressed."

"Give me one good reason."

Evans's jaw tightened. Carmody's eyes gave him away, and somehow I could hear everything they weren't saying clear as day.

"Give me a minute," I said.

Without another word, I went upstairs. Erica was still asleep, and I wrestled with whether to wake her. No. She didn't need to see this.

I pulled on some clothes. As I was about to leave, she sat up.

"Hey." She had a sweet, tired look about her. Her hair was an adorable mess.

"Hey, baby. Just stay here, okay? Evans is downstairs. I'm sure it's nothing. Take your time getting dressed."

She frowned, all the sleepiness gone from her features.

★ ★ ★

ERICA

Ignoring all of Blake's requests, I wrapped myself in my robe and followed him downstairs in my bare feet. He muttered curses under his breath all the way down. At me or Evans, I wasn't sure. I couldn't think straight. The cobwebs hadn't yet cleared, and now we had the police and the FBI at our door.

Evans was in the foyer, Carmody a few feet away. Evans's face twisted with a self-satisfied smile that sent my insides writhing. Something was wrong. I could feel it.

"What's going on?" I asked.

Carmody pulled out a pair of handcuffs and took a tentative step toward Blake.

"Blake Landon, you're under arrest. You have the right to remain silent."

Something in his posture almost seemed apologetic next to Evans, whose entire being reeked of hatred toward Blake.

"No. You can't do this." The sound was broken as it left my trembling lips.

"We can and we are. Here's the warrant." Evans shoved a folded piece of paper at me.

I looked at it, unable to read any of the words. The paper shook in my hands. This wasn't happening. This had to be a dream. Except I knew it wasn't. They were arresting Blake before my eyes. My whole body hummed and heated with adrenaline. My palms prickled and the usual sickness I felt this early in the morning had multiplied. I held my stomach, trying to suppress the urge to retch.

Carmody twisted Blake's arms behind him and finished reading his Miranda rights. Blake winced when the cuffs clicked loudly, cinching his wrists.

Tears burned and brimmed in my eyes, blurring my vision. "He didn't do this."

"Tell it to the judge." A grim smile curled Evans's lips.

I strode past him toward Blake. They couldn't take him. Not today, not ever. Before I could reach them, Evans caught my arm and yanked me back.

Fire ignited behind Blake's eyes. "Do *not* touch her."

"Then tell her to calm down," Evans shouted, more at me than to Blake.

"Blake," I sobbed, twisting helplessly away.

Evans tightened his grip, tugging me back. I yelped, scratching at him with my nails to free myself.

Blake's voice bellowed, ricocheting through the room. "She's pregnant, you bastard. Get your goddamn hands off her!"

Carmody placed a firm hand on Blake's chest, his eyes large and alert. Evans released his hold, narrowing his eyes as he gradually positioned himself between Blake and me.

I was trembling from head to toe. From the adrenaline, from the sheer panic of watching the man I loved being taken away from me. Tears fell unbidden down my cheeks. "Blake...don't leave me. Please, you can't. Tell them the truth."

His lips parted, but no words came.

"Let's move." Carmody pushed him toward the door.

Jaw tight, eyes vacant, Blake followed without a word.

The door closed and I dropped to my knees, no longer able to hold back the agonizing sob tearing from my chest.

★ ★ ★

BLAKE

The vision of Erica, tears streaming down her face, was burned into my mind. She was all I could see. And over the slamming and voices and commotion, I could still hear her desperate cry after the door closed behind us. I pressed the heels of my palms against my eyes, unable to rid myself of the pain that lanced through me every time the scene played out in my mind. I took several deep breaths and reached for hope—hope that this nightmare would soon end and I could get back to my wife.

I'd been booked and was waiting for Dean to show up after bailing me out. But the hours bled together with no word from him. Night fell and sleep never came. Not because of the sorry excuse for a bed I was lying on. Not because of the noise of the station and people being shuffled in and out of holding cells through the night. But because my brain was firing through every scenario and every possible solution.

Anyone would have been on edge here, but I'd been

here before, and with every second that ticked by, I remembered what that experience had been like. I'd been young and full of confused emotions—not the least of which was the fear that I was going to spend the rest of my adult life behind bars. They'd held me for days while I wrestled with that very plausible reality.

Assuming they'd found enough evidence to charge me with rigging Daniel's election, I'd be facing the same fears all over again.

Exhausted but no less overwhelmed, I was moved to the courthouse for the bail hearing in the morning. They placed me in a small room where I waited for Dean. I tapped my fingers on the table rhythmically, waiting for him, waiting for answers.

He finally showed up in his suit, his typical put-together self. Not a slicked back hair was out of place, but the tension rolled off him in waves. Nothing about his body language was reassuring.

"Thanks for coming out," I muttered.

His expression was tight. "I tried to arrange for bail yesterday. No dice."

"You want to explain to me why the fuck I'm here to begin with?"

He sat down, unbuttoning his coat as he did. "Who's Parker Benson?"

I frowned. "What?"

"Parker Benson. The guy you did some research on the night before they confiscated everything in your office. Ring a bell?"

"He's dating my sister. I wanted to know who he was."

"Okay, well, some people might just use Google or

pay for a legitimate background check. Apparently you accessed his bank records and hacked his university email account. None of that was legal."

I leaned in. "Are you fucking kidding me? That's why I'm here?"

"I told you they would look for anything, no matter how small or irrelevant to the matter at hand. And *you* said you were careful with these kinds of things."

"I was." I replayed the late night in my mind, assured that I had been.

"So how did they find out?"

For the first time in a while I was speechless.

"They must have tampered with my computer while I was gone, so they could trace my activity after I came back from the honeymoon. I had no idea they could be watching me at that point. Fucking hell."

"The good news is they still don't have anything on the election. They're holding you for this and hoping to get more. But this, technically, is enough to get you into some deep shit."

I sat back, sinking deeper into my denial. "It's not enough."

"It would be nice if that were true, but I think we both know better. They aren't going to make this neat and tidy for you."

A knock on the door signaled that we had to move on.

Dean stood. "You're up. Let's get your bail set and get you out of here."

Twenty minutes later, we were facing the judge.

"We are requesting bail," Dean said.

The prosecutor looked to be in her fifties. She was

petite with short blond spiral curls framing her face. As soon as she opened her mouth, though, I knew she was here to nail me to the wall.

"We're asking that Mr. Landon's bail be denied."

Dean shook his head, seeming perplexed. "This is a nonviolent crime, Your Honor."

The prosecutor continued. "This man is a walking weapon. All he needs is a computer to commit his next crime and compromise sensitive information."

"My client has a clean record," Dean argued.

"Not three months ago he was brought in on assault charges."

"Which were promptly dismissed."

"Not surprising for a man with his reach," she countered.

The judge peered at her above her glasses. "Are you questioning the integrity of the court, Counselor?"

"Of course not. All I'm saying is that this man is under investigation for rigging a state-wide election. None of us can know what he's capable of."

"The accusations made against him with regard to the election are as yet unfounded and have no bearing here," Dean argued.

"I disagree. Mr. Landon is a known hacker, and we are only beginning to uncover what could be a host of fraudulent activity. In one evening he was able to hack into the mainframes of a major banking institution and a state university. He has vast informational and financial resources. He is *not* a man to be underestimated."

"All of this is speculation," Dean noted.

"Considering the charges being brought against him

today, anyone's identity and personal information is at risk, including yours, Your Honor."

"Bail is denied."

"Your Honor—" Dean began.

He was cut off by the short bang of the gavel. "This court is dismissed."

Dread swam in my veins, punctuated by a sob that I immediately recognized as my mother's. I turned and she was several rows back. My father's arm was around her shoulders, tucking her to him. Fiona was tearful, and I guessed she probably didn't know the half of it. Fucking Parker.

I wanted to blame him, but the truth was I only had myself to blame. Other than a few unanswered messages from what appeared to be one-night stands from many months prior, Parker had checked out fine. And here I was because I'd let my concerns get the best of me.

The rest of my family looked like they were at my goddamn funeral. Then there was Erica. Stoic. Her jaw set firmly. Her eyes were tired and swollen. Under that strong facade I knew she was as devastated as I felt. The knot in my gut grew, bringing a kind of numb rage with it.

Turning to Dean, I glared at the man who rarely flinched but had the decency now to look apprehensive.

"Fix this."

"That's what you pay me for." He sounded confident, but his eyes told another story. They darted away from me, roaming over the bustling of the courtroom.

My attention shifted back to Erica, who was moving out of the courtroom with the rest of my family. Her back was to me, and everything inside me wanted to go to her. I wanted to hold her through this storm, knowing we'd get through it together somehow. But we weren't going to be together. We were going to be miles apart, spending every night wondering about the other.

I swallowed hard and watched her walk away, feeling completely gutted.

The bailiff approached, and I leveled a cold look at Dean.

"Move accounts to Heath. Do whatever you need to do. I need to know Erica's going to be taken care of if this goes sideways."

"Consider it done. I'm going to work on getting you out of this mess first though."

"I'll be fine. She's your priority."

"You're the priority, Blake. If Erica can handle you, she's strong enough to get through this. She'll be all right."

The bailiff cinched the cuffs around my wrists. As the cold metal circled my skin, my heartbeat spiked and my body grew uncomfortably warm. I'd go willingly, but this was the third time in two days I had to wrap my head around the restraints, and I harnessed all my willpower not to fight against them.

Something about this time felt final. Like the rapid clicks sliding into place was a sound I should get used to.

Dean's mouth kept moving, but the part of me that might have cared about what other assurances he could give was dying. Erica was a fighter. I wasn't sure that I was anymore.

CHAPTER SIXTEEN

ERICA

I stepped out of the flow of people and retrieved my phone from my purse. Blake's family was huddled outside the courtroom, speaking with the lawyer. I would have been with them if I'd had any faith in the legal system to fix this injustice.

With trembling hands, I pulled up Daniel's number, dialed, and let it ring. His voicemail picked up. I ended the call and dialed again. When he didn't pick up again I listened to his voicemail all the way through. Brief, cold. Like the man behind it.

"Daniel, it's me, Erica. I know you don't want to talk to me." I closed my eyes, fighting the turmoil that threatened to compound on the nearly excruciating pain I now felt. "But I really need to talk to you. It's important. And if you don't call me back, I'm just going to keep calling. If you know me—and despite everything, I think you know me pretty well now—you know that I don't exactly give up easily. Thanks."

I hung up, and with one last glance toward Gove and the somber faces of our family, I turned to leave.

The heavy wooden doors of the courthouse gave way with a push. Outside a handful of reporters rushed at me. Their questions came at me all at once. Their voices carried over one another. Daniel—Blake—the election—my involvement.

"Do these new charges against your husband have anything to do with the governor's election?"

"Do you have any comment on Fitzgerald being stripped of the win?"

My already foggy brain couldn't process what had just happened inside the courtroom, let alone formulate answers to fill their news reports. I tried to bypass them, and the only thing that broke through the mayhem was the sound of my name. Then I saw Marie maneuvering between two men. Her eyes were wide, expressing a mix of frustration and concern.

She reached out to me. "Come with me."

I caught her hand, and we walked quickly toward her car. The reporters finally gave up after we got several paces away. I sat in the passenger seat of her sedan, closing out the cold and noise with the door behind me.

One look at my mother's best friend and my tears began to fall. She reached across the front seat to hug me tightly. I buried my face in her coat and squeezed her thin frame, trying to keep myself from falling apart completely.

"I saw the news this morning and I came as soon as I could."

I sniffled and sat back. "Thank you."

"I knew things weren't looking good for Daniel. The man would sell his soul for a win, but I had no idea Blake could be involved."

I wiped my eyes. "He wasn't. He didn't have any-thing to do with the election. He's the only suspect they're looking at though, so they're making his life hell and holding him for this charge."

Anger flooded my veins. I hated the woman who'd stood between Blake and getting bail. For all her determination, she had no idea how much pain she was inflicting by keeping us apart. I balled my fists, trying to hold on to the anger, if only to ease the devastating pain that lingered just beyond.

"Why didn't you call me?"

I shook my head and stared down at my lap. "It's all been too much. It's too much for anyone to fix."

Alli had been at the house most of the night, trying to comfort me into a place that more closely resembled emotionally stable. The last thing I wanted to do was start spreading the news when I was still short on answers.

We'd talked through as much as we could and we both agreed to meet with Sid after the hearing to see if he might be able to find the code. I didn't want to ask him to put his own freedom in jeopardy, but my desperation was growing by the minute. Beyond that small sliver of hope that Sid might be able to help, I was struggling to see any light at the end of this dreadful tunnel. We were no closer to finding Trevor than we had been when I'd come home from Dallas.

Arguably, I was still in shock that Blake had been led away in handcuffs only a day ago. And now this...Now he wasn't even going to be able to come home to me.

"They denied his bail, Marie. I can't even see him. I don't know what I'm going to do now. We were going to try to get to the bottom of this together, and now he's not even here."

Marie brushed away the tears that kept coming, hushing me softly. She did that until my sobs slowed. I hiccupped, trying to catch a full breath through my misery.

"Baby girl, look at me. It's going to be all right," she whispered.

I stared into the beautiful caramel irises of her eyes. Her hair fell in long twists around her face. She was a beautiful woman with a beautiful heart. But when it came to the hard realities of the world, she could be naïve. I'd seen her heart break too many times to believe she could stop this freight train of hurt that I was riding right now.

"I see fear in your eyes, but I see your fire too. I know you want Blake to be the strong one. When it comes to protecting you, I believe he always will be. But he needs you now. He needs you to be strong."

Strong. What did that even mean in the context of what was going down now? I considered myself strong. Flawed, sensitive, sure. But when times got hard, when life served up its worst, I'd always found a way to pick myself back up.

I'd been a strong person all my life, but somehow going it alone was different now. I took responsibility for my own pain, my own struggles and circumstances. Now I shared those with Blake. As much as we'd like to battle our demons alone, when one of us was hurting, so was the other. We'd joined our joys and our burdens.

And nothing could release us from the ways we were bound together now...

"I'm pregnant, Marie."

A mix of joy and concern filled her eyes. "Oh my God. Oh my *God*. Erica, why didn't you tell me?"

"I only found out a few days ago. We had an appointment on Monday, and everything looks good. We weren't going to start telling people yet."

More tears came, raining over that remembered happiness. How could this all have fallen apart so fast? When it seemed like Blake and I couldn't be any stronger or happier, circumstances had come in and threatened to take it all away.

Marie was silent for a long time. When she spoke, her eyes glistened. "I can't imagine what you're feeling right now, honey."

I pressed my fingers against my eyelids, trying to stem the tears that simply kept coming.

"I can feel Patricia looking down on us right now."

I looked up, Marie's face blurry through my tears. Through all of this, I hadn't thought about my mother, but suddenly I could feel her too . . . through Marie's love.

"And I know that she's happy, beaming with joy. What you're going through isn't easy, and my heart is breaking for you, Erica, but this is a blessing you've been given for a reason. Hold on to it. Fight for it. Let this be your reason to stay strong for all of you."

A spark of hope lit inside me. I reached for it, but I was so far from any kind of comfort. My tears had slowed and I sucked in an unsteady breath. "I'd like to believe that having her here right now could make things better somehow. I just don't see how it could get any worse."

She brushed away an errant tear and tucked my hair back. "Why don't you come back home with me for a little bit?"

I looked down and twisted my wedding bands around my finger over and over again without answering her.

"You shouldn't be in that big house all by yourself. Come stay with me. Even if it's only for a day or two. A change of scenery can't hurt."

I'd only just come back home. But she was right. Every second in the house reminded me that Blake wasn't in it.

"I should go back. Blake's parents are close by if I need anything," I muttered.

"I know, but they're dealing with their own grief over this. Let me take care of you for a little bit until Blake can come home. You're tired and overwhelmed. I know how you are. You'll sit with this and make yourself sick over it. Stay with me and we can talk it out."

Maybe she was right. I nodded, surrendered to the idea. "Okay. Let me go home and pack a bag."

"Want me to drive you?"

"No, that's okay. I'll go with Clay and have him give me a ride to your place a little later. I want to talk to Blake's parents and see what the attorney said."

I still had to swing by the office, too. As hopeless as I felt, I couldn't go hide out at Marie's, convalescing until this blew over. I had to pursue every lead I could until it brought me closer to the truth.

"Okay. Call me when you're on your way or if anything comes up."

"I will. Thank you." I sighed heavily, unburdened of some tears, but feeling no lighter.

Marie caught my hand and held it tight. "I'm always here for you. No matter what."

I thanked her again, stepped from the car, and let her drive away. I found Clay on the other side of the parking lot. He drove me back to Marblehead and dropped me at Blake's parents' house. I paused at their door, wondering if I should knock, but decided to just go in.

Fiona, Catherine, Alli, and Heath were in the kitchen.

"What's Parker going to say?" Heath asked.

Fiona pinched the bridge of her nose. "I honestly don't know what to say to him. I can try to explain that Blake was just trying to protect me, but obviously this is a huge invasion of privacy."

The door clicked shut behind me and I walked in.

"Erica, honey. Come in." Catherine motioned me over.

She hugged me when I was close enough. My whole body tensed. I couldn't cry anymore. I'd decided last night that I was done crying, yet I'd already broken down today.

She released me with a shaky breath. "Come on. Let's go sit down."

She ushered us to the living room, where we all sat. Greg's figure caught my attention. He was on the deck, leaning against the railing, his back to us.

The water was angry today, blending into an unfeeling gray sky. Sometimes I would wonder what it might be like to be out there, stranded in the midst of the waves and the cold, at the mercy of a merciless Mother Nature. That's how I felt in this moment. Maybe I wasn't alone in that either.

My heart ached for Catherine and Greg. Today had been devastating for me. I couldn't imagine what this was doing to them. And they didn't know about the baby yet. Alli and Heath knew, but I was glad now that we hadn't told the rest of the family. Knowing Blake's freedom was in jeopardy, I couldn't share the news with them now.

"What did the lawyer say?" I asked.

"He's got his work cut out for him," Heath said. "The police traced Blake's computer activity when you all got back from the honeymoon. We all know he hacked Parker's accounts. Obviously he wasn't trying to be malicious, but they're going to try to nail him on it."

Fiona's phone rang. "That's Parker." She shook her head and set the phone to vibrate. "I can't believe Blake would do this. What the hell was he thinking?"

"He was only looking out for you, Fiona," Catherine said.

"He should know better. My God, how many times does he need to learn his lesson?" She threw her hands up, as angry as I'd ever seen her.

"This is what he does, Fiona. You know he doesn't always follow the rules," Heath said.

"He invests in real estate and software development. I didn't realize he made a habit of illegally hacking into people's affairs."

Catherine shook her head, her eyes glistening again. "All these years, and I can't believe we're right back here again. It's a nightmare. A living nightmare."

Alli was silent beside me. My hand rested on my stomach. I wasn't sure if I was reassuring the baby that everything was going to work out, or if I was silently asking it for reassurance. In this room surrounded by family, I felt like we were a team of two.

"This is who he is," I finally said. "I don't like it any better than any of you do, but frankly he can't help that it's so easy for him to do these things. It's a talent—an unethical one, maybe. But it's who he is. It's why none of us will ever want for anything. You can't vilify him for that."

Silence fell on the room. Catherine blew her nose into a tissue and left the room without a word. She returned with a bottle of wine under her arm and both hands full of wineglasses.

Heath gave her a concerned look. "Mom, it's not even eleven o'clock."

"I couldn't care less," she muttered.

I heard the front door open and close again, and a few seconds later, Parker was joining us in the living room.

Fiona's eyes lit up. "Parker... What are you doing here?"

His lips were tight. "You're not answering my calls. I was worried."

She tucked her short brown hair behind her ears and avoided his stare. "I guess we need to talk."

He winced. "I already know about all of it. Your brother is a nosy bastard." He shot a knowing look among all of us. "And I don't give a shit. I care more that I haven't seen you or spoken to you with all this going on."

As her gaze fluttered to his, her lower lip trembled. "I'm sorry. I thought you'd be angry."

His eyes fixed on her, as if she were the only person in the room. "Fiona... this doesn't change *anything*."

She exhaled audibly and stood up. He reached for her. She took his hand, and he pulled her into a tight embrace. They stood that way a moment before a flushed Fiona led him swiftly away from the room and us.

Catherine sighed and shook her head. "Thank goodness," she muttered under her breath as she began to pour the wine into glasses.

"I'm going to go make myself some tea, if you don't mind," I said when she set a glass in front of me.

"Let me make it for you, dear," Catherine said.

"I can get it," I insisted and disappeared into the kitchen.

A minute later, Heath came up beside me and took a mug from the cabinet for himself. Catherine's and the other's voices were a mere murmur. Fiona and Parker were nowhere to be seen.

"You okay?" he asked, helping himself to the tea bags.

"What do you think?"

His light hazel eyes were filled with the concern I shared. "Gove will get him out of this, Erica. Blake isn't the first wealthy guy to get out of a legal bind."

I closed my eyes and rested my hands on the counter. "I'm tired of people telling me that everything is going to be okay. I'm tired of walking through life with this blind faith that everything will magically work out. That somehow I can trust everyone to care as much as I do, to do their jobs, to find the truth that no one seems to want to find as badly as I do."

His jaw tightened. "Gove wants to start moving some of Blake's assets over to me and you, in case things get worse."

"No," I said simply.

His lips thinned. "Do you want to have faith, or do you want to start planning for the worst-case scenario?"

"Neither. I want to fix this." I paused and faced him. "And I will."

"Let Gove do what he needs to—"

"You want to motivate me, Heath?" I looked up at

him, my jaw resolute. "Then tell me *no*. Tell me I can't, or that I shouldn't."

"All I'm saying is that I know that more than anything Blake wants you safe and taken care of."

"If he wants me taken care of, he can come home and do it himself. Otherwise, I'm taking care of myself, and I'm going to get to the bottom of this if it's the last thing I do."

Before he could respond, my phone dinged from my pocket. I pulled it out. A text came in from a local number I didn't recognize.

I have what you're looking for. Park Street station.

I read the text over, my heart racing. Was it Daniel?

Heath finished making our tea, while I contemplated what to write back.

E: When?

One hour. I'll find you.

I checked my watch. As long as we didn't hit traffic, Clay could get me there on time.

"I have to go," I said suddenly.

Heath frowned. "Where are you going?"

I ignored his question and went toward the door. "Tell Catherine I'm sorry. I had to run."

I hurried home, packed an overnight bag for Marie's, and directed Clay to drive us into the city. He pulled us up to the Park Street station with five minutes to spare.

"Wait for me here," I said.

We made eye contact in the rearview.

"You need me to go in with you?"

"No, I'll be fine." This wouldn't work with Clay hovering.

He turned in his seat, eyeing me cautiously. "I've known you long enough to know the look you get when you're doing something Blake wouldn't want you doing."

"If it were up to Blake, I'd never leave the damn house. I'm just going to meet someone quick. I'll be fine. I promise."

He hesitated. "It's my job to keep you safe, Erica."

That was the second time he'd used my name. Both times had gotten my attention. I appreciated his concern but I couldn't let it get in my way right now. "It's a busy station, Clay. If I'm not back in ten minutes, you can start worrying, okay?"

He turned back and dropped a hand on the steering wheel. "Five minutes."

I rolled my eyes but didn't waste another second booking it down to the trains. Park Street was a busy station, even busier at the lunch hour. How would this stranger find me in the crowd?

I stood awkwardly, trying to seem natural, which was impossible when two trains came and went without me. More people crowded on the platform, waiting for the next train. I scanned faces and froze when I landed on one I recognized.

Shit. I turned and started walking toward the stairs that would bring me back out of the station. I wanted to run but moved slowly enough to seem natural. This could not have been a worse time. I silently prayed that he hadn't seen me and I could escape unnoticed.

"Erica!"

The man's voice was barely audible over the screaming of the approaching train.

I kept walking, until a hand came around my wrist and kept me from going any farther. I looked up into Detective Carmody's eyes, shaded under a baseball cap. He was in street clothes, but there was no mistaking his face. My heart pounded wildly. I yanked my hand back, feeling something small and hard against it. Opening my palm revealed a tiny black thumb drive. I shot my gaze back up to the detective, but that quickly he was gone.

A rush of warm air blew through my hair as the train pulled away.

CHAPTER SEVENTEEN

BLAKE

They'd moved me to a county jail that afternoon. The almost ritualistic process of moving me from place to place and room to room helped keep my thoughts off this morning's events. The vision of Erica's face, so hurt, was imprinted on my mind. But now all I had was time and I couldn't get her out of my head. I felt like someone had ripped out half my insides and told me I could live without them.

Except I couldn't fathom how I'd live without Erica for any extended period of time. I could live without money, possessions, or success. But I couldn't live without that woman.

At lunchtime I sat down at an empty table and moved my food around the tray. It wasn't so much disgusting as completely inedible. I dropped my fork and opened the small carton of milk that reminded me of a hundred school lunches I'd endured.

I guzzled it down and glanced around me at the offenders who sat at other tables. I couldn't help but draw parallels. This was far from the school cafeteria, but I wasn't going to fit in any better here than I had as an angsty adolescent. I convinced myself that I had nothing in common with these people. I had every intention of keeping to myself. Who knew how long I'd have to call this place home?

"Hey."

Max sat down across from me, wearing the same uniform as I was. He set his tray down, as if meaning to stay.

I sat back and glared. A fine pale line branched across his cheek and instantly I knew it was from the beating I'd given him. The last time I'd seen his face, no one would have recognized him. I balled my fists, reliving the memory and seriously contemplating putting it into action all over again.

"What the fuck do you want?"

He wrinkled his brow. "I don't want a damn thing from you. We're both in here. I figured you might want to see a friendly face."

"Just because we both happen to be here doesn't mean we're anywhere close to friendly."

"Yeah, well, it doesn't hurt to have allies." He glanced around the room before looking back to his food.

"If you want allies, keep looking. I'm fine on my own."

"Whatever," he muttered.

We were silent for a while. Unable to ignore the roar in my stomach, I took a bite of my cardboard lasagna and chewed over the hatred I felt for Max. People at the other tables spoke among themselves, ignoring us. True enough, Max didn't seem like he belonged here any more than I did. He didn't look like the pretty boy he once was though. His blond hair was overgrown slightly. The pallor of his skin was not its usual unnatural glow.

"You're looking pretty rough. No spa in here, huh?"

He squinted. "You're one to talk."

"Yeah, well, I never cared too much about appearances." I scrubbed my hand over the stubble on my jaw. I hadn't shaved yet. Didn't figure that mattered much now.

"It showed."

A hollow laugh escaped me, at the irony of us here, at how I could feel the fight slipping from me with each passing day. I pushed the tray away, unable to stomach another bite.

There we sat. A billionaire and an heir to one, clad in shapeless blue uniforms that relegated us to the lowest rung of society. Money helped, but we couldn't buy our freedom.

I'd known this. I learned the very real lesson years ago, and as a result, I'd always been exceedingly careful. I found the information I needed, but I was cautious with whom and how I meddled when I skirted the law. The irony was that I sat here now, in front of a man I detested who deserved nothing more than four cement walls around him for the rest of time.

That empty defeated feeling crept over me all over again.

"If Michael could only see us now."

Max's lips grew thin, all signs of his desired camaraderie gone. "He cares a lot less than you think he does, you know."

"You're saying that because he cut you off. Giving you what you deserve doesn't mean he doesn't give a shit about anyone else."

"You don't know him," he bit out.

"I've known him half my life. I know him pretty damn well."

"You had a glimpse. You've only seen the good."

Michael was more than good. In fact, *good* wasn't a word I'd use to describe him. Focused, shrewd, discriminating in his actions and choices. He couldn't choose his children, clearly, and Max would never be able to forgive him for choosing me over him when it came to business.

"You're his child, and you act like one. I'm sure he'd show a different side of himself to you. One I probably wouldn't like either."

He let out a weak laugh. "You look at me and all you see is a fuckup because that's what he wanted you to see. I would have done anything for him, for a chance to learn from him and be a part of something more. He purposefully kept me away from opportunities that would have helped me excel, and then he handed those same opportunities to you. He threw it in my face."

"Maybe he did, but that doesn't excuse the mistakes you've made."

"The only mistake I made was turning my hatred onto you. It should have been him. It should have been him all along."

"You turn your hatred onto anyone who gets in your way, lest you forget."

He dropped his fork and pushed his tray away. "Listen... I'm sorry about Erica."

The words hung in the air between us. Ridiculous, small words. "You're sorry?"

"What do you want me to say? I barely touched her. I'm doing time here for nothing."

I saw red. Every muscle coiled, ready to fight.

"You used her to get to me. And my fist was the only reason you didn't get any further with her. You know that as well as I do, you sick piece of shit. You have no fucking idea what she's been through."

"She slept around, Blake. Mark even fucked her. Just because she's your wife doesn't mean she doesn't have a past. I mean, she was asking for it the whole time she was dealing with Angelcom. What kind of woman pitches a room full of men and—"

I lunged across the table. Gaining a grip on his hair, I slammed his head down onto the table between us. I held him down by the neck. Rage coursed through me.

A gurgled cry left his throat. "Let me go!"

"Mark raped her, you stupid son of a bitch."

He struggled against my hold. The noise in the room fell, though never went completely silent. Still, I felt the eyes of onlookers nearby on us. But something wild and reckless had taken hold of me. Where else, if not in this hell of a place, could a man like Max face the kind of wrath he deserved? If it came at my hand, so be it. The measly time he'd serve wouldn't be enough. A lifetime wouldn't be enough.

He struggled and I loosened my hold only to slam him down harder, feeling the tendons in his neck bend under my grip. I bent, hovering over his ear.

"Do you have any idea what it's like for me to not be able to touch my wife because she thinks I could be you? Or him?" I paused, letting my ragged breath feed the surge of adrenaline pumping through me. "I should have finished you that day. I should have ended you and your pathetic existence. You're goddamn lucky Michael pulled me off."

He grimaced. "He didn't want to."

"Because you're a worthless piece of shit, and even Michael can't deny it now."

"You! Hands the fuck off!"

I snapped up, eyes narrowed at the approaching guard. Much as I may have wanted to give him and any number of others the same treatment I'd given Max, the guard was twice my size with a billy club in his hand that I could only assume he used with some regularity.

"Don't fuckin' look at me that way, rich boy."

I released Max and stood back from the table. Max retreated to the bench, hands to his throat as he gasped for breath. Whatever consequences might come, I'd face them and I'd do it again. If being here afforded me nothing more, it might be the chance to give Erica justice from this side of the wall. That was a purpose I could get behind.

The guard took Max by the back of the neck, matching the hold I'd had on him.

"What the hell!" Max yelled, his arms flailing helplessly until he tumbled to the floor.

"Get up," he barked.

"I didn't do anything. He jumped me!"

The guard leaned down, hoisting the stick high in the air. Max flinched back about a foot.

"First thing, you don't know what the fuck it's like

to be jumped. Second, you're in here for attempted rape, so you should get your pussy ass up or you're going to find out."

Terror flashed behind Max's eyes as he scrambled to his feet. A quick scan around the surrounding tables revealed a host of menacing glares eating up Max's present vulnerability.

"Get the fuck up before someone makes a lesson of you."

Max took his tray, got rid of it quickly, and retreated to an empty table at the far end of the room.

The guard leveled a dead stare my way. "Watch yourself," he warned.

★ ★ ★

ERICA

One step into the office and the concerned looks on everyone's faces told me that they already knew something was very wrong.

James's blue eyes peered up at me from behind his computer before he rose. "Erica, I heard about Blake. Are you okay?"

I stepped past him and set the thumb drive on Sid's desk. Sid tugged his headphones down around his neck.

"I have a new project for you," I said.

"What's this?" He glanced between the drive and me.

"I'm not one-hundred-percent sure, but I'm guessing it's the code that was loaded onto the machines that tallied false votes in Fitzgerald's favor."

He pursed his lips. "Do I want to know how you got this?"

"No. Your job is to look at it and find a way to prove Blake didn't write it."

He blew out a slow breath. "That's all, huh?"

When I didn't respond, he put the drive into his computer and started tapping keys. His eyes darted back and forth over the screen while Geoff, Alli, and I stared expectantly.

"Yes, looks like these are the binaries." He looked up. "Give me a few hours to sift through this. I'll let you know what I find."

I pulled up a chair across from his desk and sat down, crossing my legs at the knee. I eyed the mess on Sid's desk. The surface was decorated with no less than a dozen energy drink empties and a few stacks of paperwork. He lifted an eyebrow when we made eye contact.

"Blake's in jail, Sid. I'm not leaving here until you find something."

Geoff spoke up. "Can I take a look?"

"Let me make a copy, one sec." Sid tapped a few more keys and removed the drive. "Here," he said, handing it to him.

A few eternal minutes passed when Sid spoke again.

"Well, this is a good sign."

"What?" I asked, sitting up straighter.

"Looks like the code that originally ran on the machines was modified by an outside program."

"What does that mean exactly?"

"Basically, someone attached a virus by using a zero-day exploit to Blake's code to inflate Fitzgerald's votes on the day of the election. If Blake had written this himself, I seriously doubt he'd use this method."

"Why do you say that?"

"Why attach a program to your own code when you're capable of writing one comprehensive piece of code that does the job?"

Hearing that made me loathe Evans all over again. If he'd had people looking at this, they should have suspected the same. Maybe that was why Carmody had given me the drive. I wanted to ask him why he'd given it to me, but I figured there was a good reason he hadn't stuck around long enough for me to ask.

"Okay. That's a start, but we need a way to prove Trevor did this."

"Um"—Geoff's expression was tight with concentration as his fingers flew over the keyboard—"maybe we can't put Trevor's name right on this code. But Blake's is already on it, right?"

"Yes, the encryption routines are his. Everyone including the authorities know this," I said.

"Okay. Then theoretically we should be able to prove that two different people wrote the two pieces of code. It's kind of like handwriting analysis, or distinguishing fingerprints. Code patterns can be analyzed the same way."

"You can do that?" I asked.

"There are legit programs out there, but since this is, uh, sensitive, I have a friend who's got a homebrew version of his own written. I can have him run this through his program, compare the two versions and highlight the discrepancies."

"Let's do it," I said without hesitation. That's what I

needed, something concrete. Everything outside of the charges they were holding Blake on now was based on conjecture.

"If I had something else that Trevor and Blake wrote, that would help so I could compare the two," Geoff added.

"There are logs from when Trevor started attacking Clozpin," Sid said. "If we can prove the virus isn't Blake's code, we should also be able to prove that whoever hacked our site and any number of the others in Blake's fleet were the same person," Sid said. "I don't have the Clozpin server logins anymore though, unfortunately."

James spoke up. "Mine still work. I've been snooping on their progress since I left. Hang on, I'll send them over."

Sid chuckled. "Amateurs."

I was about to ask how long all this would take when my phone rang. Daniel was calling me.

"I'll be right back." I went to my office and closed the door behind me. "Daniel, hi."

"I got your message," he said.

"Thank you for calling me back."

"I told you not to call." His tone was less than warm.

"Well, I don't listen very well."

"Obviously. There's too much heat right now. The election aside, the feds are up my ass thinking I'm behind all of this along with Blake. You don't want to get mixed up in this any more than you already are."

"They arrested Blake."

He cleared his throat gruffly. "I'm aware."

"He didn't do this."

"You'd better hope to God he didn't, Erica. I'm not

going to bother telling you how much money I've sunk into this campaign. This isn't just money. This is a life's work, and if he came between me and—"

"I know who did this, and I need your help to find him."

For all the hurt Daniel had caused, all I wanted to do was smack him in the head for how single-minded he was being. Finally, *finally*, I was making progress and he was still hung up on Blake's supposed guilt.

"Erica, I don't have time for this."

"I don't care if you have time for this or not. I'll never ask you for anything ever again. I'll stay out of your life forever if that's what you really want. I'm just asking for this one thing." The words came out in a rush, before I had a chance to realize what I was promising. But the truth was that I'd say anything and do anything to get Blake out of this, and Daniel could be my last hope to find Trevor.

He paused. "We shouldn't be talking like this. It's not safe."

"Fine. Then let's meet."

He sighed. "Where?"

I thought for a minute, spinning over the best options. Daniel was probably right to be paranoid, but I was grateful he was agreeing to meet me. Seeing him face-to-face required more than privacy, though. I needed him to really hear me. I needed to say things to him that I'd bottled up for weeks, and this might be the last time for that.

"Let's meet outside the city. I'll text you the address."

"Fine."

An hour later, Marie and I were standing in her

kitchen. Her hands were curled over the edge of the counter. I shifted my weight between my feet and checked my watch again.

"Why here?"

The distress in her voice made me regret the decision to invite Daniel over to her place to talk. It was a crazy idea, yet something told me this could be the perfect place to really get through to him in a way that I never had been able to before. I hoped too that having Marie nearby would give me the strength I needed to face him again.

"Right now he thinks Blake ruined his chances to be governor. I need to convince him otherwise, and we needed a safe place to talk."

She released her grip on the counter and crossed her arms over her chest. "Erica, I warned you about him. He's dangerous and you'll never be able to trust him."

"Yes, you warned me. In my defense, I had no idea what to expect from inviting him into my life. Saying 'I told you so' at this point doesn't help. He's here and right now, I need to get through to him if I'm going to have any chance of getting Blake out of this mess. You told me to fight, and that's exactly what I'm doing."

She sighed. "I just worry about you. Richard..." Her throat moved with a swallow. "He died getting tangled up with Daniel's affairs."

True enough, Marie's ex-lover had met an untimely end by getting too close to the investigation around Daniel and his stepson's supposed suicide. I still remembered the determined look in his eyes moments before his life ended and mine irrevocably changed at the end of a gun.

Maybe in a way Richard had been as headstrong as

I am. He was a reporter and that was his job. He wasn't Daniel's daughter, though. I pitied the man who crossed Daniel, but deep down, I believed he cared about me, if only because he'd once loved my mother.

A knock sounded at Marie's front door and she jolted. "That's him."

She stared toward the door and hesitated. "Are you sure you want to do this?"

"I need to talk to him, Marie, and I need him to trust me."

She nodded quickly and walked to the door, opening it to Daniel.

He blinked rapidly, looking her up and down. He was dressed casually in khakis and a blue shirt.

"Hi, Daniel."

His shocked look morphed into a wince. "Marie?"

A small smile tugged at her lips. "You remembered."

"Of course. How could I forget?"

He seemed different suddenly. Uncomfortable, almost vulnerable. Not the Daniel I knew. Any version of him.

"It's good to see you again," he said.

I knew she wasn't happy to be seeing him again, and I hated to put her in this situation. My mother had made her promise not to tell me about the identity of my father, and yet here he was, knocking on her door. And she had every right to be protective. Daniel was not a man to be trusted.

She stepped to the side and gestured for him to enter. "Come on in. She's waiting for you."

He came inside and our eyes met. "Erica." His tone was serious, but not as aggressive as it might have been if we'd been alone.

"Hi. Have a seat."

We sat down across from each other in Marie's living room while she went upstairs to give us privacy.

"Interesting choice for a meeting place," he said, once she'd left.

"Call it a show of trust."

Letting him know that Marie was still in my life was a risk, but a little part of me believed it could be a reminder too—an important one. This election debacle would be a turning point for him, no doubt, but it wouldn't be the first. He'd made a choice a long time ago. He'd chosen to turn away from the woman he loved and the child she carried. He'd made the choice, or maybe the choice had been made for him, all for the opportunity that had so recently slipped through his fingers. He'd made a choice that would lead to this place and time, yet despite all his dreams and grand ambition, nothing had gone according to plan.

"I trust you. I don't trust your husband." He offered a tight smile.

"Do you really believe Blake did this?" I asked him the question without anger or persuasion. I genuinely wanted to know if he could believe what I knew to be untrue.

"I'm not ruling it out. He's never been a big fan of mine."

"And the same is true for you. Why would he incite your anger when he already knows how much you distrust him? How would that benefit him or me?"

He shook his head. "You can't deny that he wants me out of your life."

"You *were* out of my life."

"Blake is an extremely wealthy man. I'm sure you know this by now. I may not have the kind of money he does, but I have power. What this has done is not only sabotage the powerful position I had won, but it's threatening everything I've built outside of this election. My reputation at the head of the firm. As a community member. I'm on boards. I have sway that has taken me this far, and that foundation has been shaken." He gestured, pressing his fingertips to the coffee table between us. "That foundation, Erica, is my value, and every day that goes by, it's being stripped away. That puts me under people I've never had to answer to before so they can get what they want from me, and your husband would be among them."

My earlier patience had grown perilously thin. I groaned, halting his ridiculous tirade. "Goddamnit, Daniel. He didn't do this," I insisted, trying to keep my anger in check. "Beyond that, whoever believes their *value* comes from their political power seriously needs a vacation. Is that really how you see yourself? That's what you bring to the world?"

His jaw tightened and he regarded me coolly. "All I can tell you is that whoever is behind this will pay for it. One way or the other. I'm not the only one who had an interest in me winning. And I'm not the only one who wants answers."

"If you want answers so badly, help me find them. I know who did this. I found him once, and I need your help to track him down again so the FBI can bring him in. As long as they believe Blake did this, they'll think you were involved in some way. Helping him helps you too."

He was silent a moment. "Who are you looking for?"

"His name is Trevor Cooper. He's someone from Blake's past—a hacker who used Blake's code from an old project to rig the machines. I honestly don't think any of this has anything to do with you. All he wanted was vengeance on Blake, and unfortunately you paid the price."

"If all this is true, why aren't the police looking for him?"

"Because they don't know he exists. At least not until I find him. That's why I need you."

"This sounds like an elaborate story, Erica. Is Blake spinning this? I didn't think you could be this gullible, but maybe being in love has blinded you."

My anger flared again, and I struggled to keep from yelling. "Love hasn't blinded me. It's made me see more clearly than ever before. And yes, I will do whatever I need to do to clear his name. And you're going to help me."

He muttered a curse and rubbed his neck.

I wasn't going to win this by berating him. I wanted to. It felt good to. But I needed him invested. I needed him to feel a fraction of the desperation that I now felt. I wasn't sure if he was capable of it, but I had to at least try. There were still so many things I'd never said to him.

"Daniel." I waited until he looked up, meeting his blue-eyed gaze with mine. I took a breath and hoped to draw in some courage with it. "Blake is going to be the father of my child. You said once that wouldn't matter to you . . . Is that still true?"

He grew pale and stared at some invisible point on the floor. In his silence, I carried on. I struggled to keep my voice steady as my heart skipped.

"I'll admit that I brought you here because I wanted

you to see Marie again. It scares me a little bit to bring you into her world, however briefly, because I can't ever know what you'll do. But somewhere in your cold, power-mongering heart, I know you care about something other than this goddamn election. I hoped that for a minute you could open your eyes and see that she's been like a mother to me since Mom died."

"I'm grateful she's been here for you," he said quietly, still avoiding my gaze.

"Me too." I closed my eyes a moment, trying to speak over the knot in my throat. "After the shooting...I was scared to death that I'd never have a chance to be a mother. I thought about it so much. More than anyone would ever know. I wished for it, and then, by some miracle, I was given that chance. And the most incredible part is that I was given a chance to share that experience with a man that I love deeply, with every piece of my soul." My voice broke, but I pushed on in a whisper. "And I want to do better. I want to give this child more than I had. More than this."

My turned-up palm moved between us, a small gesture that meant to encapsulate the emptiness that had existed between us, over the years of his estrangement and the emptiness that still remained.

"You will. I have little doubt."

"Then this child needs a father, because I know what it's like to have to live without one. There will never be anyone else to fill that place but Blake. I had to grow into someone else's heart. I'm grateful for my stepfather, but you were supposed to be the one. He knew that, and so did I."

My heart ached in my chest and my eyes brimmed with tears. Everything that I'd held back for so long, from before I'd even known who Daniel was, threatened to spill out of me. How could I despise him and still want him so much was a mystery I'd never understand. I could only hope the sentiment resonated someplace within him too. If this connection was worth anything, I prayed it could mean something to him now.

His head fell into his hands. He ran his fingers through his graying hair. I wanted to see his eyes. I imagined them dim with regret. At least a part of me wanted them to be. Did he regret it, all of this?

"I *am* sorry, Erica. You'll never know how much."

His quiet words hit my heart.

"I can't do this alone, Daniel. I'm strong enough… maybe I could, I don't know. But I can't fathom it. I've been given a chance to have something I thought had been taken away. And now the love of my life could be taken away too. I need your help, please."

He sighed. "Okay."

My heavy heart fluttered back to life. "You'll help?"

"If I can. I'm not sure what you expect me to do. I'm under a microscope too."

I pulled a piece of paper from my pocket and handed it to him. "You can start with Margaret Cooper. She's Trevor's mother. She's how I found him last time, but they're off the grid again. That's their last known address and anything else that might help. If I can find her, or if you can, maybe I can find Trevor or convince her to lead me to him."

He stared at the paper, his face expressionless. "You're asking for information."

"Yes."

His face went tight. "Information comes at a price."

I parted my lips as I imagined what he might want. "I have money—"

"I don't want your money. I'm telling you that I'm not like you. The people who find information for me don't walk into a room and ask nicely. People could get hurt."

I rolled that thought over in my mind a few times. I remembered Trevor's mother, the way she came at me. If she hadn't been so drunk, maybe she would have made it far enough to hurt me. I'd been stupid to go to their home alone, and maybe I was being stupid again now to ask this of Daniel, but I was running out of options.

"I don't care what you do as long as it gets me Trevor's location. Find him, and you won't ever have to hear from me again."

He nodded and stared back at the paper. He moved it rhythmically back and forth between his finger and thumb. "Is that what you want?"

My breath caught in my chest. "What are you saying?"

He shook his head and moved to stand. "I don't know. I should go."

"Daniel—"

Stuffing the paper in his pants pocket, he rose. "I'll see what I can find. I'll be in touch."

"You just got here." I followed him to the door.

"Margo started packing her things this morning. I

need to get back and try to talk some sense into her. The fact that I left to see you won't help my case."

"I'm sorry."

Regret swam in his eyes. "Me too."

★ ★ ★

Early the next morning, the sound of my phone ringing woke me. I picked it up, rubbing the sleep from my eyes.

"Hello?"

The reception was scratchy, and then an operator asked if I would accept a collect call from the county jail where I knew they'd been holding Blake. My heart pounded loudly in my chest, both in anticipation of hearing Blake's voice and with the unwelcome reminder that he was still being held there. I accepted the charges and heard a click.

"Erica?" Blake's voice seemed far away.

"It's me." I closed my eyes, struggling for words when all I wanted was to feel him with me. I wanted to speed to wherever he was and take him back home where he belonged. "How are you doing?"

"I'm okay." There was no life in his answer, and I fought the sudden urge to cry. I didn't want him to hear me breaking down. I had to be strong...

"I miss you so much. When can I come visit you?"

He was silent for a long time. "I'd rather you didn't," he finally said.

"What do you mean?"

"I don't want you here, okay? I miss you. Jesus..." He released a shaky breath. "I miss you more than you can possibly imagine, but I don't want you to set foot in this place. Do you understand me?"

I sat up in bed as fresh worry sobered me. "Is everything okay? You're scaring me, Blake."

"I'm fine. It's nothing to worry about. Being here... you seeing me this way... That isn't a memory I want for either of us."

"But what if—"

"How are Mom and Dad?"

What if you can't come home? was the question neither of us wanted to contemplate. I took an unsteady breath, decided to respect his wish, and mercifully changed the subject.

CHAPTER EIGHTEEN

BLAKE

"What the fuck is this?" I sifted through the stack of papers Evans had dropped in front of me.

"Looks like it's a detailed analysis of the code."

Evans was on the other side of one of the small round tables reserved for inmates and their visitors. I'd secretly hoped for another visitor, but I was glad that Erica had respected my wishes and not come. I wanted to see her, if only for a few minutes. I wanted the chance to comfort her in any way that I could, even if it was on the other side of a piece of glass, but I also didn't want her to see me this way.

Max had been right about one thing. I'd never paid much attention to my looks, at least not the way he did. I had a decent collection of vintage T-shirts that I could easily replace with a closet full of three-piece suits to wear to work every day, but I didn't care about putting on airs the way others did. I never had. I knew who I was, and I didn't need glamour to back up the wealth I'd accumulated or the success I'd earned without all that superficial crap.

Still, with the wealth, I'd grown used to the finer things. Spending my days in a concrete box with access to only the bare necessities was a far cry from my real life.

Real life, or old life? Damn, I'd fallen too far, and I didn't want Erica to know it.

I looked like hell, and I felt even worse. I couldn't protect my family from in here. I couldn't take care of everything and everyone who needed me. And I sure as hell wasn't winning any beauty contests.

I shoved away those thoughts and tried to concentrate on the details annotated between the lines of code, some of which I recognized as my own. Some was clearly not. What it amounted to was a fairly solid evaluation that I had not, in fact, written the entirety of the code used to manipulate the votes.

I slid the papers back to Evans. "Took your techies long enough to put that together."

"They didn't."

I lifted an eyebrow.

"Someone 'anonymously' sent it in. Any ideas?"

I shrugged. "You're the experts. You tell me."

"You're in jail and you're on your way to doing some time, so why don't we cut the shit. Who's Trevor Cooper?"

I stared. I assumed the notes I'd just skimmed through were enough to convince the police that I wasn't guilty, but I could tell Evans wasn't giving up the fight that easily. I was going to have to draw this out with crayon for him to believe I wasn't at the center of this.

He went on. "Gove is telling us he's some sort of cyber-rival of yours? From where I stand, it seems like you coordinated this effort with someone else and now you're trying to toss the blame onto him."

I let out a dry laugh but otherwise held my silence.

"Damnit, Blake, start talking."

"I can't get a word in edgewise. And why bother when you think you've got it all figured out already? I'd hate to burst your bubble by filling you in on the details, otherwise known as the truth."

He sat back in his chair and worked his jaw. "I don't like you, Landon."

"The feeling is mutual."

"I don't underestimate your intelligence, however."

"I can't say the same about you."

He grimaced, and I knew his patience was wearing thin.

Now was the time. I wasn't holding on to any hope that Evans would hear reason, but at least he was asking questions. Dean had told him about Trevor, and there was enough proof distinguishing his code from mine in front of me that Evans might have to follow some new leads if he had any chance of making a case out of this.

Beyond all that, things couldn't get much worse. Every day I spent in jail was a day without Erica, and I wasn't ready to martyr myself for Brian's kid brother, no matter what had happened in the past.

I drew in a steeling breath, preparing to tell him the whole story. "Fine. What do you want to know?"

"Let's start with Trevor. How do you know him?"

"It's safe to assume that you are aware of all the details surrounding M89, correct?"

Evans relaxed back, that shit-eating smile back on his face. "For the sake of conversation, let's assume that."

"Fine. When Brian Cooper committed suicide, he was survived by his mother and one brother, Trevor."

Evan's smile slipped a bit. "Continue."

"I don't have to tell you my story. I developed Banksoft, and I've invested in a number of my own projects since then. A few years ago, I noticed a few of my sites being targeted by a hacker or possibly a group of hackers. Nothing serious. Nothing that my team couldn't work around. Mainly a nuisance."

"And you think that was Trevor."

"I know it was him. He credited this new generation of M89 every chance he got. I never spent much time trying to track him down. It seemed like more effort than it was worth, but Erica found him through his mother and confronted him about everything. He all but admitted it, but promptly went off the grid again. He's a shitty programmer, but he's good at staying under the radar."

"Okay. Say this is all true. Why would he get involved in rigging an election? Is he tied to Fitzgerald in some way?"

"His only connection to Fitzgerald is through me and Erica. He doesn't care about money or prestige. He's built his life around avenging Brian. And what better way to avenge his dead brother than to see his former cohort behind bars for the very same thing that made Brian hang himself? Fitzgerald's election was just the vehicle to implicate me."

Several empty minutes passed while I tried not to think about the life that both Evans and Trevor had been wishing for me. A life behind bars, maybe not forever, but long enough to miss a thousand precious moments I'd never get back. Moments with Erica and our child, the family that we were so close to having. That Trevor might be able see this plan through made me sick.

I curled my hands into tight fists, pressing them into the tops of my thighs. Evans's voice cut the silence.

"How do I know you're not just feeding me a load of shit?"

I leaned in with a glare, more irate than ever that after holding all of that back until now, his immediate response was skepticism.

"Let's get something straight, Evans. If I rigged this fucking election, which I didn't, you'd have never known it. Second, if by some miracle your band of geniuses found a way to tie it to me, I'd own it."

He snorted. "You're prideful, I'll give you that."

"Call it what you want, but having my name associated with any part of this bullshit is insulting. I brought a dozen of the most powerful Wall Street scumbags to their fucking knees when I was thirteen years old. You think I can't rig a voting machine undetected? Give me a fucking break."

Red seeped into Evans's cheeks, and he adjusted his shirt collar around his neck. "So if you're telling me the truth, and Trevor is behind all of this, where would I find him?"

I shrugged. "Figure it out."

"You want out of here, Landon? Or do you want your kid visiting you behind bars?"

I bit down hard on all the things I wanted say to Evans. "I wouldn't be behind bars if it wasn't for you. Now you're trying to squeeze me to do your fucking job for you, is that right?"

His nostrils flared. "You think about it. Think long and hard about it."

His phone rang then, a shrill annoying sound. He answered and held the phone to his ear. "Evans." He stared past me. "You did? Where?" A second later he stood and the chair scraped loudly against the concrete floor. "I'll be there in ten."

He shot me an inscrutable look and left.

★ ★ ★

ERICA

I'd spent the next couple nights at Marie's house, and I was glad for it. Even though I was still distraught with missing Blake and worrying about our future, I appreciated having her near. The same kind of carefree spirit and tender heart that made her love quickly and bruise easily made her a person who was comfortable and natural to be with. Warm and unassuming, she never judged, never let her worries compound mine.

I was a long way from relief, but the progress I'd made with Sid had given me hope. We had anonymously sent Evans the analysis compiled thanks to Geoff's contact. While I waited for any word on that, I also waited for Daniel to reach out to me.

I'd run our brief conversation over and over again in my head. He'd seemed genuine. Genuinely pissed about his situation, and also genuinely sorry that he'd failed me so miserably. Hopefully he'd be genuine in wanting to find Trevor, because he was the key. He was the shadow who'd haunted our lives for too long. Sometimes I couldn't believe that I'd managed to find him once. I cursed myself over and over for letting him slip away. I'd been rash going to him on my own. I should have waited for Blake's help.

Maybe we wouldn't be here now, facing the prospect of a future divided.

In the mornings, I went to the office. Having the simple routine and the company of the people at work was a small comfort. I spent most of the day trying to learn more about other computer fraud cases and comparing our situation to others. Most of the time, doing so only left me more anxious.

Alli knocked on my door in the midst of one of those moments. "Hey, you okay?"

I spun in my chair and faced her as she lowered into the seat across from me. "Sure. Just going through emails."

"How are you feeling?"

I slid my finger along the edge of the desk. "That's a loaded question, Alli."

"Sorry. I meant physically."

I shrugged. "Nothing I can't handle."

She nodded and didn't speak for a while. "Have you been to see Blake?"

I shook my head wordlessly.

"Any particular reason?"

I couldn't go an hour without thinking about Blake. We'd spent a month together, twenty-four hours a day, seven days a week, and it hadn't been nearly enough. I longed for his presence more than anyone else's, and still I couldn't bring myself to have Clay drive me to visit him when he'd specifically asked me to stay away.

"He doesn't want me to."

"When has that ever stopped you?"

Ignoring his wish had crossed my mind. Sometimes Blake didn't know what was good for him, but a part of me was scared to see him so vulnerable too.

"I think I'm waiting," I finally admitted.

"What are you waiting for?"

"It's like I'm waiting for him to just come home. And when I realize that he's not, I feel like I'm waiting until I can fix all of this somehow."

"I understand why you feel that way, but we have no idea how long this process is going to take. No matter what's happening in his case, you're still married and in love. He needs you."

"I know he does, and believe me, it's killing me. The day of the hearing, he looked so hopeless. The only time I've ever seen that look in his eyes was after I was shot. He's always so strong, so incredibly determined. But he couldn't hide the fact that he thought I might die right there in front of him that day. If that's how he feels, like there's no hope, I don't want to go see him until I can give him hope. And I don't feel like I can do that yet."

Sadness swept her features. "Any word from the police?"

I shook my head. "Gove called me and said they were 'looking into it,' but no word yet."

She released a tired sigh. "Let me take you out to lunch."

"I'm not really hungry."

"Listen, I'd love to take you out and kill a few martinis, but you're out of commission for a while. You should at least be able to indulge in some amazing food from time to time. I found this great little Indian place a few blocks away. Their naan is absolutely mouth-watering."

My stomach offered a little rumble of assent. "Okay."

A little over an hour later, thanks to a tasty lunch rich in carbohydrates, I was carrying a food baby along with our actual baby. I patted my stomach, which seemed silly and natural all at once. No one would know that I was pregnant, but I looked forward to the day when that wasn't the case.

We were walking back toward our office when I ran into Risa walking out of a deli with another familiar face, my old friend Liz. Liz and I had been roommates my first year at Harvard, but after I'd moved, we'd grown apart. She'd been the one to refer Risa to me when I was looking to hire for Clozpin, but we hadn't kept in touch since then.

Now the two women were standing in front of us, dressed in dark slacks and dressy tops. Bags that no doubt contained their lunches hung from their hands. Liz was the first to speak.

"Erica, how are you?" She came up to me and gave me an awkward hug.

"Fine, and you?"

"I'm great. Still crunching numbers at the investment firm, but whatever. At least I have company now." She grinned and gestured to Risa, who stood tensely beside her.

I wasn't sure how much Risa had briefed her on our falling out, but apparently it wasn't enough. Risa had betrayed my trust and threatened my business, two offenses that were nearly unforgivable in my book. She'd attempted to make amends months ago, and a small part of me pitied her for making such terrible decisions when it came to inviting Max into her life, but she'd brought them on herself. I'd never be able to trust her again.

She seemed to be reading my thoughts when she spoke up. "I heard about Blake. How are you holding up?"

I shrugged, not quite knowing how to answer that.

How I was holding up wasn't much of her business. Also, I wasn't holding up as well as I wanted to, especially when tears burned behind my eyes at the mere mention of Blake.

"Well, it was great seeing you. We're late for a meeting, though." Alli glanced at her oversize watch and hooked her arm in mine, coaxing me away.

"Um, Erica. I was hoping we could catch up sometime." Risa set her bag down to look through her purse. She retrieved a business card, confirming that she too was employed at the same firm that had hired Liz right out of school.

With Liz among us, I didn't know what to say. Polite convention told me to say *sure*, but I had no desire to speak to Risa. She was incredibly far outside the circle of trust, and there was no way in hell I was letting her back in.

Alli plucked the card from her hand. "Cool. We'll see you two around then. Have to run!"

We hurried down the street to our pretend meeting.

"Sorry, I went deer in headlights for a minute. Thanks for rescuing me," I said as we approached the office.

"Not a problem. I was rescuing the both of us. I have nothing to say to that woman after what she did to you. I don't imagine you do either."

"Nothing good anyway." I slid her card into my jeans and tried to ignore the fact that she now worked a few blocks away, and it was only a matter of time before our paths crossed again.

CHAPTER NINETEEN

ERICA

Clay drove me to Marie's again that night. When I walked through her front door, my gaze immediately landed on the figure sitting on the couch across from my dear friend. Daniel stood and walked slowly toward me.

"Is everything okay?" I asked.

"Here." He withdrew a piece of paper from his pocket and handed it to me.

"What's this?" I asked as I unfolded it.

"That's where you'll find him."

"Trevor?" Relief washed over me, along with a potent rush of adrenaline. Could it be possible that Daniel had really found him?

"He's holed up in an apartment in Roxbury above a convenience store. It's a rough area, so proceed with caution."

"How did you find him?"

"The same way you did. Through his mother."

"She just *told* you?"

His lips thinned into a grim line. "No. Not exactly."

I felt the blood drain from my face. Oh, God. What had he done?

"Everyone has a price...Hers was much lower than I would have expected."

"Do I want to know what you really mean by that?"

He cracked a smile. "If the little prick hadn't cost me the governor's seat, I might take pity on him. A few grand and couple bottles of Vicodin was all it took. Seems like he was neglecting her habits, so she wasn't feeling too maternal when my friends came to chat with her."

"Oh."

Sadly, nothing about that scenario surprised me. The woman had looked like a train wreck the first and only time I'd seen her. Like Daniel, if Trevor hadn't singlehandedly threatened to ruin everything I held dear, I might feel sorry for him, knowing that was the woman who'd raised him.

"How do you know he's really there?"

"I had someone watch his apartment to make sure he was there. Short kid, black hair?"

"Yeah, that's him."

"We hung around long enough to make sure the address was legit, but I didn't want him to get spooked and disappear again. I figured I'd let you take it from there."

"Thank you."

The paper shook in my trembling hands. Before I could think better of it, I threw my arms around Daniel and buried my face against his shoulder, stifling the tears that wanted to burst free—tears of overwhelming relief. His arms came around me. His chest expanded with a deep breath before he tightened his embrace the smallest amount.

"Thank you so much," I whispered.

We broke apart, and he avoided my eyes.

"I better go," he said quietly. He glanced back at Marie with a nod.

"Bye, Daniel," she said.

"Goodbye."

Then he left, down to the street to where Connor was waiting for him by the black Lincoln that used to fill me with dread every time I saw it.

See you around, I thought to myself. But I wasn't sure if I would. I'd promised him he'd never seen me again. Is that what he really wanted? Is that what I wanted?

I knew the answer, but I didn't have time to dwell on it. Not now, when we were so close to ending this.

As soon as Daniel's car disappeared down the street and I got my emotions under control, I dialed the number that had anonymously texted me a few days before, hoping to hear Detective Carmody's voice on the other end.

"Carmody," he answered abruptly.

"Hi, this is Erica Landon."

He hesitated. "What can I do for you?"

"I found Trevor. He's in the city. I want you to bring him in."

"Where is he?"

I swallowed and glanced down at the paper in my hands. I held it tightly, like it was a precious thing. If Trevor was really there, and if the police could apprehend him, it truly was.

"Erica, are you still there?"

"Yes. I have the address in front of me. I just need you to promise me something first."

"What?"

So much hung in the balance. We couldn't mess this up. If Trevor caught on and disappeared again, I might never find him again. Not until it was too late...

"I have to know that you're going to do this right, Carmody. I'm scared he's going to slip away and I'll never find him again."

"If he's there, I'll bring him in."

I wanted to trust him. He had the authority to take Trevor down, and he was my best and possibly only chance to achieve that. The fact that he'd gone out of his way to help me find Trevor made me trust him more than anyone else, but it also made me suspicious of his motivations for doing so.

"Why did you help me?"

He was silent for a long time. "Listen, it's nothing to get sentimental about. I'm not on anyone's side here but the truth. The way Evans was going with this, I knew we weren't anywhere near it. Obviously he's on a vendetta for the agency, and I had a feeling you could get us closer."

I closed my eyes, grateful he'd done what he had. If he hadn't... I couldn't even think about it.

"Just promise me."

He released a noisy breath. "Erica, if Trevor is wherever you say he is, and we can find evidence that points to him being behind this whole operation, I'm not going to let him out of my sight. You have my word."

"Okay," I finally relented. I rattled off the address, willing my heart to slow. I heard rustling on his end of the phone followed by silence.

"Are you going today?" I asked.

"I'm getting in my car right now."

"Thank you."

The phone clicked, and I waited.

★ ★ ★

BLAKE

"Today is your lucky day."

I took a seat across from my attorney, wanting to smack the optimism off his face. Nothing was lucky about my current predicament. "I highly doubt that."

"They found Trevor."

I stilled. "How the hell did they manage that?"

Dean shot me a slanted smile. "Another anonymous tip. Between that and the code, I think Evans's curiosity was piqued. Regardless, Carmody was the one who got the tip and brought him in. Wasn't easy either. I guess he tried to run. He got banged up a little when Carmody took him down."

"Wow. I can't believe they really have him."

They'd managed to catch a ghost. A shadow. But I couldn't give them all the credit, or even the lion's share of it. Erica had to have tipped them off.

Damn, how did she do it? First the code and now this. I couldn't imagine anyone else could have pulled it all off so quickly. Anyone who underestimated my wife was a damn fool.

My face split with wide grin.

"Needless to say, he's not cooperating," Dean continued. "But it doesn't really matter, because they found a mountain of incriminating evidence on his machines. Source code galore. For the voting machines, a bunch of your sites and Erica's. It's all there and more. They're still wading through it all now."

"I guess that means I'm off the hook now."

"For the election tampering, yes. But they don't want to budge on the fraud charges with Parker unless you deal."

"Deal?"

"They want your cooperation to help prosecute Cooper. They want a full statement and any supporting evidence you can provide about his activities with your business. And they may want you to testify."

"Fuck," I muttered. I could handle the statement and providing evidence, but I didn't want to face that little prick in court. Something about it felt beneath me.

"We've come this far, Blake. You should count your lucky stars that we have, and not without risk. God knows what Erica had to do to track down that code, *and* Trevor. If you don't do this..."

He dropped his pen and pinched the bridge of his nose. He didn't have to say it. If I didn't do this, I was a self-destructive, self-absorbed idiot.

"What are they offering?"

He gave me a tired look. "A reduced sentence."

Any relief I felt was quickly replaced with fresh dread. "You mean I'll still have to do time. No fucking way. No deal."

"Probation, Blake. I can get you out of here tomorrow. Stay out of trouble for a few months and other than your record, it's like this never happened." He shoved a hand through his hair, mussing its careful placement. "You think I'd let you do time? Give me little fucking credit."

I released a frustrated sigh. "Fine."

He stilled. "You'll do it?"

"I'll do it. Where do I sign?"

★ ★ ★

As unaffected as I wanted to be, my heart damn near sang when I was able to put my own clothes on after out-processing. I assessed myself in the small mirror hanging on the wall where I changed. Even though I knew I wasn't, at least I appeared to be the same man Erica had last seen.

My glasses rested on my nose. I tossed my hand through my hair, which was due for another cut. I hadn't seen Erica all week, and while I wanted to race home to her as fast as humanly possible, I was also apprehensive about what she would say when I finally walked through the door again.

She was the one who'd set me free. But even if she was the same warm Erica welcoming me into her arms, I knew I wasn't the same man she'd last seen. This latest brush with the law had been painfully eye-opening. I could be prideful at times, but knowing that I wasn't the only one whose future was at stake had humbled me.

I passed through the last security door and entered the sterile entryway of the jail. Before me, Michael Pope emerged from the waiting area. He was dressed in an expensive pinstriped suit. He was sporting a nice tan and his graying blond hair was trimmed neatly. For the first time in my life, I felt a little inferior in my current condition.

I walked toward him. "What are you doing here?"

"Thought I might give you a ride."

"I wasn't expecting you." Dean had agreed to meet me and drive me home, but he was nowhere in sight.

"I know. I spoke with your attorney already. I let him know I'd take you home." Michael nodded toward the doors. "Ready?"

"Never been readier."

The cold air outside hit me and I inhaled deeply, more grateful than ever for freedom.

Then it occurred to me that Max was also here, locked up, breathing the stale air that I'd been breathing for the past several days. "Did you see Max?"

"He didn't want to see me." Michael's face was calm, expressionless. "Maybe next time."

We climbed into the back of the only black town car parked in the lot. I gave his driver my address, and we drove away from the hell I solemnly swore I would never know again.

I sank back against the seat. Leather, a hint of scotch, and Michael's subtle cologne, a scent that I'd always associated with him for as long as I'd known him, permeated the cool air of the car. For me, they were the smells of a civilization, luxury, and a life I'd worked hard for and wanted back. Yet as Michael naturally represented all those things, he was ominously silent.

"I appreciate you being here, Michael, but I can't imagine you flew all the way from Texas to drive me home. What's going on?"

"No, I came to town to speak to Trevor, actually."

I frowned. "Why the hell would you waste your time with him?"

He folded his hands on his lap and held my stare. "When the police got hold of him, I thought I might need to intervene."

I scanned his face, searching for clues. Something wasn't right. My gut knew it. He shouldn't be here, and he shouldn't be wasting a minute of his day on someone like Trevor.

"Why would you need to intervene?"

"When things went south with Max, I hired Trevor." He cleared his throat. "I took him off the books and closed down Max's operations first. Then I put him to work."

What in the ever-loving fuck? "You hired him?"

His eyes lit up a little. "I saw promise in him, an opportunity to turn him into something more. There was something about him that reminded me of you, and I took a chance. The same way I took a chance with you once upon a time."

"I'm nothing like Trevor."

He cocked his head and made a small sound of dissent. "A younger you, perhaps. You and Cooper have more in common than you might think...Angry, confused, driven toward a mission that had no focus. I could have tried for retribution after learning what a nuisance he'd become of yours. But how do you discipline a rogue like him? You don't. You can't. So instead I tried to change him. I tried to make him what I made you. I gave him a project. New focus."

My thoughts reeled at a million miles an hour. Erica's first instinct to go to Michael had been right. She just didn't know it. Still, I couldn't believe Michael would go to the effort of hiring Trevor. Michael had been a great mentor, but I had no idea he was looking for new recruits.

"The things you did for M89 a decade ago were remarkable," he continued, clasping his hands in front of him. "Cutting edge, really. If you hadn't gotten caught, banking software wouldn't be what it is today. You identified the shortcomings in what was out on the market. Maybe you didn't realize it at the time because you were still so young—not quite the capitalist you are today—but because of what you did, everyone with money to protect had an interest in solving this problem. Bankers' phones were ringing off the hook. People wanted to know how their money was going to be protected. You created fear. And people respond to fear."

"Banksoft was an easy sell for you."

"Absolutely. In a way, it was priceless. Banksoft was the most expensive software acquisition in history up to that point. That wasn't a fluke. Because how much would you pay to protect your wealth?"

He glanced my way, but I was silent and still, sensing there was more that he wasn't telling me.

"Let me ask you another question. Can you put a price on the integrity of the vote that determines the men and women who will run our country, at any level of government?"

And there it was. A bitter smile twisted at my lips.

"By your math, the price goes up considerably after someone compromises a faulty system. Is that your new business model?"

He nodded slowly. "It was. I figured the same principal would apply to the voting software I wanted Trevor to build out for me. And when the time came, I'd have the solution ready to sell to the highest bidder. But instead of waiting for demand, I created it. I wanted scandal. Some news."

"Glad I could help you out." I ground my teeth, already seething from what Michael had revealed. The way he perceived Trevor made me question everything I'd ever respected about Michael. How could he see promise in a person who'd done nothing but vandalize my efforts?

He sighed. "Blake, I didn't want to send you to prison."

I let out a caustic laugh and shoved a hand through my already messed-up hair. "He used my fucking code. That didn't concern you?"

"I didn't know the first thing about encryption routines until the FBI came calling. I'd given Trevor access to whatever he needed. Whether that was code or money. I brought him into the fold, the same way I did you. People like you respond to trust when no one else believes you deserve it."

I worked my jaw. "People like me, huh?"

"Don't be so sensitive, Blake. That's how I won you over all those years ago. I trusted you . . . implicitly."

"I trusted you too."

A flicker of emotion passed behind his eyes. "I know, and perhaps I failed you there. But I needed your trust to teach you all the other things first."

"Why the governor's election? Why Fitzgerald?"

"That was an easy choice. His attorneys turned their backs on Max when we went to them for representation. Do you have any idea how many hundreds of thousands I've dumped into Fitzgerald's firm?"

"So this was about vengeance."

"Not at all. This was about creating an opportunity first. Vengeance was an unexpected benefit. A bonus, if you will."

"And when I was implicated and the FBI came to you, you still wouldn't give him up?"

"If it had been simply a matter of protecting you, I would have. But I was concerned Trevor might turn and try to implicate Max to get back at me. The last thing I want is my only son doing more jail time. He's a goddamn fool, but he's my son. It was easier to keep Trevor in the shadows than expose him for what he'd done."

I shook my head and stared listlessly out the window. "Unbelievable."

"You know as well as I do that when you start letting emotions get in the way, you lose control of the situation. It's a weakness and a vulnerability that will catch up to you, sooner or later."

Michael had taught me that, and at the time, it was a principle that made sense. I was all emotion when he'd met me. I needed hard lines. He'd simplified everything with the laws of business and showed me how to use my talents within a framework that was both legal and lucrative. Don't fight the problem from the bottom, he'd say. That's a waste of time, not to mention dangerous. Find their weaknesses and root out the solution from the inside.

And that's what I'd done with the payoff from Banksoft. Instead of punishing the people responsible for the injustices I saw all around me, I built companies that answered those problems with solutions that didn't exist yet.

Ironic, when my mentor was paying a hacker who'd done everything in his power to disrupt all my efforts. I curled my fists tightly, counting down the seconds until I'd be home and this fucked-up conversation would come to an end.

"I can see that you're taking this personally, Blake. But

you have to understand that after a certain point, this was damage control. Something I've had to do a lot of when it came to Max. I'm disgusted with what he did to Erica. I really am. But I wasn't about to lead this investigation to him."

"I thought you didn't let emotions get in the way."

"I don't. Max and I are different that way. Every business decision Max has ever made has been emotional. Fueled by vengeance or pride. Trying to get my attention or tear you down because you'd always gotten so much of it. Max never understood why I brought you into the fold...why it couldn't have been him instead. He was too young, of course, but it was never a matter of having faith in his abilities. There was nothing he could do to change the fact that he was my son, so he had to be sidelined."

"He hates you now. You know that?" I remembered our brief interaction in the cafeteria. Before I'd wanted to rip Max's throat out, I'd registered the smallest inkling of sympathy for him. Without Michael's protection, he seemed so lost. I'd never forgive him for what he did to Erica, but an unmistakable feeling of shared betrayal tugged at me. Max had betrayed me a hundred times. I'd expected it, and half of the time, I'd seen it coming. But Michael had always had my respect and my trust. His betrayal cut deeper. It cut right through me.

"Regardless, he'll inherit the empire I've built, and he'll thank me. Maybe not right away, but eventually he'll understand that in order for me to have come this far, I couldn't allow my emotional attachments to rule my business decisions. There's no greater attachment than a parent to his child."

Michael seemed older in that moment. No longer the young, ambitious mentor I'd always known. But someone who had changed before my eyes. And suddenly I wasn't the young man he'd coaxed out of a troublesome period. I had grown, and I had lived. More than anything, I'd learned. In this very moment, I was still learning.

I pushed at my forehead, the beginnings of a headache emerging.

"You seem surprised, but if you strip away all the emotion you're feeling right now, this is what you would expect or even do."

"It's never something I would do."

"This isn't betrayal. This is business. If you look at your life, you've done the same thing. The way you handled Heath, for example. You marginalized him from your affairs. You've always exercised a level of control over your world that impressed me." He paused. "With Erica...she's good for you, I think, but she's a weakness. You're changing for her."

I riled at the mention of her name. How dare he even presume to know what she was to me?

"She's worth changing for."

He nodded. "It's normal to feel that way. Love and passion will do that. Clearly you have both with her, and I'm happy for you. It does pass, though. You're married now. She's pregnant. She'll focus on your family, and this obsession you have for each other will settle. You'll find your way back to yourself."

No. Nothing could temper what I felt for her. That she carried our child now only added fuel to that flame. "The last thing I want to do is find my way back to myself when I've already found the best part of myself in her."

"I have faith that you will. I've invested in you more than anyone else in my life. I have a pretty good track record of making sound investments." His satisfied smile dimmed a bit. "Except for this whole situation with Cooper... Too much pride, I think."

"Him or you?"

"Maybe both. I wanted to cheat and jump ahead a few spaces. Of course you know all about that."

"Do I?"

"Moonlighting as a hacker? You don't consider that cheating?"

"I'm not hurting anyone."

"You've never sought out information to position yourself more favorably in a business deal? You've never used that information to discredit or eliminate competition? You can dress it up in whatever white-collar terms you'd like, but we both know it's cheating. And that's fine, because anyone who isn't cheating at least a little bit isn't making it very far."

"You didn't make it too far with this one."

He glanced out the window. "No. Unfortunately, Trevor had more of Max in him than you. All emotion and no control."

"And what makes you think your new prodigy isn't going to tell the FBI that you put him up to this?"

"He won't be telling anyone." He shifted his gaze back to me. "I'm sad to say they found him hanging in his cell this morning."

My blood went cold, stilling like ice in my veins. Michael's confessions had rattled me to the core. But the vision of Trevor, a boy I'd never met, hanging in a cell not unlike the one I'd just left, was incredibly vivid in my mind. My stomach writhed and I couldn't shake the sick feeling that swept over me no matter how hard I tried. We were less than a mile from the house and I'd had more than I could take.

"Let me out here," I said to the driver. He pulled to the side of the road and I stepped out. A light rain had begun to drizzle down but I didn't care. I carried forward.

Michael got out and circled the vehicle. "Blake, wait."

"Enough!" I shouted and doubled back to face him. "Call it business. Call it keeping everything under control. Whatever the hell you want to call it that makes sense in your warped fucking version of reality. It's nothing but a goddamn game. And you're deluding yourself if you think you own the board and can move all the pieces however you like."

His lips drew back in a bitter smile. "I do own the board, Blake."

I took off my water-stained glasses and stared at him. Resentment and pity for the man in front of me mingled with my anger, creating a potent brew.

"Maybe you do, Michael. And if that's the case, consider this my final act of forfeiture. We're through. I'm not playing anymore."

"You're willing to throw away our entire relationship over this? Is that what you're telling me?" There was a hint of challenge in his voice and I didn't like it.

"That's what I'm telling you."

His jaw tightened. The mirage of warmth and kindness had vanished. "Do not cross me, Blake. If I taught you anything, I taught you that." His voice was low and edgy, laced with threat.

Maybe at a different time in my life, I would have heeded it, but not today. Not when I'd been so close to losing everything. I'd been turned inside out. Everything I knew to be true, every tenet of wisdom Michael had instilled in me had to be questioned.

"I'm not crossing you, Michael. But I am walking away. If you think that because you took me under your wing ten years ago I'm going to worship you for the rest of my fucking life, you're wrong. I'm not pandering to you the way everyone else does. I made my money, and I'm using it to work on things I believe in. I'm making a life with the woman I love. And I don't need to find my way back to myself. This is it, right here. This is who I am, and I don't need to play God with people's lives and count my money all day long to feel like my life is worth something. So get in your goddamn car and go back home."

With that, I turned and made strides toward home. After a few moments, the black Lincoln drove past me. I walked faster, fueled with relief that Michael had left and a powerful urge to get home to Erica.

The rain came down heavier. Cold driving rain that saturated my clothing and seeped into my skin. It couldn't numb the chaos inside me. And it couldn't wash away the blood on my hands.

CHAPTER TWENTY

ERICA

I paced the living room. What was taking so damn long? Rain pelted against the window, obscuring the clear view of the ocean. Gove had called me this morning, letting me know to expect Blake soon. I'd wanted to pick him up myself when they let him go, but he insisted I wait. He wanted to be the one to break the news to him about Trevor.

Leave it to Trevor to take matters into his own hands.

My heart broke for Blake when I thought about what he must be feeling. Relief to be free, but now the guilt he'd harbored for Brian would double if he let it. I wanted him home so I could talk him out of that way of thinking. But it wouldn't be easy. I was up against Blake's darkest memories, and history had just repeated itself.

I'm not sure what we could have done differently. Carmody had said he wouldn't let Trevor out of his sight, but I couldn't take that literally. None of us could know that he'd seriously consider suicide as a way out. The police barely had a chance to question him before he'd taken his life.

It was almost as if Blake had seen this coming from miles away, and turning away from any path that would lead to Trevor's incarceration was his way of avoiding the inevitable. Yet, he couldn't have known. And here we were still . . .

I'd wanted truth and I'd wanted justice, but Trevor's death was still tragic. Like Mark's, his life meant no less than anyone else's despite his transgressions.

The sound of rain falling filled the room when Blake came through the door. He was soaked through. I stood, frozen in place. He shut the door and leaned against it, his chest heaving under his breaths.

"Erica."

The pleading in his voice made me run to him then. Our bodies crashed, and I wrapped my arms around him. I slid my hands through his damp hair, curving over the nape of his neck and down his chest where his shirt clung to him. My heart raced and swelled. I whispered his name, like a dream. He was home. Thank God, he was home.

He held me so tightly around my ribs it almost hurt, but I didn't care. I held him back. When I finally pulled away, my heart twisted at the sight of those incredible green eyes boring into me, brewing with emotion. I feathered my fingers over his lips, over the prickly hair along his jaw. My love . . .

Seeing him had sent a rush of adrenaline through my body, warming me, but Blake was still cold. The moisture from his clothes had started to seep into mine.

"You're soaking wet."

I pushed back a little, separating us enough to unbutton his shirt. I skated my palms down his chest and back up, pushing the wet garment over his shoulders. He wrenched it off the rest of the way and pulled me back to him roughly, capturing my mouth in a savage kiss. He was all taste and need, and I was engulfed in it, unable to feel or see anything but his urgency, his all-consuming presence. My pulse hammered in my veins, but he still trembled against me.

I broke the contact, breathless but scared for him. "Blake, you're shaking."

"Doesn't matter," he murmured, moving his hands all over me.

I put my hands over his, trying to slow him down.

"You're going to get sick, Blake. Let's get you warm and dry."

He stilled, and the fire in his eyes blazed. "I need you...please."

The desperation in his voice destroyed me, and I wondered if the cold was making him tremble against me. Whatever it was, I wanted to take that look away, and whatever pain had caused it.

I nodded quickly, and then his mouth was at my neck, sucking and biting. I felt the edge in every touch as liquid desire snaked through me. He pushed my shirt up and over my shoulders. Tugging at my jeans, he got them past my hips before I stopped him.

"Let's go upstairs," I said.

I led him toward the stairs. My breath caught when he came at me again. Tangled in each other's embrace, we almost made it.

"Here," he rasped.

We stumbled at the first step, and he took us both down to the floor. His hands were everywhere.

"Now." He yanked my jeans and panties off and hauled me over to him so I straddled his hips.

He pulled me down against his chest, anchored me to

his mouth, and ravaged me with one breathless kiss after the next. A knot of heat grew within me, starting low in my belly and weaving down my limbs and to the throb between my legs. Desire was thick in my veins.

"Tell me what you need, Blake." My body was soaring under his touch and I was racing for more.

Raw emotion flashed behind his eyes. "You. You're the only one I need. You're the only one in this whole god-damn world I need."

Ripping open his fly, he shoved his jeans down just past his hips. He grasped his firm length and lowered me down onto him. My head fell back at the sweet pleasure. Lifting his hips, he rooted deeply, joining us completely.

A hoarse cry tore from him. One that brought tears to the corners of my eyes. I could feel his pain, his struggle.

Eyes closed, jaw tight, he began to move me over his cock. I clenched against his penetration, overwrought and aroused. Pain hit my knees with every thrust, but I didn't care. I only cared that we were connected, loving one another, giving each other what we needed.

He worked me over him in urgent glides. I met his pace, churning my hips to feel him everywhere. He bucked up and held me firmly, fusing us together with vigorous, shattering drives. Every one struck at the heart of me, and I cried out. The sound echoed off the walls and melted into the next desperate cry that left my lips as he claimed me over and over.

I trembled, mindless in this rapture.

"Erica..." He wet his lips.

His hands left my hips and trailed down my arms. Our fingers threaded hotly together, and I leaned down, bringing us chest to chest. A searing kind of energy radiated there and everywhere our bodies touched.

I'd never experienced anything this intense in my entire life. And I was lost in it, fully submerged.

Our gazes locked, and the intensity in his eyes seized my heart.

"I love you, Blake," I whimpered against his lips, a tear escaping down my cheek.

I could live in this moment forever, I thought. Painful as it was, Blake was showing me a part of himself I'd never seen. This raw vulnerability. And I was as grateful for that as I was to have him here with me, taking his pleasure and giving me so much more.

His expression was taut, almost pained. He tightened his grasp and his biceps tensed along with the rest of his powerful body. Heat licked down my spine, and I cried out as he did. We crashed over, together.

★ ★ ★

Little by little, life returned to normal. Over the next few months, Blake and I threw ourselves into work. He let me into his projects and I let him into mine. Blake turned most of his focus to a voting software project that would undoubtedly fill an unmet need. I could appreciate too that every line of code was an unspoken victory over Michael's foiled plan.

He hadn't heard from Michael again since their long ride home, and even though Blake didn't say much about it, Michael's betrayal weighed on him. It had broken something inside of Blake—maybe something that needed to be broken so it could heal the right way.

Despite all the hurt we were working through, we had a bright future to look forward to. I was growing and glowing, and every day was a step closer toward having our family complete.

I found myself falling in love with him all over again. I fell in love with the broken parts and the parts that had healed and changed for the better.

Ours was a hard love. We'd fallen hard into it, and we'd fought hard to keep it. Our kind of love didn't ask nicely. It took. It ravaged. It consumed the heart whole and asked questions later. The rewards were soul-deep and all-consuming, sweeping through like a wildfire.

I sat alone in a little bistro near the office. Light danced off my rings as I ruminated over the journey life had led us on these many months. We'd been hurt, threatened, and betrayed. We'd found love, forgiveness, and hope. We'd run the gamut of emotions and experiences, and we were still holding strong, ready for the next adventure.

Risa pulled a chair from the table and settled into it across from me.

"Hi," she said with a tentative smile.

She wore fitted black pants and a matching blazer over a simple white shell blouse. She'd always been the picture of style when she worked for Clozpin, but she had adopted a decidedly more corporate look the past couple times I'd seen her.

My thoughts returned to why I'd finally accepted her invitation to meet. "How are you doing?"

"Okay, I guess."

"How's work?"

She shrugged. "Um, it's fine. I guess I never thought

I'd be working at an investment firm. But life is full of surprises."

"I can attest to that."

Her deep blue eyes softened a little. "You've been through a lot. I'm sure it's been difficult, but I admire you all the more for it."

She sounded genuine, except she'd caused a significant amount of the drama I'd endured.

"So why did you want to see me?" I asked, drinking from my water glass.

She hesitated before responding. "Sorry, I never thought you'd really agree to meet with me again. I'm a little off balance I guess."

I hadn't wanted to see her for a long time either, but after stumbling upon her card one day, a thought had occurred to me—one I hadn't been able to shake since.

"Well, here we are. Indulge me."

She drew in a steeling breath. "Okay. I want something that you probably will never give me, I know that. I want another chance to work for you."

"Clozpin is gone. If I trusted you enough to work with you again, your love of fashion would be wasted on anything I have going on at the moment."

She worried her bottom lip a second before releasing it. "Listen, I made a huge mistake. I know I lost your trust, and I may never get it back. I can make excuses all day long. I could try to explain that in the end, I realized how completely Max had manipulated me. I could try to explain the things he had me do...to prove my loyalty to him." She looked down at the table, avoiding my eyes. "I think all it would do is convince you of my lack of mental strength against someone like him, and that's hardly a job qualification. But what I want to tell you, more than all of that, was that I was really happy working for you. We clashed sometimes, I know, but I felt alive for the first time in a long time while I was there, and I haven't felt like that since. Every day I wake up and drag myself to a job I don't hate, but one that I don't love either. I regret everything I did to mess things up for you."

I was silent for a long time, taking in all that she'd said. "Do you really mean all that?"

"I have nothing to gain by lying. I know you're too smart to bring me anywhere near another venture of yours. I guess I'm just getting it off my chest. It's been weighing on me. If nothing else, I wanted to clear the air and tell you how I felt. I can't change how you feel, but it hurts to think you will always hate me for the mistakes I made."

"I agree that you made some really poor choices. And some of those were because you were misguided, but I don't hate you, Risa."

Her gaze flickered up to mine.

"You look good," I said.

"Oh...thanks." She looked confused, tucking her sleek hair back nervously behind her ear.

"When we met, after Max attacked me, you didn't seem like yourself. You looked like he had put you through the ringer."

Her face fell. "You have no idea."

"What did he do to you?"

She sat back and fumbled with her napkin. "I don't know if I can talk about it," she murmured.

"You can't, or you don't want to?"

She shook her head. "I guess I want to believe that he can't hurt me now, but two years can go by and that could all change."

"You're afraid of him?"

"Even if I weren't, I'm not sure I'd want to talk about what happened between us. It's…embarrassing… shameful."

"Was he violent with you?"

Pink painted her cheeks, and her eyes seemed to glow against the flush of color sweeping over her skin. "Sometimes. Never in a way that anyone could tell. He was…careful. He never left marks anywhere that people could see."

"Why didn't you tell anyone?"

"I—I don't know. I didn't think anyone would believe me, I guess. He's rich, good-looking. Charming. Who wants to believe a man like that beats his girlfriend?"

I closed my eyes and didn't like the vision I saw there. No one, not even Risa, deserved to be treated that way. I knew firsthand what it was like to fall prey to his violent streak. I didn't think I could despise him any more than I already did, but Risa's admission had done that. I didn't want to ask, but I had to know more.

"You seemed taken aback when I told you what he did to me," I said, pushing her to tell me more.

Lips thin, she drew tiny circles into the tablecloth. "I was, I guess. Sounds strange to say, but a small part of me was jealous. Even though things were crumbling between us, that he wanted you sexually was really hurtful. I had fallen for him. Loved him. How else could I have stayed as long as I did? I knew things were fucked up, but I was still under his spell in a lot of ways."

"Did it surprise you that he wanted to rape me?"

Her eyes were serious before her gaze dropped to her lap. "No," she said barely above a whisper.

I swallowed over a fresh wave of emotion. "What did he do to you?"

She squeezed her eyes tight. "I can't talk about this, Erica."

"Why not?" I knew why, but I had to press her.

"You don't understand—"

"I understand perfectly."

She opened her eyes and the fear I saw there inspired me to say the words that she struggled to say now. She wasn't alone, and that was how I'd felt for so long. No matter what she'd done to me, I could never really shake the thought that Max had carried out his plans for me on her, possibly more than once, and disguised the wrongdoing under a promise of love.

"When Max attacked me at the engagement party, it wasn't the first time I'd been through something like that. His friend Mark MacLeod raped me my first year at college. He took my virginity on the dirty ground behind a frat house while my friends partied without me inside. Liz was there. You can ask her."

Her eyes brimmed with tears. "I had no idea."

The memory worked its way through me, like a small earthquake that eventually faded into the distance. Every day it had a little less power over me.

"You wouldn't, because it's a hard story to tell. I felt

the way you feel. Embarrassed. Ashamed. I spent the rest of my college career looking over my shoulder, waiting for the day when I'd see him again. I never knew who he was until I recognized him one night at a bar. And Blake was the first lover I ever told about the whole experience. When Max attacked me, it all came back. Years of pretending like I'd healed and had moved on came crashing down on me. The only real solace came when I made my statement to the police. That was one of the hardest things I'd ever done."

"I can't imagine."

She wiped at her eyes, and I took a deep breath, remembering how difficult that choice had been for me. But because I'd done it, Risa and the rest of the world were safe from him. At least for a little while.

"Do you really want to work with me again?"

Her eyes brightened. "Yes." She said the word emphatically, hope lighting up her face.

"Okay."

"Okay?"

"Yes."

Her jaw fell. "Wait. Are you serious?"

"I've thought about it a lot. I can see that you made a mistake. I want to protect myself from people who would do what you did to me, but I also want to believe that people can change and be better."

"I will, and I am. I promise you."

"I hope that's true and that my instincts on this aren't completely wrong. I want to hire you back at your original pay. I have only one condition."

"Absolutely. Whatever you want."

I drummed my fingers on the table a couple times, wondering if she would really do it. If she had the strength to, I knew I was making the right decision.

"Risa, I want you to go to the police and tell them what Max did to you."

The earlier flush of color left her cheeks. "I—I can't do that."

I leaned in, holding her gaze. "You can."

Her lip quivered.

"Risa... You can do this. And I'll be there to help."

"Okay," she said, with a whisper.

EPILOGUE

Crisp cool water washed up on my feet. I scanned the sand below for something that would catch my eye. Any little treasure she would like. The pull of the tide made a divot around a shell. I bent and captured it. Finding it unbroken, I washed it clean with the next wave.

"Mommy! Look what I found!"

Tricia ran toward me, breaking her stride with playful, excited leaps. Her swimsuit was a shock of neon colors among the otherwise muted tones of the ocean side. Her fine blond hair fell long down her back, bright against her sun-kissed skin.

"What did you find, honey?"

She stopped abruptly in front of me, holding up a long, slightly mangled feather, no doubt once belonging to a seagull.

"Wow, that's beautiful. Can I clean it for you?"

She hesitated a moment before handing it to me. "Okay."

I washed it in the water, smoothing the gray and white fronds until they more closely resembled their original form. As soon as I finished, Tricia reached for it eagerly and ran back to where Blake sat several feet away in the sand. I followed behind, sizing up the sand castle progress that had been made.

"Daddy, this can be our flag."

The excitement in her voice was contagious. I reached

for a distant memory on the beach at the lake with my mother and Elliot, when such small triumphs could fill my young heart. Witnessing her wonder was a gift, one I was grateful for each day.

A concentrated frown left Blake's features as he gazed upon our daughter and her new treasure.

"Perfect." He reached for the small feather.

She held it back. "No, I wanna."

He sighed. "All right. Where do you want it?"

She sat on her knees and shimmied closer, sending an avalanche of sand into Blake's carefully constructed moat. "Here," she said, planting the quill into the soft sand at the top of the castle Blake had spent the better part of an hour crafting.

She sat back, eyes bright. Blake's mouth lifted into a small smile, admiration and love plain on his features.

"Perfect."

He reached an arm around her, tugging her close to his side. They admired their handiwork when the sound of a car door closing interrupted them. In the distance, a man walked toward us.

Tricia's eyes widened, and she scrambled to her feet and out of Blake's arms. "Poppy!" she squealed.

She ran toward Daniel with the same leaps and bounds as before. He caught her little frame and tossed her into the air before catching her and holding her up on his hip. A smile tugged at my lips, but all signs of the love in Blake's eyes had vanished.

I rose as they approached.

"Hey," Daniel said, his voice low but jovial. He leaned in, kissing me on the cheek.

"How was the trip?" I asked.

He smiled fondly, his gaze falling on Tricia. "Ah, not bad. Well worth it to see my princess."

"Poppy, I want to show you something." Her pale green eyes widened with excitement, and she wriggled free from his embrace.

"What do you want to show me, sweetheart?"

She caught his hand in her small one and tugged him down onto the sand. He laughed, and she began cataloging the pile of shells and debris she'd accumulated over the afternoon.

Blake stared off into the horizon, and I searched for a way to break the tension that always came between them.

"Are you hungry, Dad?" Food was the cure-all, surely.

"Sure, I could eat in a little bit. No rush though."

"I'll go fix us something," I said quickly.

Blake stood and brushed the sand off his board shorts. "I'll help you." He shot Daniel a questioning stare, eyes cold and jaw tight. "You okay with her?"

"We're fine," he answered mildly without making eye contact. "Aren't we, sweetheart?" His voice softened when he spoke to Tricia. Carefully, he pushed a strand of hair back from her sandy face.

Tricia began burying Daniel's now bare feet in the sand and decorating them with shells. Seemingly content leaving her in Daniel's care, Blake took me by the hand, and we headed back up to the beach house.

"You should try to be nicer to him, Blake," I chided softly.

"I'm plenty nice," he mumbled, the impassive expression on his face communicating just how it pained him.

We'd made so many memories here on the Vineyard. I knew Blake would never forgive Daniel for the things he'd done, but letting myself forgive him, finally, had allowed me to appreciate the memories Tricia was sharing with him now. She'd always have Blake's family, who so lovingly and regularly spoiled her and her cousins. Alli and Heath had two little boys close in age now, and on the surface I couldn't ask for anything more than the love they brought to our little family.

Marie, now a year into a new and promising romance, was never far and always eager to dote on Tricia too. But selfishly, with my mother gone and Elliot so far away, seeing Tricia experiencing a small part of my family meant more to me than Blake could realize.

Daniel wasn't the father I'd always imagined. He was deeply flawed, but he'd come a long way from when we'd first met. Many would claim behind closed doors that he'd fallen from grace, but I knew better. He was better off than he'd ever been.

Not long after losing the governor's seat, he'd also lost Margo. The death of her son combined with the humiliation of Daniel's loss had proved too much for her to take. They divorced within the year. Then the controversy around Daniel's rumored involvement in the botched election had put strain on the law firm he ran. Reluctantly, he let go of it all and opted for an early retirement.

All his lofty aspirations, the grand plan, reduced to a simple life in a quiet coastal town in Maine where he'd started spending most of his time. The political machine of his life had come to a screeching halt, and with that supposed failure, he was able to live the way he'd never been allowed to live before. Finally, he was free of the life that had made all his decisions for him, ever since he'd been my age. Success was only a word, something that meant less next to the promise of some simple happiness. Now he at least had a chance for that.

Tricia seemed to make him happy, happier than I'd ever seen him. His eyes would light up at the sight of her, or glisten with emotion when she nestled up beside him after she'd tired herself out with her boundless energy.

I glanced back. His and Tricia's outlines were small in the distance now. Maybe he didn't deserve her, or us. Maybe his transgressions were too great, but I wouldn't stop believing that he could be worthy of forgiveness, worthy of a second chance.

Blake and I rounded the corner of the wraparound deck. He twisted on the outdoor shower that started a waterfall of cool water cascading down over him. I stared, appreciating the rivulets gliding over his gorgeous body. Five years hadn't changed an inch of him. He was still mouth-watering, breathtaking in every way.

He paused, catching my stare. He held out his hand. I took it, and he pulled me under with him. I sucked in a quick breath at the shock of cool water. But then Blake's lips were on me, melding our mouths in a slow, passionate kiss. I lifted on my toes, giving myself over to it.

He groaned, the vibration tingling my lips. "Let's go inside."

I couldn't miss the suggestion in his tone, or his arousal pressed against me. I tensed, recognizing the hesitation I'd never have wrestled with before becoming a mother. "What about Tricia?"

"She'll keep him busy out there for a while."

"A while?" I glanced back toward the beach even though they were out of sight where we stood.

A small touch guided my focus back to him, mischief and lust twinkling in his eyes. "Long enough for me to thoroughly devour you."

I fought a smile. "Tempting."

He shot up his eyebrows with pretend shock. "Tempting? That's all?"

"Quit." I laughed and pushed his chest.

He didn't budge an inch, his arm firmly banded around my waist. "Nonsense. We've got at least twenty minutes, and nothing's going to stop me from making you mine."

"That's not a lot of time," I teased.

He traced his tongue over his lower lip. "I can work quickly."

My breath rushed out as he grabbed the hem of my now drenched white linen cover-up. Lifting it over my head, he exposed the less modest bikini I wore beneath. He tossed it to the ground, the wet fabric slopping against the wood deck with a thud. His hands roamed over my wet skin, down my sides to my hips.

"God, you're beautiful. Why do you wear that thing anyway?"

"I don't know," I lied. I cast my eyes down, trailing my fingertips down the rigid columns of his abs.

Between the scar and the pregnancy, unlike Blake's, my body wasn't what it had been years ago. To anyone on the outside, under the thin garment, I was the same girl with the same body. In private, the scars had become reminders of what I'd been through. The trauma that had threatened to take away my dreams, and then, ultimately, the pregnancy—the gift that we'd been given with our daughter. I should have worn those scars with pride, but couldn't bring myself to.

Being able to have a child was a gift we'd receive only once. We'd tried again, to no avail. She was our miracle. The sunshine that lit up any dark day. A beautiful, perfect reflection of the love that we'd fought so hard for.

Brushing the backs of his fingers across my cheek, he tipped my chin up. "Don't cover yourself up, baby. I love your body. I don't want to see you hiding it."

"I'll try," I promised.

He skimmed up and down my arms, down my chest, lingering at the edges of the fabric that covered my breasts.

"Then again, I'm not sure if I'd be able to control myself seeing you this way all summer. I've hardly any willpower as it is."

A second later, he'd pushed one triangle of my bikini top to the side. My breast was heavy and tight in his grasp.

"Blake." His name left me like a mixed warning. Anxiety mingled with the prickle of desire humming under my skin.

He hushed me, erasing my objection with another deep kiss. I wrapped my arms around his neck as he moved us out of the water and against the wall of the house. I was pinned by his hard body, my thigh hitched high over his hip so I was open to him. His tantalizing touch trailed down the length of my body, over my belly, and farther down. I gasped when he slid into the front of my bikini, cupping me firmly. His mouth left mine and found my breast. Sucking and laving, he teased the tight peak while his fingers coaxed the arousal between my thighs.

I bit my lip, holding back a moan.

"I want to hear you," he whispered between breaths, sucking me harder, nibbling my tender nipples until I couldn't hold back any longer.

Arching with a whimper, I sifted my hands through the wet strands of his hair. I held him to me, held on as the waves of pleasure washed over me, growing in intensity by the second, like the steady rising tide. Gradually, my sense of the time slipped. The sounds of the beach fell away, and Blake took over my senses, playing me like a song he knew well, one he'd never forgotten.

"Oh, God." The stuttering cry left my lips as I shuddered violently against his ministrations.

"Ah, there you are," he murmured.

My head fell back as I caught my breath, my heart racing in my chest. I relaxed my grip on his shoulders. My nails had left white and then red marks on his tanned skin.

"Wow," I uttered between jagged breaths.

The warm salty air filled my lungs and settled on my damp skin. Every sensation pulsed through me. The brush of his legs against mine, his palms curving around me from behind, drawing us closer. Our hips rocking together, his lips soft against my neck. When he drew back, his green-eyed gaze was filled with wanting and something else, something deeper that never failed to rob me of breath. A kind of shattering love that he was capable of sharing only with me.

"Blake...I love you so much." The words spilled out of me, an easy and automatic proclamation, but one that never lost its meaning as time wore on between us. The words meant nothing less than they had when we'd first uttered them. They only ever meant more.

"I love you too." His gaze flickered over me. "And I'll never get tired of putting that look on your face. I love seeing you that way, all pink and flushed, with stars in your eyes when you let go. Makes me feel like I'm the center of your world, if only for a minute."

With a shaky hand I traced the dark wing of his eyebrow, down his beautiful nose and across his full etched lips. The work of art that I shared my life with…one I would never tire of, one I refused take for granted.

"I'm not sure if there's such a thing, but if there is, the center of my world is our love, Blake. Every joy…everything beautiful in my life I have is because of our love."

He closed his eyes, drawing me closer until our foreheads touched. He slowly lifted his, capturing me in a deep, soulful gaze. "You'll always have it."

BONUS SCENE

*Go back to where it all started . . . Now we get a
special chance to see exactly what Blake
was thinking when Erica first walked into
the Angelcom boardroom.*

BLAKE

I leaned against the wall of the elevator and watched the
numbers change as I approached the top floor of the Angelcom offices. I closed my eyes, wishing I had a few extra
hours to keep them closed.

The doors opened with a ding, and, a few steps
beyond, Greta sat behind the large reception desk that bore
the Angelcom name and logo. A home away from home,
this office was where some of my best ventures began.

Greta smiled warmly as I approached. "Good morning, Mr. Landon. The other investors are meeting in conference room B this morning."

I nodded and checked my watch. I was already five
minutes late. I enjoyed the smallest satisfaction knowing
we were meeting with one of Max's recruits today and my
tardiness was no doubt pissing him off right now.

"You look tired. Can I get you anything?" Greta's
brows knit together.

"Thanks, I'm good."

I shoved a hand through my hair. I'd been up half the night thwarting a cyber attack on a platform we'd launched only a few days ago. Whoever was targeting this one was goddamn persistent but ultimately unsuccessful in taking us offline. I took another sip of my jumbo iced coffee and made my way toward the conference room down the hall.

The other investors were in place already, seated around a large conference table that faced Boston's skyline. I dropped into the empty seat next to Max and locked in on the beautiful blonde sitting across from me.

"This is Blake Landon," Max said to her. "Blake, Erica Hathaway. She's here to present on her fashion social network, Clozpin."

"Clever name. You brought her in?" I asked without breaking my focus on her.

"Yes, we have a mutual friend at Harvard," he replied.

I nodded slowly. Prior to this meeting, I'd had the pleasure of a much more physical introduction to the girl, who looked all woman now in her suit and a soft teal blouse that played off her mesmerizing blue eyes. Eyes that I couldn't tear my attention from now. Something in that moment of recognition made the long night and the rough morning fade into the background.

Erica Hathaway.

I licked my lips and watched her follow the movement with her eyes. A small flush worked its way across her chest and up to her cheeks. This was the second time in a row I delighted in her visible physical response to me.

The spark went both ways, and I almost cursed myself for not following through on my attraction to her. By the hazy look in her eyes when she'd stumbled and I'd caught her against me at the restaurant the other night, I could have asked her out for a drink, which could have turned into more. But Michael had been in town, and I couldn't blow off dinner with him for a quick fuck.

At least now I had a second chance.

She fidgeted with her jacket, avoiding my stare, and stuttered into her presentation.

Meanwhile, I let myself dwell on all the ways the night could have ended. Then I redirected my wandering thoughts to the present and all the ways I could make good on those missed opportunities by spreading her out on the rather sturdy table separating us now. I ran my tongue along my lower lip, wondering what she might taste like. The memory of her body, warm under my palms, pressed tightly against me, just got a little more potent now.

I couldn't help smirking every time we made eye contact and she hesitated over her words. She looked uncomfortable, definitely nervous. Not unusual for a first pitch, or any pitch for that matter. I should have wanted to make her feel more at ease, but all I could think about was how she'd respond under pressure. I interrupted her mid-sentence and hammered her with rapid-fire questions about her business model, which she answered with more grace than I'd expected.

So Erica wasn't just a pretty girl. She was smart, and the fact that she'd made it to my boardroom meant she was determined too.

Satisfied, I waved her on to continue.

As Erica spoke, I debated which I wanted more—a slice of her business or the memory of her under me, screaming my name.

Too bad I preferred simple. Uncomplicated. Otherwise I could have had both. I wasn't in the market for breaking hearts, and mixing business with pleasure was a fast track to that end.

My phone lit up with a text, interrupting my laser focus on Erica and her presentation. My ex Sophia was coming into town in a few days. The emoticons appending the text made it clear she wanted to do more than see me. I smiled inwardly at her persistence. I should have wanted everything she offered, but I couldn't bring myself to take her to bed again. After everything we'd been through, we were better as friends.

And not when I had a tasty morsel like Erica Hathaway right in front of me.

I shot a text off to Sophia, letting her know I'd be in Vegas and would miss her visit. I dropped my phone back to the table as Erica wrapped up. I couldn't miss the mix of relief and fear that flashed behind her eyes. Vulnerability, with a little flash of fire.

When she concluded, I asked, "Are you seeing anyone?"

I knew I was going to hell as soon as I uttered the words. The shock of pink that hit Erica's cheeks confirmed it.

"Excuse me?" Her voice was unsteady.

"Relationships can be distracting. If you were to get the funds you need from this group, it could be a factor that affects your ability to grow."

I could have majored in bullshit, if I'd found college worth the effort. Except she wasn't buying it. All her vulnerability had vanished. Now she was all fire, a reality that sent a rush of blood south. Unfortunately for her, or perhaps fortunately, the promise of taking her to bed was winning out in my internal battle.

"I can assure you, Mr. Landon, that I am one hundred percent committed to this project." Her eyes narrowed as she gazed steadily at me. She tilted her head a fraction. "Do you have any other questions pertaining to my personal life that will influence your decision today?"

I had all kinds of questions pertaining to her personal life that I intended to get to the bottom of as soon as this meeting was over.

"No, I don't think so. Max?"

I turned to Max, who quickly prompted the rest of the investors to voice their interest either way. Erica drew an unsteady breath and clasped her hands in front her, so tightly her knuckles went bloodless.

Then, one by one, the others passed.

She swallowed hard, and I could sense her preparing for the very real possibility that she'd leave this room unilaterally rejected. What Erica didn't know was that Max had stacked the room with men who rarely invested in web-based startups. This alone told me he wanted her for himself.

Then all eyes were on me and the room fell silent. I leveled a steady stare in Erica's direction.

In that moment, I decided I wanted her for myself too.

"I'll pass," I said.

DISCUSSION QUESTIONS

1. Over the course of the series, Blake and Erica's love has evolved, grown, and strengthened. How would you describe how their relationship has changed? What is it about them and their journey that makes their love unforgettable?

2. *Hard Love* is the only book in the series told in dual perspective throughout. What was it like to get into Blake's head? Did spending time with his thoughts change how you saw him or understood his character?

3. Early in the story, you're given the chance to read a moment of passion and punishment from Blake's point of view. Did your understanding of his desire for control and trust change after reading it from his perspective?

4. What was it like to see Blake at his most vulnerable or when he willingly gave up the control and fight that he'd always had? What did those moments illuminate about his character?

5. *Hard Love* brings about a major change for Erica and Blake when they find out they're expecting

a baby. What was it like to experience this news with them, from each of their perspectives?

6. When Erica forgives Risa and gives her a second chance, they share an emotional moment together. What does this conversation illuminate about both of their characters? Why do you think Erica chooses to forgive Risa?

7. The Hacker series has introduced many supporting characters, along with Blake and Erica's love story: Alli and Heath, James and Simone, and Geoff and Sid. What do you think the future holds for these characters?

8. As this series came to an end, what did you think of how it concluded for Blake and Erica? Thinking back on all that they have been through together, was all of that worth it to get Blake and Erica to the ending they have in *Hard Love*?

ACKNOWLEDGMENTS

This book is for my little rug rats, S., A., and E., who, even though I refuse to accept it, will not always be so little. Though it may not be obvious to you now, I promise that every single day that goes by in our crazy hectic lives, I find myself overwhelmed with pride, awe, and more love for you than I'm able to truly express with words. Thank you for sharing your mommy with her characters and readers and for accepting the sacrifices that we've had to make. Thank you for being excited about every little step of our journey, for being the first ones to hug me when I need it the most, and for reminding me every day of what's truly important.

I would like to thank my readers, street team, and beta readers for the incredible support! Your love for this story has inspired Blake and Erica's journey more than you can possibly know. I am forever indebted to you for being such an enormous part of making this dream of mine come true.

I am excited for the opportunity to finally and formally credit my literary agent, Kimberly Brower, and the support of the Rebecca Friedman Literary Agency. Kimberly, thank you for finding me, for reading and loving my books, and for agreeing to hop on this crazy roller coaster ride of a writing career with me.

My gratitude goes out to the many people at Hachette

Book Group, Grand Central Publishing, and Forever Romance who have helped bring the Hacker Series books to my readers with great dedication and efficiency. Thank you, Leah Hultenschmidt and Jamie Raab, for seeing the series' potential and for bringing new energy to the publishing and distribution effort. Thank you also to the many foreign publishers and the ladies at Bookcase Literary Agency who have shared that enthusiasm by bringing Blake and Erica's story to the rest of the world.

As always, big props go out to my talented editor, Helen Hardt. It's crazy to think that it's been two years since I sent you the first draft for *Hardwired*, and here we are six books later! I know I always promise every crazy deadline will be the last, but I think you know me better by now. Thank you again for your flexibility and your always thoughtful red pen.

I could not have confidently navigated the judicial system of my fictional world without the legal expertise of Anthony Canata, Esq. and my long-time business counsel, Michael Gove. Michael, I'm grateful to have had you by my side through some of the most challenging times of my life. Thank you for your continued friendship and always sound advice.

Much of Blake's natural genius and technical expertise has been inspired by Luc Vachon, my "real-life" Sid, brilliant friend and former colleague, who only uses his powers for good. Thank you, Luc, for your amazing brain, which never fails to inspire the people around you to imagine what's possible. And after years of harassing you about it, please accept this acknowledgment as my final acceptance of your inability to come to work before the noon hour.

Thank you to my Waterhouse Press team, for taking care of business while I went underground for weeks at a time to be a writer instead of a business owner. David Grishman, thank you for taking the reins and allowing me to retire from being *the boss*. Kurt Vachon, it's hard to imagine completing any major project without the regular stream of cute baby animal videos that you provide, in addition to the never-ending technical support that keeps everything running smoothly behind the scenes. Shayla Fereshetian, somehow you bring my chaotic world into order, and you do it with such passion and positivity. A thousand times, thank you! Fair warning, if anyone ever tries to steal you away from me, I will cut them.

Mia Michelle, my sweet! Thank you for being my novel-writing doula once again, for your unfailing support, and for being such a beautiful soul that I'm so blessed to call a friend. Chelle Bliss, your work ethic boggles my mind and has been a true inspiration to the professional procrastinator in me. Thank you for the regular check-ins, for sending me great writing jams, and for being so incredibly real.

Thank you to Remi Ibraheem, for your friendship and amazing guidance. Thank you to the many friends I've made along the way, and the ones who have journeyed with me through this crazy experience with positivity and encouragement.

As always, thank you, Mom, for listening and for helping me believe the things that sometimes feel impossible are always within reach. I could not have survived this journey without your steady support and selfless love.

Above all, I would like to thank my husband, Jonathan, except the words *thank you* will never be enough. I could never imagine writing a story about two characters so passionately in love without knowing that kind of crazy love for myself. Thank you for being my champion, my best friend, and the love of my life.

ABOUT THE AUTHOR

Meredith Wild is a #1 *New York Times*, *USA Today*, and international bestselling author of romance. Living in the White Mountains of New Hampshire with her husband and three children, she refers to herself as a techie, whiskey-appreciator, and hopeless romantic. When she isn't living in the fantasy world of her characters, she can usually be found at www.facebook.com/meredithwild.

You can find out more about her writing projects at www.meredithwild.com.